〜〜〜

Who is the lady setting London astir?
All is about to be revealed.

Notorious rake Leo Wade is not one for house parties—he'd much rather pass the time in London's gaming halls . . . and ladies' boudoirs. But when his gambling instinct leads him to believe the enchanting and utterly impossible Miss Susanna Leland is the anonymous model of a shockingly immodest painting . . . he braves country tedium for a chance to prove the lady's secret.

With one foot already firmly planted on the shelf, Susanna cares not a fig for propriety. But even she never imagined she'd become caught up in a ridiculous game of cat and mouse, and certainly not with the most wicked man of her acquaintance! Susanna has absolutely no intention of letting Leo confirm his suspicions, no matter how persuasive he can be. . .

Until sweet temptation becomes too much to bear, and they both learn that the price of trust may just be worth every scandalous secret.

Romances by Gayle Callen

EVERY SCANDALOUS SECRET

GAYLE CALLEN

AVON

An Imprint of HarperCollinsPublishers

AVON BOOKS
An Imprint of HarperCollins*Publishers*
10 East 53rd Street
New York, New York 10022-5299

Copyright © 2011 by Gayle Kloecker Callen
ISBN 978-0-06-178345-6
www.avonromance.com

First Avon Books mass market printing: October 2011

Avon Trademark Reg. U.S. Pat. Off. and in Other Countries, Marca Registrada, Hecho en U.S.A.
HarperCollins® is a registered trademark of HarperCollins Publishers.

Printed in the U.S.A.

10 9 8 7 6 5 4 3 2 1

To Theresa Kovian, longtime Packeteer and good friend. You've never given up on your writing, and now have grown in new directions with new challenges. You'll always have my admiration and respect.

Every
Scandalous
Secret

Chapter 1

Hertfordshire, 1846

This was not the first time Mr. Leo Wade arrived at a house party without an invitation; however, it was the only time he had arrived anywhere with the intention of catching a spinster.

"I seem to be interrupting," he said cheerfully, looking about as if intrigued by the identity of the guests arrayed in the Marquess of Bramfield's elegant, marble-columned drawing room.

But he only cared about Miss Susanna Leland, cousin to the Duke of Madingley, artist, bluestocking, and a spinster by any definition. She was sitting by herself, spectacles flashing a momentary reflection of candlelight. Not his usual quarry, and that was proving most interesting.

Their gazes clashed, and he knew she'd begun to think herself safe from him, that he hadn't followed her from London. If he expected dismay, he was pleasantly surprised not to receive it. She looked over her spectacles at him, her cool brown eyes briefly narrowed as if he were a peculiar sort of insect. Her unfashionable dark red hair was pulled severely back into a chignon at the base of her neck. No ringlets for Susanna. Her face was almost pretty in a plain sort of way, with cheekbones that would have been dramatic had her mouth not been a bit too wide. Her ordinary gown began at the base of her neck, leaving not a hint of womanly cleavage. Though her figure looked average and not overly endowed, a corset could hide much.

If the painting hanging in his London club was correct, much was certainly hidden.

And he was prepared to discover it all.

Viscount Swanley grinned at him and left the side of his father, Lord Bramfield. Swanley was a tall, gangly, dark-haired man, perpetually cheerful and able to overlook Leo's many sins, if not participate. They gave a quick nod to each other for etiquette's sake.

"Good to see you," Swanley said, then glanced back at his mother. "My lady, did you invite Wade without telling me?"

Lady Bramfield, plump with her settled life, forced a smile from beneath her crown of gray-streaked untamable curls. "I regret to say I did not, but his appearance here surely rectifies my mistake."

She exchanged a glance with her husband, tall as his heir, Swanley, but rather stooped, as if he spent so much of his time bending over to talk to people that it had become a permanent condition. During their momentary silent communication, Leo waited, confident of the outcome.

"You must stay at our house party," Swanley said. "There are birds to shoot and pretty girls to watch"—he added the latter in an undertone—"and card games where I'll certainly best you at last."

Leo chuckled and resisted the urge to send impassive Susanna a triumphant grin. "As long as watching pretty girls is treated as a sport and not a step toward marriage, then you can count on my companionship." He shuddered. "I've avoided these house parties because they're usually a veritable marriage mart."

Swanley laughed. "You have to marry sometime, Wade. Why resist the inevitable, when it can be so pleasant?"

Leo snorted. "My brother has the title and all the duties attending it. I'm in no hurry to join him in marital shackles." For a moment, memories swamped him of the constant fighting his parents had engaged in, the disdain, the bitterness. Nothing he and his brother and sister tried ever made things better. His brother's recent marriage still seemed too good to last, so Leo watched it from afar, feeling almost guilty, as if he were awaiting their unhappiness.

Lady Caroline, their host's daughter, walked to Susanna's side, towering over the other ladies, her dismay with his presence very evident. She whispered something in Susanna's ear, and although his quarry nodded, she revealed nothing else. He rather liked the way he couldn't read her every emotion. Made it more of a challenge.

"You have arrived just in time for dinner," Swanley was saying.

Leo turned his most humble smile on Lady Bramfield. "I do regret the inconvenience, my lady. Swanley always said I should drop by if I was traveling north from London."

"I hope we are not keeping you," Lady Bramfield said quickly, glancing over at the innocent young ladies in her charge.

Though she obviously wished him gone to protect her flock, she couldn't know that Susanna was not so innocent. "Nothing that cannot wait," he assured the marchioness.

To her credit, her fixed smile didn't change.

Several of the younger men moved among the ladies although one chap stood off by himself awkwardly. A mix of gentlemen and nobility, none so highly ranked that they would think themselves too lofty for such a gathering. He wasn't certain that the mix was ideal, but if these were the eligible men Bramfield wanted his daughter and the other unmarried women to choose from, who was Leo to protest?

"Ignore Greenwich's frown," Swanley said in a quiet voice. "He's a windsucker."

The earl was frowning at Leo as if in warning, marring his distinguished looks, while his wife, with hair unnaturally dark for her age, whispered animatedly in his ear, her affronted gaze never leaving Leo. Then Leo spotted Lady May, their pretty blond daughter, who fluttered her lashes and her fan at his notice. "Ah yes, she must be the lamb to my wolf, if the earl's demeanor means anything."

But Greenwich didn't need to worry—Leo hadn't

arrived to peruse possible lovers, certainly not among the debutantes. Susanna was his main mission, the subject of a wager he'd proposed with his two closest friends. Recklessness was nothing new for him—desperation was. He'd been feeling bored with a life that had always provided such amusement and excitement. Each day had become almost . . . predictable. Surely a wager against three beautiful women should get him over this strange restlessness that had recently invaded his thoughts.

His arrival necessitated rearranging the procession into dinner, and now that the numbers were uneven, shy Mr. Tyler walked alone at the end.

Susanna, noticing what Leo's arrival had done to the other man, gave him another disapproving stare. He grinned at her, then held his arm out for Miss Norton, the niece of their host, with sandy hair and a freckled face that blushed prettily when she gaped up at him. Susanna and her escort walked just behind them in line.

There was already a seat for Leo at the table, as if he'd been invited all along, and he proceeded to enjoy dinner. He kept up a lively conversation with many of the guests except Susanna, who spoke calmly to the gentlemen on either side of her.

Leo bided his time, conversing with the men over port and cheroots after dinner, until at last they rejoined the ladies in the drawing room. The older ladies looked up with fondness to their husbands, while the younger ladies betrayed a bit too much eagerness.

Leo walked purposefully toward Susanna. He felt the change in the air, the way people tried not to watch his progress across the room. He could tell by the set of her shoulders that Susanna felt their stares, but she turned away to talk to one of the young ladies at her side—Miss Randolph? He thought he remembered the way Miss Randolph spoke in a half-whispering voice that betrayed her zeal.

When he stopped in front of Susanna, she raised an eyebrow as if she couldn't fathom why he'd approached her. The minx.

He hadn't imagined he could enjoy himself as much as he had five days ago, when he'd seen her dressed as a boy, but tonight was almost proving its equal in entertainment.

"Miss Leland," he said, bowing to her.

Her curtsy was fluidly feminine. "Mr. Wade."

"Would you do me the honor of taking a turn about the room?"

She gave him a polite smile, and when she would have simply walked at his side, he held up his arm, forcing her to touch him—to confront the reality of the situation from which she'd tried to flee.

People continued to converse as they moved away together, but he knew it was all speculation about why he'd chosen to bestow his attentions on spinster Susanna rather than debutante beauty Miss Randolph. The girl's parents were the only couple who watched him with naïve interest. The others would soon set them straight.

Susanna's hand was featherlight on his arm. They

walked before the long expanse of French windows looking out onto the dark terrace. No one could overhear them now.

"It was rather easy to find you," Leo said softly.

She regarded him calmly, her face half-lit with the lamps of the room, the other half in the shadows of the night.

He continued, "Your maids were quite eager to help an eligible gentleman who was so distraught over missing you." He patted her hand before she could speak. "Do not be displeased with them. I am persuasive."

"Really?" she inquired, one eyebrow lifting. "It remains to be seen if that extends beyond innocent maids."

"I am eager, too. Surely you could tell by the way I followed you into Hyde Park."

"You could have simply called on me rather than skulking in wait to accost me in public."

"Far more difficult for you to reject me."

"But reject you I did," she said brightly. "I was sketching."

"And you have quite the skill for it." He smiled down at her, even as he effortlessly guided her through a turn and started back along the length of the windows.

"Flattery, Mr. Wade? I do believe that is beneath you where a wager is concerned."

"And so is 'skulking' after you, but it served my purpose. It maneuvered you to this house party, away from the protection of your family, didn't it?"

If she was startled, she hid it well, keeping a pleasant expression on her face.

"Did you think it was all *your* idea to flee London?" he continued.

"I did not flee; I accepted a long-standing invitation to attend this house party. Unlike you," she added dryly, "who rudely appeared without invitation."

"I, too, had a long-standing *personal* invitation— luckily for me." He grinned, but although she looked faintly amused, she did not return his smile. Most young ladies would have, his charm being what it was, but Susanna was unlike his usual quarry.

"And so what do you intend to do?" she asked, her curiosity out in the open.

"If I told you, I would lose the advantage."

"You have no advantage, Mr. Wade. You are trying to gather proof to win a scandalous wager. Of course, I will not be helping you."

"Of course not—that would defeat the purpose. You can't even bring yourself to speak aloud what occurred that night. I believe there was a painting, and you were—"

"Please be quiet." She directed a pleasant, distracting smile at other guests. "I don't talk about it because I do not wish to be overheard. Gossip spreads far too easily."

"Then prepare yourself for many secret discussions, Susanna, for although I'm competing with two of my friends"—he lowered his voice to a husky timbre—"I am also competing with you."

He bit off the last word as Lord and Lady Greenwich strode by, their lined, patrician faces identically disapproving, their glances at Susanna full of sympathy and poorly veiled curiosity. He knew he'd practically cultivated such treatment, but to his surprise, it didn't make Susanna distance herself from him.

When the couple was far enough away, Susanna said, "I do not care to compete with you, Mr. Wade."

"That is obvious by the way you fled London."

She looked at him with the toleration of an adult to an incorrigible child. "Believe what you wish. It only goes to prove your arrogance."

"You're not the only one who fled, of course." When she remained silent, he continued, "Your sister Rebecca mysteriously decided to visit an elderly relative."

"No mystery there, sir. Our great-aunt Rianette is doing poorly. Rebecca is visiting, as is her duty."

"While you enjoy a frivolous party."

"If you knew anything about me, Mr. Wade, you would know that 'enjoy' is an erroneous word."

He studied her with curiosity. Ladies of the *ton* lived for these sorts of social events—but then again, Susanna was not proving herself a typical lady. "Fear not for your sister's welfare. She is certainly not alone. I am quite positive that Julian followed her."

Susanna blinked at him. "I do not believe that. The Earl of Parkhurst is far too busy to . . ." She trailed off, once again unwilling to say the words.

He was never unwilling to be reckless. "To win a wager over—"

She pinched his arm, and he chuckled.

"We'll have to discuss the details sometime, but I can be patient," he said. "As I was saying, Julian entered this *unnamed* wager freely enough—which did surprise me, I'll admit. He's not known for the same frivolity I am."

He thought the corners of her mouth twitched, but he couldn't tell if she betrayed amusement or impatience.

"But then you knew that," Leo continued.

"I beg your pardon? I barely know either you or Lord Parkhurst—except by reputation."

He deliberately winced. "A salvo fired in my direction. But not a direct hit. You assumed that by the three of you going your separate ways, we gentlemen could not marshal our resources against you."

"I assumed no such thing," she said demurely.

"But of course you left your cousin, Lady Elizabeth, behind."

"I did not. Her mother was feeling poorly, and she wished to remain in London."

"So then you *did* encourage her to leave."

He felt the flexing of her fingers on his forearm, but she did not snatch them away from him. How could she? Conversations were almost absent as they'd become the focus of the evening's speculation. He saw the way Susanna glanced at their audience, knew she was weighing her options, already guessed that she did not speak without thinking. What a challenge to face such a woman—the boredom and restlessness that had lately crept up on him was already dissipating after mere minutes in her presence.

"You have me at a disadvantage, sir. I cannot defend myself in such a public place."

He leaned down toward her. "I cannot believe a man ever has you at a disadvantage, Miss Leland."

Her eyes, which he'd thought of as plain brown, stared up into his, and he glimpsed pinpricks of gold, so unexpected. They regarded each other for a moment, then both stepped back, as if by mutual agreement.

Leo bowed his head and whispered, "Then I'll find you in a more private place where we can continue our discussion."

It was a promise—it was a threat.

A full quarter hour had passed before Susanna felt her excited breathing return to normal. Lady Caroline Norton, daughter of her host, watched her with restrained curiosity as they sat side by side on the sofa. Caroline was very tall for a woman and seemed to prefer remaining seated, where she could look a person in the eyes. She was sympathetic to Susanna's sister Rebecca, throughout her constant childhood illnesses. Caroline was one of the few friends who didn't gradually distance herself, and Susanna never forgot such a kindness.

But now she anticipated that Caroline would use the connection to ask about Leo Wade. Susanna wasn't used to questions about a man's interest in her, or at least not since the disastrous year of her coming out. Thank goodness that Lady May decided to treat them all to a fast rendition of a sonata by

Handel on the pianoforte. Susanna smiled politely and let her mind drift, calming her curiosity and confusion.

But nothing helped her stop thinking about Mr. Wade and the very unusual challenge he presented. Out of the corner of her eye, she watched him talking to Lord Swanley, both of them using their hands with animation, drawing in several other gentlemen as they all laughed. But Mr. Wade stood out, with his wavy hair and the sideburns that emphasized his angular cheeks. Though not as tall as Lord Swanley, he had enough height to make him rise above most of the other men. With his lean, compact build, she found herself thinking that his clothing restrained him, hid his true nature. She could easily imagine what lay beneath, the long line of muscle that smoothly intersected with the next, molded over bone, the functionality of the human form capable of its own kind of beauty.

She flushed, then looked down at her fingers, which she'd been twisting together, forcing them to relax before anyone else noticed. Often, she found herself studying the subjects she would draw just like this—but that could never include Leo Wade. She did not want to even attempt to capture those green eyes, full of mischief and laughter. The world was a place he played in—he had no intellectual interests that she'd ever heard of. He cared little for propriety or decency.

And he was chasing *her*, she thought, surprised to feel a touch of exhilaration rather than dread.

Mr. Wade had such a scandalous reputation in Society, that even she, an unmarried woman, had heard some of the rumors. More than once, he'd snuck a member of the demimonde into balls held by the most prominent of peers. He gambled and drank almost every night away. He lured ladies onto shadowed terraces and appeared unmasked at Vauxhall Gardens, only to disappear into the darkness. Susanna knew well enough what sort of assignations happened in such a scandalous place.

But how could she pass judgment? Not six nights ago, she'd tried to steal a painting off the wall in a gentlemen's club—wearing boy's clothing to hide her identity. She could have groaned her mortification. But she and her sister and cousin had been desperate, forced into a reckless adventure that had ended with them being caught by Mr. Wade, Lord Parkhurst— and Peter Derby, the man she knew the best of the three, and the last she had wished to see.

The men were foxed, the lot of them, or they'd never have challenged each other to that scandalous wager, that even now she could barely think about let alone discuss aloud. Susanna had been trapped into accepting.

After that, she'd known Mr. Wade might follow her from London—but never guessed he'd so boldly manage an invitation to an exclusive event! Only part of her felt dismayed—another part felt a sense of elation that he would risk censure. Even though he was considered a scoundrel, he'd never done quite enough for people to forget that his brother was Viscount Wade, an influential member of the House of Lords, regardless of his blindness.

When would Mr. Wade use up the passes Society seemed to keep giving him? He won so often at cards that more than once there'd been rumors of cheating, which he'd amiably denied, and proof had never been discovered. No challenges to a duel for Mr. Wade.

And the women—she'd heard that he had mistresses through the years, even more than one at a time! Again, his preference for loose women was not all that unusual in the *ton*, but his openness about it surely was. Although there were highly moral peers who would not invite him to their dinners, others— including industrialists—had no such problem. Mr. Wade didn't care where he enjoyed himself, as long as he did.

If only she could stop looking at him.

It was the artist in her, she assured herself. There were other men equally as handsome to admire. She had not come to the Bramfield house party simply to evade Mr. Wade. She had promised her brother Matthew that she would give the eligible gentlemen another chance to impress her, and she never went back on a promise. Matthew and his wife Emily had risked much to be together, including a false marriage and a secret elopement no one in the family would ever know about except her. Susanna would have been content with her life, her art, her work for her father, until she saw the special happiness that the two of them shared, imagined all of her family having children but her. The future had suddenly seemed lonely, with her the only one without a partner to share it.

Yet she hadn't imagined how complicated it would be when she arrived at Bramfield Hall two days before, without a female member of her family to keep her company. It had been difficult to find common subjects of discussion even with the women, let alone the men. Hour after hour in the company of other people was wearing on her, and sometimes she had to escape for a moment's solitude. Thank goodness she had her art as an excuse, something most people could almost understand.

The men in attendance at the house party were perfect for her beginning foray in husband hunting. She knew Albert Evans, a neighboring landowner near Madingley Court, the ducal palace she'd been raised in. He wasn't much taller than she was but had an honest country face. He'd never shown a bit of interest in her—not that she'd shown any in him. She could change this. He'd courted her sister-in-law Emily when it seemed her brother Matthew was dead. Obviously, Mr. Evans was looking for a wife.

And then there was Lord Keane; he was a handsome man, with his dark good looks, full lips, and broad physique that spoke of an athletic nature. But there was something about the way he seemed to secretly laugh at everything around him, and not in a pleasant way.

Viscount Swanley, as the heir to a marquisate, could obviously appeal to a titled lady, but Susanna did not consider her own connections exalted enough. Her father was a professor, after all, even if her cousin was a duke.

She'd already discovered Mr. Frobisher's propensity for chatting, when he wasn't nervously polishing his spectacles. He was eager and pleasant, and perhaps they'd find something in common to discuss.

As for Mr. Tyler, he was still standing alone by doors open to the torchlit terrace beyond. He'd been there before dinner as well. It was early summer, not exactly hot enough to need the breeze of an open door. He had wavy brown hair that fell haphazardly across his forehead and an absent stare, as if he were thinking of something else. Perhaps he didn't like house parties either; they might have that in common.

Mr. Frobisher and Mr. Tyler were country squires seldom in London. But that did not bother her in the least; she preferred the countryside, with its gorgeous scenery just waiting to be captured by her pencil or brush.

Here in Hertfordshire, she would be able to paint new landscapes and bring back memories—and sketches—to fuel her art for some time to come.

She hoped to bring back a fiancé, too.

When Caroline began to clap, Susanna did the same, realizing that Lady May had finished playing the pianoforte without Susanna's hearing a note.

Then Caroline turned to face Susanna, their knees brushing. Her bright blue eyes settled inquisitively on her face.

"So . . ." Caroline said, tilting her head.

Susanna smiled. "So?"

"Mr. Wade?"

Susanna willed herself not to blush but felt the warmth in her cheeks. It was . . . strange to imagine discussing something personal with a woman not her sister or cousin. "I know him no better than you do, Caroline."

"That was a long conversation for someone you do not know well." She leaned closer and whispered, "Perhaps he admires you."

Susanna restrained herself from rolling her eyes. "He gave me no indication of that. He knows my brother and wishes to meet my cousin Madingley. He probably wants to challenge him to a card game, just to say he defeated a duke."

"It could be about business or politics."

Susanna shook her head. "Mr. Wade? Never."

Caroline stopped asking questions but still glanced at Susanna occasionally with a curiosity she didn't bother to hide. Susanna would hold her secrets close. She could never tell another soul about the scandalous wager and what had led up to it. Too many lives could be ruined.

Chapter 2

A s was her custom, Susanna was up at dawn, and she felt a bit guilty ringing for Caroline's maid so early after a late night. Marie had blond curls that fell from confinement across her neck or down her cheek. Yawning, she tucked the hair back behind her ear and looked into the wardrobe where Susanna's clothes hung on display.

"Miss Leland, tell me ye brought more than this."

Susanna blinked in surprise at her forthright speech, even though Caroline had laughingly warned her in advance. "Is something wrong, Marie?"

"O' course not, miss, but ye've not purchased new gowns in some time, I see."

"They are serviceable and flatter me well, or so I'm told," Susanna answered in confusion.

"Yes, miss, that makes perfect sense."

And she said nothing else, only laid out the gown Susanna chose. Once or twice while she worked on Susanna's hair, she opened her mouth as if to speak, then closed it. Susanna did not question her again.

She wouldn't force the girl. Too many people treated servants as if they only existed in service.

The breakfast room was deserted at first, and Susanna ate contentedly as she read the *Times*. When she heard male voices in the corridor, she tensed, then questioned her own reaction. Eating the last of her toast with deliberation, she reminded herself that Mr. Wade would not give up easily. Perhaps she didn't want him to, she realized, never having played such a game with a man before. Of course, she needed to be concerned that others might discover their connection.

Would he risk the censure of her brother or her male cousins? She didn't know.

Several young men entered the breakfast room, and all greeted her politely. Mr. Evans gave her a special smile of familiarity, but then he'd probably bestowed that on every female member of her family, with their long history in Cambridgeshire. Mr. Wade came in at the end of this group and attempted to conceal a yawn. His eyes look shadowed, as if he didn't relish the morning, but this did not surprise her, with his well-known preference for an evening's entertainments. Lord Keane and Lord Swanley went to the buffet, while talkative Mr. Frobisher approached her directly.

"Miss Leland, my, you are awake early."

"Country hours, sir," she said, nodding briskly. "Others would do well to arise. Much can be accomplished—not that I am accusing anyone of being lazy," she added quickly, realizing she sounded too bossy and opinionated, as her sister would be quick to point out.

But Rebecca wasn't there. Mr. Wade was the one who rolled his eyes and smiled as he turned away.

Thankfully, Mr. Frobisher himself beamed at her. "Yes, yes, at home I am usually out inspecting the fields. A good brisk walk invigorates the blood."

"I like to walk as well. I am off to explore the park as soon as I'm finished here."

But if he heard the invitation in her voice, he ignored it.

"We'll be walking the fields as we shoot," Mr. Frobisher said.

"Hunting? What good exercise," she said, feeling foolish.

"Not so good for the birds." Mr. Wade brought a loaded plate to sit down beside her.

She stood up. "I'll leave you gentlemen to it, then."

"And what are your plans for the day, Miss Leland?" Mr. Wade asked.

She glanced uneasily toward the Lords Swanley and Keane, who debated the merits of kippers versus ham but did not notice Mr. Wade's bold curiosity.

"Nothing that would concern you, sir," she said, smiling. "I do believe a brisk walk is in order."

"Wait, and I shall accompany you."

Without hesitating, she called, "Lord Swanley, Mr. Wade just told me that he wishes to accompany you on your hunting trip."

"He's changed his mind, then?" Lord Swanley said happily.

Mr. Frobisher cleared his throat and studied her with bemusement through his newly polished spectacles.

Mr. Wade smiled. "Miss Leland insists I go. I do believe she thinks my solicitude to her is unnecessary."

Lord Keane eyed her as he whispered something to Lord Swanley. How long would it be before Mr. Wade's attention to her made every other man who might be at all interested, back away—or worse, inspired gossip?

Yet something deep inside her reminded her that she was changing her life, taking risks, living on the edge, rather than at home in safety. She met Mr. Wade's knowing eyes, allowed him to see just a hint of triumph in her own, then nodded to them all and left the breakfast room.

The walk was everything that invigorated her. The park itself was beautifully maintained across rolling fields, full of elaborate gardens and even a maze. A summerhouse stood empty beside a small lake, and several rotundas dotted the grounds, each designed to look like Roman temples. Susanna mentally filed away several perfect locations for sketching and painting, knowing just where she would bring the other young ladies.

She left the manicured park itself and walked up a long hill through tall grass that whipped about her skirts with each stride. She passed Mr. and Mrs. Randolph heading down, and waved to them, realizing that they must have arisen even earlier than she—and they had a daughter to look after late into the evening.

At the top of the hill, she shielded her eyes and turned all about, admiring the countryside, from Bramfield Hall, with its mellow stone and tall windows reflecting the light, to the distant woodland past the river. She heard muffled gunfire, and knew the hunting party would be bringing home game for the kitchens. She almost saluted in their direction, feeling a jaunty satisfaction that she'd eluded Mr. Wade.

But it was only the second day of their quiet battle, and she wouldn't get too overconfident.

At last she returned to the hall and instructed the servants to set up a half dozen easels on the terrace. As she was standing in the shade, sharpening her pencils with a penknife, Lord Bramfield approached with his sister-in-law, Mrs. Norton, a quiet woman who seemed always in his shadow, especially since her husband's death a few years before. Susanna had heard more than once that she didn't allow her daughter to do anything without Lord Bramfield's approval, no matter how long she had to wait to secure it.

Susanna found herself smiling easily at Lord Bramfield. He had always been a friend to her family, so fascinated by her father's anatomy research that he often patronized Cambridge University just to have discussions with the professor. When he'd joined a biology society, she'd thought him the most wonderful man to give her father someone to converse with among the *ton*. She'd always treated him as a doting uncle, and now he looked at the various easels she'd set out and beamed at her.

"Painting, Susanna?" he asked.

"Your daughter very kindly requested that I give art lessons while I was here."

Lord Bramfield tsked and shook his head. "You are here as a guest, my dear. You should not be put to work."

"I so enjoy it, my lord. Lady Caroline knows me too well, knows what I like to do most in all the world."

Mrs. Norton covered her smiling mouth, a shy gesture. "And you are quite talented, Miss Leland. Isn't she, my lord?"

Lord Bramfield grinned. "It seems many people have heard of her artistic abilities."

"Not so many," Susanna said. "Your family dotes upon me, it's true, but as for the rest of Society, I concentrate too much on my art for a lady."

Mrs. Norton nervously looked up at her brother-in-law as if awaiting his reaction.

"I imagine it only matters if your parents approve or not," he said.

"'Approve' might be too strong a word," she said ruefully. "'Tolerate' is more accurate."

"Nonsense. A gift like yours comes about rarely." He lowered his voice. "And look how beneficial it has been to your father."

Mrs. Norton stared quizzically from one to the other, but when Lord Bramfield didn't elaborate, Susanna chose not to either. What was the point of dwelling on another of her bluestocking preoccupations, especially when there were young men about?

As an assistant in her father's laboratory, she'd put her artistic skills to good use, sketching his dissections, which helped when he was lecturing his students. She'd temporarily withdrawn from her father's service at her brother's request since young men would hardly understand her devotion. But when she found the perfect husband, she would convince him that her life's work was too important to give up.

Mrs. Norton suddenly stiffened. "Oh, dear, Lord Bramfield, that . . . young man is approaching."

Susanna knew whom she meant before she even looked. Mr. Wade was coming across the gravel paths of the park, his gun tucked under one arm, a full leather bag in the other. She felt another frisson of excitement, ready to match wits with him. He took the broad marble stairs up to the terrace two at a time, looking so confident in himself. She would make him lose some of that confidence.

"Mr. Wade," Lord Bramfield said, gesturing with his head toward the bulging bag, "I see you're helping our cook."

"Yes, sir, your park is well stocked. I could hardly miss my aim, there were so many birds."

Lord Bramfield nodded, then glanced at Susanna. "The two of you spoke together at length last night."

Susanna opened her mouth to remark on their passing acquaintance, but Mr. Wade beat her to it.

"I could not waste such an opportunity, my lord. I had no idea that Miss Leland was here—and to think I only came to Bramfield Hall by chance!" He smiled down at her, dimples winking in his cheeks.

"Really, Mr. Wade," Susanna said, raising both hands. "Do not tease Lord Bramfield so."

"Then you are an admirer of hers?" Lord Bramfield asked.

"I am," Mr. Wade said sincerely. "I've seen beneath her façade to the woman she hides."

Susanna knew what he referred to and had to admire his wordplay.

Lord Bramfield glanced at her. If he was surprised at Mr. Wade's response, he only said, "Then, Mrs. Norton, I suggested we leave the two young people to talk." He waved and strolled away, his sister-in-law clinging with devotion to his arm.

Susanna went to the balustrade and watched the two walk down into the garden.

"We are hardly alone," Mr. Wade said softly as he came up behind her.

"But they think we want to be," Susanna mused. "Well done on your part."

He laughed softly, even as she went back to sorting her pencils.

"Surely you must head to the kitchens with your bounty," she said.

Mr. Wade whistled for the attention of a footman at the drawing-room doors. The man in his powdered wig and knee breeches gingerly took the bag between his two fingers and began to walk away.

"I wouldn't go through the house, my good man," Mr. Wade called. "Dripping blood, you know."

The footman grimaced even as he bowed and continued down the terrace.

"You could have gone yourself," Susanna continued. "I will be too busy in a moment to play our little
game."

"So that's why you put me into the hunting party
this morn."

"You cannot blame me—you pleased our host,
whom you're imposing upon."

"He doesn't think I'm imposing."

"He doesn't want you for a son-in-law either."

If her words pricked him, he didn't show it, only
tilted his head as if awaiting her next salvo.

"And that's what this party is about," she continued, lifting her chin. "Respectable men treating
women . . . respectfully."

"Ah, I see."

He took a step closer to her, and she gripped the
balustrade to keep from backing away, then pretended to look out at the park. Though the sun was
high in the sky on this lovely English day, something
in her felt uneasy, being so close to him. She wasn't
frightened of him—perhaps she was concerned
about what could happen if she weren't careful. She
was walking a very delicate course, where one mistake on her part could bring her utter ruin. And not
just her—her sister and cousin, too.

But she'd never played such a game with a handsome man before. The lure of it was surprisingly
strong.

"I'm not respectable," Mr. Wade said.

He was speaking so close to her she could feel the
faintest touch of his breath upon her lips.

"I make merry too late into the night, I part fools from their money, and I enjoy myself with ladies."

"Ladies?" she echoed dryly. "Surely not a description of *all* the women you consort with."

"Every woman wants to be treated as such," he said gently. His gaze swept her face. "Don't you, Susanna?"

She licked her lips, feeling the faintest bit lightheaded. "Don't I what?"

"Want to be treated as a lady?"

He slid his hand until it just touched hers on the balustrade. She gave a little jerk, surprised at her reaction.

"I *am* a lady, and I hardly need your confirmation."

"I'm not certain a lady would do what you and your fellow conspirators were doing in a gentlemen's club not six nights past."

She stiffened. "We were desperate. The painting wasn't supposed to be there."

"So I heard. Something about its being destined for a private French collection?"

"The public wasn't supposed to have seen it," she whispered, experiencing again the fear of being discovered that had overwhelmed her that night.

"You took a grave risk, Susanna. You trusted the artist."

"He is my friend." She heard herself defending Roger Eastfield even now.

"Your 'friend' needed money more than your friendship."

How could she answer that? It was true. But right

now she had to be so careful with her words, remaining faithful to the story she, Rebecca, and Elizabeth had settled on.

Mr. Wade was too close to her, in full view of everyone from curious gardeners to Lord Bramfield.

"Mr. Wade, this is not the time to—"

"If it were up to you, you'd never make the time, Susanna. But unless you want to flee this cozy artistic scene you've created, you're forced to stand here and talk to me. Do you care what they think? You've already proven how little you regard Society. You posed nude for a portrait—or so you claim."

Chapter 3

A little voice inside Leo's head had been halfheartedly urging him to stop, to save this confrontation for a more private moment. Susanna stared up at him, her generous mouth slightly parted, her breath coming a bit too fast.

He could be driving her away—but he didn't think so. She wasn't immune to men, as so many had long assured him. Perhaps that assumption was easier for such men to imagine than trying to court a prickly woman with interests so unlike other ladies'.

She wasn't what any man expected—she wasn't the kind of uncomplicated woman Leo someday wanted in his life.

But for right now, due to circumstances she'd begun, they would be together for the next three weeks—the deadline for the end of the wager.

Her lips pressed together. "Mentioning the portrait in public will not help your cause."

"You won't let me mention it in private. I should have come to your rooms last night."

She tensed but didn't back down—and he was once again finding himself surprised by her.

"You would not dare enter a lady's rooms."

He gave her his slow, intimate grin.

Her pale skin blushed, and the glow made her quite striking, lightening her brown eyes.

"You would not dare enter *my* rooms," she amended.

"Why not? According to you, you are a woman who removed her clothing and posed very scandalously for a painting."

She balled her hands into fists, openly facing him now. He knew he should stop provoking her, that if anyone was still watching, they made a strange tableau.

"What do you mean, according to me?" she asked softly. "I *am* the model."

He rubbed his chin and frowned. "Strangely, your sister and your cousin claim the same thing. How touching that you all support each other so completely that you'd risk scandal and the ruin of your very pristine reputations."

Was she the model? That was the central question, of course. Julian, Peter, and he had been drunk enough to make a wager out of it. They'd each chosen the woman they most believed it of, then wagered that they could find proof, all within a month. And if the month passed, and none of them could produce actual evidence, the women won the right to the painting. The men were supposed to buy it for them and hand it over.

But it wouldn't come to that, Leo knew. Someone would prove one of the women was wild enough to risk—everything.

At first he'd chosen Susanna as a lark—she'd been prissy and uptight from the moment he'd seen her that night, questioning his intelligence at every turn. Deflating her high opinion of herself had appealed to him. She was not the sort of woman he spent much time with—bluestockings bored him.

But Susanna was different on so many counts. She'd intrigued him and amused him from the first. He'd stared at that painting on the club wall over her head, examining it for anything he could use against her. And he'd seen it, a small mole high on the model's thigh. If she were the model, as she claimed, he would need to see her thighs—and there was only one way to do that, he thought with rare eagerness.

They heard the lighter sound of feminine voices leaving the drawing room behind them.

He glanced at all the easels. "Plan to sketch a half dozen different scenes all at once?"

Susanna opened her mouth, then glanced back toward the house. The first ladies were arriving with their sketchbooks. Miss Randolph and Miss Norton paused noticeably to blush in Leo's presence, while Caroline strolled forward with her usual confidence.

"Mr. Wade," Caroline said, a smile in her voice, "joining us today, are you?"

"Perhaps I shall if you tell me what I'll be joining."

Susanna only arched a brow as the ladies began to prepare their easels.

"A painting session," Leo said at last. "Miss Leland, I should have known by your practical gown."

He watched her blink down in confusion at the green gown she wore. How could she not see that she dressed so plainly compared to the other women, with their ribbons and lace? Though he allowed for the fact that painting could be quite messy, he didn't understand why her clothing was of so little importance to her.

Perhaps that's why she'd taken them all off.

He stepped away from the lesson but did not leave the terrace immediately. He wanted to watch her in her element, having heard something about her artistic skills. Every young lady was urged to such a path, of course. And the result was usually watercolors where he wasn't certain if the rendition included people or animals.

He leaned back against the cold stone of the house and studied Susanna. She was all business now, discussing the importance of shadows and shading, and how they'd only be using pencils at first. Her voice was brisk with knowledge, but in no way did she come off sounding superior. He simply heard her love of the subject, her enthusiasm to bring the other ladies along with her on an artistic journey these next few days.

They seemed captured, too, some of them watching her with a new interest. Lady Caroline stole glances at her other guests, looking pleased that her suggestion to have Susanna teach was having a successful start. As they began to work, Susanna removed her spectacles from her pocket and donned them to look closely at her students' work.

Leo felt . . . strangely uneasy. He tended to avoid this side of the young ladies he flirted with, and for the first time, he wondered why he felt so. He encouraged their chattering about hobbies or fashion or gossip—but hearing about a lifelong pursuit, something intellectual and beyond a mere hobby, always made him long to escape.

And he did so now, turning his back, knowing he would have to find another time to get Susanna Leland alone.

Susanna moved through the rest of the day in a happy glow. Her art was the one commonality she had with other ladies, and it gave her great pleasure to discuss it in such depth. She saw their respect for her growing, and much as she usually didn't care about such things, today it felt . . . good.

And it could only help her if others were speaking about her in a complimentary way to the men.

Mr. Wade stayed out of her way, at least until dinner. The rain had begun in the late afternoon, and by the evening, the house felt warm and muggy, with all the doors and windows closed. The ladies fanned themselves after dinner, and more than one man tugged at his cravat.

Usually, Susanna would have sat by herself with a book, earning her mother's disapproving frown. It was simply . . . easier, for she never knew what to say—especially to men. But that had to change.

Marshaling her courage to speak to the bachelors, she started off with Mr. Evans, increasing her pace to reach him just as Mr. Wade came toward her.

Mr. Evans's eyes widened as she skidded to a stop beside him. "Good evening, Miss Leland," he said.

She thought he was hiding a smile at her behavior; but if he believed her eager to converse with him, it could only help. "Good evening, Mr. Evans. I was so pleased to see you here when I arrived. It seems we seldom have a moment together at Madingley Court."

Mr. Wade began a circuit about the room, watching her, even as he was called over by various guests.

"I have not attended festivities as much as I used to," Mr. Evans was saying. "My estate has required most of my attention."

She wondered if that also had something to do with embarrassment because he'd courted her brother Matthew's widow only to discover Matthew wasn't really dead.

"That is very dedicated of you, Mr. Evans," she said, telling herself she could admire such a man.

A strained silence fell between them. She hated talking about the weather—the most mundane but somehow obligatory of topics—but would resort to it if necessary, especially since Mr. Wade seemed to be laughing at her.

She turned her back on him. "What do your fields produce, Mr. Evans?"

He seemed relieved to launch into the details of grain and drought, and she listened with an interest she didn't have to feign. She *liked* hearing about people's passions, even if they weren't her own. It was simply that most of Society preferred to discuss—Society: gossip, balls, and who was at whose dinner. She didn't care about those things, and her lack of suitable response always sent people hurrying away as quickly as they could.

When his words at last trailed off, she expected him to reciprocate, to ask something about her, but instead, he glanced at his watch on its chain absently.

She was boring him, and she'd barely said a word. But she'd always been told a man *liked* talking about himself.

And there was Mr. Wade, arms spread on the back of a sofa, Lady May and Miss Randolph sitting on either side of him as if tucked beneath his wings. They looked at him with an awe that their hovering parents didn't appreciate if the frowns exchanged between husbands and wives were any indication.

Mr. Evans tugged at his cravat.

"It's a bit warm tonight," Susanna said, cursing herself for falling back on the weather. "But I imagine your crops will appreciate the rain."

"Yes."

Perhaps he thought he knew everything about her—perhaps every man did. She was different, removed from the ordinary, little caring about gossip. And she'd always liked it that way.

Until her brother had made her see that even though she'd always have a place to live, she'd be forever on the outside of his small family, or Rebecca's, once they all started having children.

"Do you like children, Mr. Evans?" The words came out of her without intention, sounding too wistful—too desperate.

He cleared his throat. " 'Course I do."

She smiled nervously. "I do, too."

He was polite enough not to flee immediately, but he soon claimed a farmer's early bedtime and retired for the night.

And Mr. Wade was watching, an eyebrow raised.

That was enough humiliation for one night, she thought, thanking her hostess for the lovely evening and taking a candle from a footman in the hall to find her way to her bed.

But in the entrance hall, she could still hear the wind and rain lashing at the windows, at the front door of the mansion. And she wasn't tired. Instead of ascending one side of the curved double staircase, she went straight, through the long central corridor of the house, to the two-story conservatory that framed the back of the house in iron and glass. Globe lamps hung along several of the paths, illuminating trees that touched the very top of the glass ceiling and disappeared as if into the darkness of night. Walking forward, feeling the wetness of fern leaves brushing her arms, she could see the rain running in rivulets down the glass, but nothing beyond, with the world in darkness.

"Do you like storms?"

She whirled about, almost dropping her candle. Mr. Wade blocked her path. His dark clothing seemed to fade into the background, leaving his face and hair lit with the golden glow of light. His eyes, ever amused, studied her.

"It is impolite to sneak up on a woman," she scolded, trying to hide the way he'd set her heart pounding.

"I was not sneaking. I could even hear the shells crunch under my feet along the path."

"Well, I could only hear the storm. And what if someone saw you following me?"

"They didn't."

"I am alone—you should not be here." But oh the excitement of it surprised her, called to her.

"Other girls have female relatives at these house parties, to make sure they're tucked in safe each night. But not you."

"That is how I'm different—I'm not a young girl. I'm far too mature—"

"And on the shelf?"

"—to be held to such strict standards," she finished, trying not to smile. "There are enough married and widowed ladies about to see to any chaperoning necessary."

"But none of them are here right now," he murmured, taking another step toward her.

The candlelight gleamed in his hair, shadowed his cheekbones. He looked teasing and dangerous all at once—it played with her nerves, setting off a tremble deep in her stomach as if he fingered the strings of a violin. She'd never experienced the like of it before.

"We didn't finish our conversation," Mr. Wade said.

"There is nothing left to talk about," she answered calmly. "I posed for a painting, but you cannot prove it to your friends."

"Not yet," he agreed pleasantly. "But I will. Until then, we can talk."

She knew he would attempt to use her words against her, but she doubted he could. Let him try to confuse her with the pretty phrases he used on gullible, green girls fresh from the schoolroom. She had asked about him before leaving London—he was not a gifted scholar, lacked even the will to be interested in his finances. But he always had plenty of coin. Did his brother give him an allowance?

In a low voice, he said, "When I first saw the painting, I came to a complete stop, unable to move."

She took a deep breath and let it out slowly. His words and the gravelly timbre of his voice had an unsettling effect on her in the shadowy dampness of the conservatory.

"There were many men as stunned as I, of course, for the painting was a new attraction. But there you were, reclining above us all, your skin golden with candlelight against a black background."

She swallowed, surprised to notice the tightness in her chest, the way she felt too warm even though the storm beyond chilled the conservatory, letting in drafts that seemed to swirl beneath her skirts.

"With your head arched back as if in ecstasy, I could not see your features. And there was that scarf, twisting about you."

The warmth seemed to pool deep into her stomach, even between her thighs. His voice wove a spell that made her feel . . . sinful.

He was closer now, his smile gone, those dimples hidden, his green eyes as watchful as the deep forest.

He didn't know anything about her—he didn't know the truth.

She smiled. "Was that speech supposed to sway me? 'Oh yes, Mr. Wade, I'll tell you everything.' Then you wasted your time and your performance."

"I wasn't performing."

She laughed softly. "But you thought your pretty words would convince me to fall at your feet and offer proof for you to win that wager."

He grinned and reached to briefly cup her cheek. "No, this is merely the beginning battle in our little war, sweet Susanna."

She let herself briefly experience the warmth of his hand before stepping back playfully. "Then you should retreat, general. Better yet—surrender."

He laughed, hands on his hips, watching her as if she'd pleased him tonight instead of refusing to succumb to his obvious ploys.

"I won't be the one surrendering," he assured her. "I'll seduce the truth from you. And you'll give me the proof I need to win."

She almost laughed again, for no man had ever attempted to seduce her. But there was something about his confident certainty that intrigued her. "This is your plan? And you didn't even try to keep it a secret, to at least surprise or fool me?" Once she might have thought his plan proved he lacked intelligence, but now she didn't know.

He folded his arms across his chest. "There's no need. As you've already said, you're a woman, Susanna, not a debutante. And according to you, you were daring enough to pose for that painting. I'll look forward to finding out what else you've done— and what you'll do with me."

She nodded in reply to his challenge, feeling another tug of amusement as she brushed by him and left the conservatory.

She was forced to hide her emotions when the maid, Marie, rose from a chair before the bare fireplace.

"Oh, Marie, I hope I did not keep you from Lady Caroline."

"No, miss, she's not even abed yet. She's often the last to sleep when Bramfield Hall is hostin' a party. So I followed you."

Susanna swallowed, feeling like a croquet ball was lodged in her throat. "Excuse me?"

"I was outside the drawing room after delivering a note to Lady Bramfield from the housekeeper," Marie said. "I saw you leave. That handsome Mr. Wade trailed right behind."

Susanna set down the candleholder, and it jittered once against the wood with her unsteady hand. "We simply looked at the rain."

Marie grinned, even as she pushed a wayward curl out of her eyes. "If ye don't mind me bein' so bold, nothin' improper will ever happen until you do something to help yourself."

"I beg your pardon?"

The maid threw open the wardrobe doors. "We can't buy ye new gowns, o' course, but we can fix the ones ye have. Lady Caroline has practically a whole room of ribbons and lace for us to choose from—and these necklines! Did yer ma insist they cover yer chin?"

Susanna gave a snort of laughter—it was turning into the strangest night. "I—I thought her neckline suggestions made me look too—desperate."

And then she laughed openly, falling back on the bed. When she came up on her elbows, the maid was shaking her head, wearing an exasperated smile.

"Oh, Marie, perhaps I need your help."

"I'm glad it didn't take ye much time to admit it, miss. I don't offer to help too many—but I think ye could be special."

Susanna's warm feeling faded a bit as she remembered Mr. Wade's blatant plan of action. He thought she'd be easily swayed, a spinster who would succumb to his well-practiced charms.

"This corset manages to endow my 'special' figure, Marie. Between us, we'll do our best. So show me what you have in mind—but let me make one thing clear. None of this is for Mr. Wade."

Looking skeptical, Marie only said, "Aye, miss."

Chapter 4

The card game went late into the night, to Leo's relief. Sometimes he had trouble sleeping, and it was best if he was totally exhausted before he went to bed. Otherwise, dark, vague dreams disturbed him. He never remembered them, was only left feeling tired and ill at ease and confused. So he did whatever was necessary to avoid them.

He was encouraged that neither Evans nor Keane had played with him before, so their pockets were quickly emptied. He assured them he'd play another night. It always went this way—his demeanor and reputation made every man think he could defeat him in cards. Even when they'd heard otherwise, they assumed his first win could only be a fluke, and next time they'd have him . . .

He grinned to himself as he retired to his rooms. The valet he'd "borrowed" from Swanley was waiting, the tub already filled with steaming water. He soaked, letting his mind wander, full of confidence that the next time would go just as badly for his opponents. He excelled at cards, never had to question himself, could always read the faces watching him, and had an uncanny ability to know what cards would be played.

His brother Simon had taught him to play long ago, he remembered, smiling faintly as he leaned his head against the back of the deep tub. They'd both been so certain that if their father could be distracted in the evenings by playing with them, that their parents' arguments would cease. He, Simon, and their sister Georgiana had come up with many different distractions over the years—games and plays and musicales—and each had only worked temporarily.

And now that Simon was blind, he couldn't play cards anymore, Leo thought, his smile fading. For just a moment, he was back in time a year, standing at his brother's bedside, helpless at the terrible headaches Simon had suffered and his despair when Simon could no longer see.

Though the family had felt altered by the tragedy—their mother's reaction the worst of all—Simon had bravely picked up the threads of his life and even married recently. It was hard to live up to a paragon for a brother, Leo thought dryly, but knew his relationship with his brother was about more than that. He'd spent his life learning to emulate Simon's ease with people, made no secret of his admiration. And it had only increased since Simon's accident.

But once he lay in bed, his thoughts moved in a different direction. The darkness made him think of the black background of that painting—of Susanna. He hadn't minded her amusement as she left the conservatory; she was using it to try to alter an inevitable outcome. His thoughts drifted to the look on her face when he'd described the painting. Her lips had been gently parted, her breath coming too quickly, her eyes wide with interest, and perhaps even arousal. The perfect beginning to his plans. He would woo her with words, with touches, until she could no longer help surrendering.

Susanna awoke at dawn with a start. She was lying in bed, a book facedown across her chest, staring up at the frilly, feminine canopy. The goals she'd been considering for this house party as she fell asleep immediately reemerged in her thoughts.

Eluding Mr. Wade's plan was something she didn't even have to worry about. She would be careful when alone with him. He had not overstepped the bounds of a gentleman in the conservatory—although he'd touched her face. It had been startling, far too pleasant.

But once he was convinced of her ability to resist him, he might grow more desperate. Five hundred pounds was a large sum of money to dangle in a younger son's face.

His words were certainly daring enough. Seduce her, indeed.

With whom did he think he was dealing? She would never succumb to his flattery. She knew the type of woman he preferred; everyone did.

She considered his description of the painting, which had made her feel strangely breathless. She didn't like to imagine men gaping at it. If the women won the wager, no man would look at it again.

Regardless of Mr. Wade and his games, she was determined to become better acquainted with the other eligible men at Bramfield Hall. But just conversing with them during the evening or at meals seemed . . . impractical. Their speech might be just as misleading as any Mr. Wade gave. She had to find out what kind of men they were. Talking to the other guests would help, of course, but she couldn't be too obvious about it. She was looking for an intellectual, a man who shared her interests, one who wouldn't think her work for her father appalling.

So how to find out which man would have the most in common with her? After all, not every man would believe that a woman, even one raised by a professor of anatomy, could threaten her "delicate sensibilities" by sketching dissections.

Her hands still rested on the book across her chest, and it gave her a sudden revelation. The library! Any man she would marry would have to frequent libraries, love reading and educating himself. She would make it a point, once or twice a day, to stop in the Bramfield library and see if she could find a compatible man.

She didn't expect to be lucky enough to find love— she wasn't the sort of woman to inspire that kind of passion in men. But respect and communication and shared interests—those were things she could aspire to in a marriage. Surely there had to be some man out there who would embody such simple requirements.

And she had several men, all at her fingertips for at least a week. It was perfect!

So on her way to breakfast, she ducked her head into the library. There was no one but a maid, cleaning out the coal grate. Susanna smiled at her, inhaled the smell of leather and lemon polish, and, with a shrug, went off to eat before taking her usual walk.

Leo hurried into the breakfast room, but he was already too late. Susanna was long gone. This rising early would be the death of him. He'd stayed up far too late, and his head still ached a bit from the brandy. But he was used to that.

As he ate his breakfast, and the other guests came and went, he resisted the urge to ask if anyone had seen Susanna. Much as he desired answers, he didn't want all the busybodies assuming he planned to marry the woman. He shuddered. Nothing a chap did would be good enough for Susanna Leland. No wonder she was still on the shelf, he thought, remembering the phrase he'd used to her face.

She hadn't blinked.

But perhaps the nights in her arms would be worth it for a future husband, he amended, his lips tilting in a half smile. If she was the model, and that painting hadn't been exaggerated . . . his thoughts drifted into memories of its shadowed beauty, the glow of her breasts, the darkness between her slightly parted thighs. A man would do much for that in his bed each night. He shifted uncomfortably in his chair, wondering why the image held such appeal for him.

He'd seen such paintings before—but none of a respectable woman like Susanna.

He gave a start, then glanced around him. The widow Mrs. Norton was sitting primly beside the widower, old Mr. Johnson. Neither spoke, although she snuck an occasional glance at the man.

At least she wasn't looking at Leo. He didn't want to imagine what his face had looked like as he remembered the painting.

He'd already bedded a model who worked for several of London's finest artists. She hadn't lived up to the beauty of their art—and certainly Susanna gave no indication that she could either. Art was meant to make one think of the highest achievements, and no ordinary woman could capture that.

"Good morning, Mr. Wade!"

He rose to his feet when Mrs. Randolph entered the room. He could see the boots beneath her plain skirts as she walked toward him and knew she was dressed for the outdoors.

"Good morning, Mrs. Randolph. The rain has stopped, I see."

"Perfect for a walk. Perhaps I'll see Miss Leland forging across the hills, as I did yesterday."

Leo only nodded, trying not to appear too interested in Susanna's whereabouts. After he seated himself, she brought her own plate and sat across from him.

"How is your brother, Mr. Wade? Such a tragedy, to lose one's sight in a fall from a horse. I imagine it could happen to many of us, yet the numbers who could flourish as Lord Wade has might be far less."

"It was an adjustment, Mrs. Randolph, but Simon has never been a man who would shirk his duties. Even when barely out of his sickbed, he was overseeing his estates, as well as my grandmother's."

"Must be difficult to be the brother of such a pillar of strength," Mrs. Randolph said with sympathy.

Leo smiled wickedly. "Such a shame he has to put up with me."

She laughed with him, but her gaze remained on him occasionally as she ate.

The men planned to fish for the morning, and Leo didn't decline, letting out a little bit of line for Susanna to become complacent with her supposed ability to elude him. Then, with a little jerk, he'd reel her in later in the day. Usually, the time spent alone with men bothered him the most about house parties, but this time, things were different. He had the anticipation of his next encounter with Susanna.

Early that afternoon, he and the other men joined the ladies on a hilltop that emphasized the beauty of the countryside broken into varied green squares by hedgerows and earthen lanes. An ancient castle rose on a distant hill, the outer walls crumbling but the turrets still pointing to the sky. Pavilions had been erected for protection from the sun, and servants took their catch of fish to fry for the meal. The older couples sat beneath the shade of a pavilion, talking together.

Several tables were piled with fruit and cheeses, as well as bottles of cider, ale, and lemonade. Leo helped himself before strolling toward the ladies.

Blankets were spread near the summit of the hill like an enormous quilt, and they sat about, legs folded demurely beneath them, skirts spread, sketchbooks in their laps.

Susanna was closest to the edge of the hill, but to the side, so as not to block the view of her students. She was gesturing to the distant countryside, but he wasn't really listening. He realized that something seemed . . . different about her. She'd tossed aside her bonnet, and its ribbons trailed in the grass. Her students hadn't followed her example—perhaps they cared more about freckles than she did.

Her hair was in the same severe style, but the breeze had blown a curl or two about her ears—or had such artifice been deliberate? While he was puzzling about that, he realized that he could see her collarbones winging out gently across her shoulders—this was almost a daring revelation of skin compared to her usual style. He found himself staring as if he could see her breasts, and his own behavior amused him.

He'd never found a house party half so entertaining.

Susanna moved among the blankets, examining sketchbooks, praising as well as critiquing. But even she must have been able to tell that her students were beginning to watch the bachelors. At last the art lesson broke up, and the ladies began to rise and make their way toward the pavilions where the men waited, offering to hold plates or drinks while the ladies helped themselves.

When Susanna did not immediately follow, Leo went to her. "Another successful lesson?"

She glanced at him without a blush or evasion of his gaze, which intrigued him.

"I am evaluating the skills they've already acquired," Susanna said, "and trying to bring some of them up to the knowledge of the others."

He removed her sketchbook from beneath her arm before she had a chance to grip it tighter. "May I take a look?"

"Would you respect my wishes if I decline?" she asked dryly.

"Probably not. Although I will make quite the show of it, so no one will suspect my dastardly rudeness."

From the light in her dark eyes, he thought perhaps she was repressing a smile. Ah, success.

He opened the sketchbook, and his own smile faded as he paged through, staring in surprise at her brief representations of Bramfield Hall, from the drawing room during a candlelit evening, to Bramfield's dogs sleeping in the sun by the orchard, to the distant track and smoke of a train heading north through the Hertfordshire countryside. She was exceptionally talented.

And then there were people—only parts of them, really. Page after page of hands and heads, expressions and poses, the fall of a young lady's unbound hair, a gentleman's thighs as he rode his horse.

Leo arched an eyebrow at her upon seeing the latter, but she only put her hands on her hips.

"That isn't you," she said mildly.

"Perhaps you're imagining me."

She rolled her eyes.

"Don't look so annoyed with me," he said. "Others might think we're having a lovers' quarrel."

"They'll think no such thing. They'll assume a woman such as myself has little toleration for men like you."

"Men like me?" he said, hand to his chest in practiced astonishment.

"You like to flirt, Mr. Wade, and everyone knows it. Your attention will only inspire sympathy for me—perhaps even from other gentlemen." She paused, head cocked in thought. "So maybe you have your uses," she added slowly.

Wickedly, Leo thought in surprise. He deepened his voice as he said, "I have many uses to a woman."

She studied him, eyes half-closed. "Yes, perhaps I could use your insistence on cornering me to my advantage."

"How will this help you?" he asked, amused.

"Sympathy, of course, perhaps even the curiosity of wondering what you find so attractive about me."

"I'm glad you think so highly of yourself." He chuckled. "So you have a purpose here, besides trying to escape London?"

"I always have a purpose, Mr. Wade, and this time, it is typical of my sex. I am here to meet suitable gentlemen."

"The fact that you admit it is refreshing."

"Why? Do you not think a woman of my age

should still imagine herself marriageable? I do have compelling connections, of course, and my dowry is not insignificant. I've put my mind to finding companionship. Mr. Frobisher accompanied me on my walk today, and he always finds a good topic to discuss."

"Companionship? What an interesting choice of words." It was difficult to imagine Frobisher letting Susanna carry her side of any conversation.

"Marriage is a partnership, and two people must suit as companions, with the same interests and expectations."

"You make marriage sound deadly dull," he said.

"Perhaps to someone like you, who needs to be entertained every moment of the day." Her brown eyes sparkled.

"And night," he added, giving her his special grin. He liked that she wasn't leery of him. "But as for *needing* to be entertained, I think you mistake me. I enjoy being entertained, and I am happy to reciprocate. I spent much of my life entertaining my family, so it's only natural that now it's my turn to enjoy myself."

She looked at him too closely, as if reading something in his words. "Entertaining your family? What a peculiar way to put your childhood, Mr. Wade."

"It's the truth. As you know me better, you'll see I don't make a habit of lying. You'll soon know me well, I promise." He offered his arm before she could say anything more. "Shall we partake of the feast? I'll make sure to save the choicest fish for you."

* * *

The Misses Norton and Randolph monopolized Mr. Wade's attention during the picnic luncheon, while Susanna ate contentedly of her roast-beef slices and pigeon pie, topping it off with jam puffs and iced lemonade. She idly listened to Lord Keane drone on about the future of the railways. The topic actually interested her, but he spoke with such superiority, as if with his investments, he had created the railway boom himself.

But just because he thought highly of himself, she didn't rule him out as a possible suitor—not that she could make him take interest in her, of course. And he hadn't truly given her a second glance, but that didn't daunt her. Most men treated her that way. The point of this party was to show them that there was more to her than they thought.

"Lord Keane," she called, "I understand your enthusiasm for the railways. It is obvious they will improve both industry and people's lives."

He turned his head and looked at her with his dark blue eyes. "Of course, Miss Leland."

She heard the faintest patronization in his tone, but ignored it. "Yet they need to put more thought to standardizing all the tracks, so passengers forced to travel different railways don't have to get off one train, then ride a carriage across town to the next."

He exchanged a smile with Lord Greenwich, who regarded her fondly, as if her sweet attempt to keep up with their quick minds was endearing.

"A narrow gauge will be standardized this year," Lord Greenwich said.

Lord Keane nodded to her. "I see you read your newspaper, Miss Leland. I don't usually meet such ladies."

She resisted the urge to stiffen, overcome with the feeling that he didn't find her quest for knowledge an admirable trait. But he could be taught a different way. "As I grew up, our large family dinner table was always full of spirited conversation about the world, Lord Keane. I enjoy such discussions."

Lords Greenwich and Keane nodded to her, and both looked behind them to something Mr. Randolph said. Susanna didn't catch their words, but saw Mr. Wade watching her, an enigmatic smile on his face. Rather than sit there feeling equal parts annoyed at them and at herself, she saw elderly Mr. Johnson struggle to his feet.

She rose quickly. "Mr. Johnson, I find myself in need of a walk. Will you join me?"

His wrinkled face further creased with a smile. "By all means, Miss Leland. The legs stiffen when one doesn't use them."

Though the other men ignored her, she felt Mr. Wade's stare as if he touched her. Constantly being under the weight of a man's stare was a new experience for her, and it was surprisingly pleasant.

She chatted with Mr. Johnson about the fine weather, his newest bull, and the flowers his gardener had just planted. She caught a glimpse of shy Mr. Tyler through the trees, kneeling at the edge of the stream as if he were trying to get a closer look at something. But she couldn't even work up much curiosity because she found herself wondering what Mr. Wade thought of her interest in the railways.

Or did she simply not want to be embarrassed in front of him? What a novel idea.

At last Mr. Johnson asked her to bring him a chair by the edge of the woods, so he could sit in peace—she thought he might actually want a brief nap. She returned to the picnic alone, meandering slowly, not at all as enthusiastic as she'd been that morn. Several of the young ladies were picking wildflowers, while the older ladies looked on in maternal contentment from the pavilion. She leaned against a tree, not quite ready to go back. Puffs of clouds floated above the expanse of farm fields laid out beneath her. She heard the older gentlemen discussing horse breeding, while the younger—

"—the painting at our club," Lord Swanley said behind her.

She froze, her fingers digging into the tree at her back, afraid to move.

Which was silly. The men had no idea of her connection to the painting. They'd be embarrassed if they realized she heard their discussion. But she remained still, hoped even a breeze didn't swirl her skirts.

"The nude painting?" Mr. Frobisher said, his voice positively gushing. "I saw it, too. Remarkable!"

"They say the model is a woman of Society." Lord Keane sounded almost bored.

Susanna stiffened, the rough bark of the tree digging into her back.

And then she heard Mr. Wade laugh, and she closed her eyes. She hadn't realized he was there—would he unthinkingly give away her secret?

"Perhaps you're only amused, Wade, because you haven't seen the portrait," Lord Keane continued dryly.

"Oh, no, I've seen it."

"Every man should," Mr. Frobisher said with a happy sigh.

Susanna gritted her teeth, her shoulders tense with worry.

"But a lady of Society?" Mr. Wade said. "Anyone who would believe that does not understand how a club earns its money. They want you to gawk and trade inspired guesses, all while you buy their drinks. It's surely a lie."

She let out her breath with surprised relief. Mr. Wade had actually deflected interest, as if he were . . . defending her.

Or defending his own side in a wager, she reminded herself. But in that moment, she felt too grateful to care about his motives.

"Why must it be a lie?" Lord Swanley asked with curiosity. "Not all young ladies are saints. Some give a man far more than he's expecting."

They all laughed. Such men would never imagine there might be other reasons a woman might be so desperate.

"Trust me," Mr. Wade said. "It's only advertising, nothing more."

Someone clapped hands, and Lady Bramfield called, "Let us walk farther. Have any of you seen our famous local ruins? A Roman temple, surely."

Voices rose in a chorus of excited agreement, and Susanna stepped around the tree, only coming to a stop because Mr. Wade blocked her way.

He was watching her with interest, those green eyes assessing, then held out his arm. "You are not so inclined to see the remains today, Miss Leland?" he asked softly.

She straightened her shoulders and placed her hand on his forearm. "Whatever would give you that idea, Mr. Wade?"

"Perhaps you heard something distressing."

There was no sympathy in his voice or demeanor, and she appreciated that.

"No, Mr. Wade, nothing unexpected, anyway. Men are a vulgar species."

"We're an entirely different species?"

"It sometimes feels that way, yes."

"But two separate species can never mate," he said, his face too obviously affronted. "How would we bear it?"

She willed herself not to blush, knowing that she was too old for such a reaction to the intimate topic. "So you know about classifying creatures by species?"

He blinked at her. "Classifying by species? I do not know what you mean."

She studied him with narrowed eyes. He was behaving too innocently, and she did not know him well enough to interpret. "Species are grouped together because of certain likenesses. But I know not all of you men are alike. And certainly the male members of my family do not mind a lively intellectual conversation. There must be other men of similar bent."

He grinned. "You are not walking with one. Have you written Keane off your list of eligible gentlemen?"

She glanced ahead, where most of the guests led. Lord Keane was escorting Lady May, and her trilling laugh probably could have been heard from the next parish.

"Not yet. Some men hide their true selves from other men."

"But not me."

"Why did I know you would say that?"

He laughed.

"So are you qualified to give advice on every man here?" she asked.

"I might be, but you won't need to return the favor. I already know the type of woman I want—though I am too young to be in a hurry to marry."

"How lucky for you. Do describe her for me."

"She'll be accomplished, of course, in every feminine art."

"I'm shocked that your first word wasn't 'beautiful.'"

"I am not so shallow."

She gave a slight cough of disbelief. "I think you simply know what to say to me." Which led her to deduce he could read people, at least down to a certain level. While that might impress her, she shouldn't be surprised. Anyone who could still move among Society after some of the outrages he'd committed—bringing women of the demimonde to a duke's ball!—had to be able to tell just how far outside the boundaries he could go. "Then do explain what sort of feminine arts a man such as yourself prefers."

"Serving tea, of course. She must have the steadiest hand."

She bit her lip to keep from laughing at him. Mr. Wade was used to being amusing—she didn't want to make it so easy for him. She did admit to surprise at how easily he had a response to everything she said, sometimes entertaining, sometimes intriguing. She wouldn't have guessed it of him.

He helped her to step up and over a fallen log on the hillside, and the imprint of his hand on her arm seemed to remain far too long. Shaking her head, she returned her focus to their conversation.

Perhaps he was being honest with her. Serving tea was certainly a necessary talent in a well-bred young lady. Susanna usually spilled hers because she was always thinking about something else.

"She should have a tasteful eye for fashion and be able to shop for hours," he continued.

"Shop for hours? Most men would shudder at such an expenditure."

He shrugged. "I enjoy seeing a woman well adorned."

"Another way we differ, Mr. Wade."

He looked at her face, then his gaze slid slowly down her body. When she stumbled over a tree root, he caught her arm.

"I would not be so sure, Miss Leland. Look at how you've garbed yourself today."

"You're not serious, sir. This gown is at least three years old."

"The horror."

She laughed. "It is a sensible style that is simple and classic."

"Hmm."

"Yet you noticed it," she said slyly, glancing sideways at him.

"How could I not? It is such an improvement." He dropped his voice. "But perhaps I prefer you in nothing at all."

She looked ahead again to keep herself from tripping the rest of the way down the hill. "I did say you were a vulgar species."

"An honest one—and you yourself do not deny what you've done."

"You're taking the conversation away from our topic, Mr. Wade. How will I ever learn the skills I need to emphasize?"

"Sarcasm? It does not become you."

"But it's so true. I can cut out silhouettes, you know," she whispered as if in confidence. "And I can embroider the alphabet in many different ways. I paste shells in picture frames."

"Don't speak too loudly. Not every woman has your artistic gifts and would be jealous."

"But that is the sort of woman you want, isn't it? You want her to be occupied with frivolous things."

"Don't forget gossip—I enjoy it immensely."

"I believe you do if I've heard correctly."

To her surprise, something flickered deep in his eyes, before he masked it.

"People are always talking about me," he said flippantly.

"And you *like* that?" she asked in astonishment.

"On the whole, it's favorable. And I'm usually invited to the best parties."

"But not all, Mr. Wade. Why is that?"

"Perhaps because I'm a second son?"

"Or perhaps your reputation precedes you."

He shrugged. "It never concerns me one way or the other. I am exceedingly fond of my life."

"You forgot one other attribute for your perfect wife—youth."

He arched a brow at her.

"Only a very young woman, fresh from the schoolroom, without any experience of life, would fit your requirements."

"I am not interested in a lady too young," he said, shaking his head.

"But you flirt with every young lady here!"

"Flirting serves many purposes, only one of which leads to a wife."

"And the rest lead to mistresses?" she asked, intrigued.

"Flirting is barely necessary for that." He grinned at her. "But flirting gives a debutante some excitement, when all she usually knows is her mother's firm hand. Don't we all need a little taste of danger, the chance to take a risk, even if it is only flirting with a wicked gentleman?"

Taking a risk—it was as if he could read her mind. "So you would never harm an innocent young lady?"

"Not deliberately, no. Does that appease you, Susanna? Perhaps ease my way into your good graces?"

"Perhaps," was all she offered.

They walked in silence the rest of the way down the hill, along a faint path through tall grass. It wasn't until they reached the bottom and swung left to follow it around that she saw the crumbling piles of tall stone that were too orderly to be random, still held upright by ancient mortar. She heard many of the guests gasp with delight.

To her surprise, Mr. Wade's arm stiffened beneath her hand. She glanced up at him, but he only smiled at her before returning his focus to Lord Bramfield. Her gaze lingered on Mr. Wade for a moment in curiosity, for something seemed . . . different about him.

"You all know we are not far from the town of St. Albans," Lord Bramfield began, rocking back on his heels as he regarded them all. "The Romans called it Veralumium. They left behind many towns like it when they fled Britain. Just last year, the St. Albans and Hertfordshire Architectural and Archaeological Society was founded to promote interest in local history and research."

"Is someone overseeing how they define 'interest'?" Mr. Wade asked.

Susanna stared up at him. She wasn't alone in her surprise, as several of the women whispered to each other, and Lord Keane rolled his eyes.

Lord Bramfield studied Mr. Wade, seeming to take no offense. "Your meaning, Mr. Wade?"

"I've heard that many wish to repair and update old buildings, and there's a debate about how much interference should be allowed before it alters the work of past craftsmen."

Lord Bramfield slowly smiled. "You're correct, Mr. Wade. The Society was formed to ensure adequate discussion before any work is done. We must protect the treasures of our past. I am glad to see you are interested."

Mr. Wade shrugged. "Not interested, exactly. I merely overheard a conversation at my club."

Lord Bramfield briefly frowned before turning back to his curious audience. Whether they were curious about relics—or Mr. Wade—Susanna didn't quite know.

"The scientists studying in St. Albans," Lord Bramfield continued, "tell me that our Roman wall here might have been part of an outpost leading toward Veralumium from Londinium. If you come closer, you can see the small remains of a mosaic floor."

Part of the wall had a flattened section, and letters were carved into it. As people rushed forward to look at the mosaic, Susanna held back, trying to make out the Latin words, which used all capital letters and no punctuation, and had also suffered the ravages of time.

She turned to Mr. Wade for help, only to find him staring off into the distance. "Mr. Wade, have you suddenly lost interest? Romans were here before our natives barely had their own writings."

He glanced at her, wearing his charming smile. "The present matters the most, living life, enjoying oneself."

"Now you sound very focused on yourself."

"Trust me," Mr. Wade said, "I know how to focus on a lady."

Now that no one was watching him, his glance traveled with heated slowness down her body.

"But the past influenced the present," she insisted, ignoring his innuendoes. "I thought you understood that a moment ago." For some reason, she felt he was deliberately distracting her.

"But why should I care? I'll leave it to the dusty scholars while I concentrate on the present—which I'm certain those Romans did."

"And their society collapsed."

"And you're comparing that to our wondrous British empire?" he asked, spreading his arms wide.

"How can you not even want to know what ancient men wrote? I can make out 'For the Emperor Titus Cae'—I think it must be 'Caesar'—then 'Vesp-' something, and 'son of' . . ."

Mr. Wade shrugged. "Simon did much of my schoolwork for me."

She stared at him as disappointment suffused her. She'd been foolish to consider even for a moment that he was something other than what he always portrayed.

Mr. Wade gave her a bow, then walked away, joining the group at the wall, to the delight of Miss Randolph, who took his arm. Her mother looked pleased, until Lady Greenwich whispered something to her. Gossip, surely—which Mr. Wade professed to love. Maybe even about himself.

Chapter 5

~~~∽∽~~~

At dinner, Leo studied Susanna from the far end of the table. Lady Bramfield had very pointedly seated him between Mrs. Norton and Lady Greenwich, rather than the young ladies. He didn't mind. The older women tended to speak to the dinner partners on their other sides, leaving him free to annoy Susanna with his gaze.

And it wasn't all that difficult to focus on her while still pretending to watch the other young ladies. Her maid had obviously done something new with her hair. It was caught up high on her head, with artful auburn curls strategically positioned as if they were about to tumble free. It made her neck seem elegantly long, graceful, as she turned to smile at something Swanley said.

And no spectacles in sight, much as he knew she kept them on her person at all times.

And then there was the gown—no striped taffeta or embroidered silk for Susanna. But the green satin was rich and evocative, simple enough to highlight the form within it. Yet the bodice was cut low and square, beneath her shoulders, with simple fabric flowers trimming the edge. Hiding the lack of deep cleavage, he guessed, but what she showed was quite delectable enough.

And then, of course, he thought of the painting, where she lay on her back and exposed each gentle slope.

If it was truly her—and he had his doubts.

She never looked at him during dinner, not once, and he knew she was still annoyed with him.

Hell, he was annoyed with himself. Why had he conversed with Bramfield about Roman antiquities, of all things? He'd drawn Susanna's curiosity, but not in the way he wished. A simple seduction was not going as he'd planned, and he felt a bit frustrated that his usual smooth efforts seemed ineffectual.

But . . . wasn't that what made this pursuit so unlike any of the others he'd engaged in in the past? That was the true challenge—that he didn't know exactly how to get to Susanna, how to seduce such an unconventional woman. Gifts and pretty words would never do.

Later, when they gathered in a larger drawing room, the rugs had been rolled back and a quartet brought in to entertain. The ladies were excited by the thought of dancing, especially the young ones. Chandeliers gleamed with candles overhead, and the French windows were thrown open for the night breeze.

He saw Susanna standing beside Lady Caroline, and her enthusiasm was not as evident, especially when Keane swept Lady Caroline away in the dance.

Leo had decided to let Susanna wait, wondering what he meant to do. But no man approached her. Tyler wasn't even all that far away, but he was looking out the window, as if he could see something spectacular in the dark, damn the man. Every young lady but Susanna was dancing, and Leo found himself bowing before her.

"Miss Leland, would you care to dance?"

She snapped open a fan and regarded him over it. "The waltz has already begun, sir."

"Then we'll join."

He took her hand, leaving the fan to dangle from her wrist as he pulled her into his arms. Within two steps, she trod on his foot.

"I know you can dance better than this," he said.

"Not when I'm nervous." She avoided his gaze.

"Why would you be nervous? It's simply *me*."

"Again."

"What does that mean?" He swept her through a tight corner, maneuvering her between two slower couples.

"We spend too much time together, Mr. Wade. People are paying attention to that."

"You mean certain men."

"No, I mean everyone," she said calmly. "Whatever you think you're doing with me, it isn't working. You risk upsetting me. Why would I want to tell you anything in such a state that might compromise myself?"

"And how will I coerce you to tell me anything, if I *don't* make you upset?"

Her laughter was almost a groan. "Can you not go play cards, like some of the other men?"

"I'll retire to that eventually. Just remember that a waltz shows off your form to the gentlemen present. It's a chance for them to watch you without appearing impolite."

She shot him a startled glance, then looked away. He remained silent, trusting in the dance itself to ease her qualms. As she relaxed, they moved more easily together. He had imagined most bluestockings as uncoordinated, another good reason for them to remain with their studies. But Susanna put a lie to that reasoning.

"You're allowing me to lead," he said at last.

She blinked up at him, chocolate eyes studying him. "I am supposed to."

"I thought you would resist being led."

"It's a dance, not an insurrection—should I define the word for you?"

He grinned. "I seem to recall asking you to spell a word for me that night at my club."

"You were teasing me during a stressful time. I did not take well to it."

When the dance ended, she curtsied to him. "This is all the homage you'll get from me, Mr. Wade," she said softly, before walking away.

He chuckled, and went to do his duty with another partner. He'd never considered it a duty before to have an awed young thing in his arms, but tonight he felt . . . impatient. He thought of Julian and Peter and wondered at the methods they were using to coerce the truth about the painting out of two reluctant women. It wasn't the money that was important to Leo, nor defeating two very worthy opponents. He'd used both of those goals at first, a way to combat his growing, confusing restlessness. But somehow this challenge had become all about Susanna, understanding her, defeating her—winning her. Having her was growing more important than the wager, than even the truth.

Susanna stood near the open windows, letting the breeze cool her damp skin. She'd danced more this night than she had at crushes of two hundred people. Though pleasantly tired, she felt satisfied with her performance. She'd danced with every man there, even Mr. Tyler—when he was practically forced by his hostess—who could only stammer about the weather and looked past her shoulder rather than into her eyes. Perhaps he was trying not to stare into her cleavage, but she was only deluding herself.

Lord Swanley brought her champagne, and she sipped it gratefully, looking up into his eyes so far above her.

"Thank you, my lord. You are rescuing a lady in distress." Was she actually *flirting* now, she thought, feeling her cheeks redden with heat. Rebecca would be stunned!

Though she smiled at the viscount, inside a lump

seemed to lodge in her throat. She didn't remember the last time she'd spent even a few days apart from her sister. Though they were dissimilar in temperament and dreams and so many other things, they shared the fierce bond of sisterhood. What would Rebecca think of how Susanna was opening herself up to the chance of suitors? Their cousin Elizabeth Cabot would be proud since she thought only marriage could give a woman fulfillment.

But Rebecca? No, Rebecca had been ready for adventure for a long time, and the wager over the painting seemed to give her a new purpose. But Susanna always knew that Rebecca would someday find a husband to love her. Susanna knew Rebecca wanted the same for her.

Of course, Susanna wasn't a success yet since no man but Mr. Wade spent an inordinate amount of time with her, but she wasn't expecting a sudden thunderclap of love.

"You look pensive," Lord Swanley said. "Would it be impolite to ask what you're thinking?"

What a refreshing change—a gentleman who considered her feelings. She looked up at him from beneath her lashes—wasn't that how Elizabeth told her to do it? "That your parents are wonderful hosts to bring in music and make this such a special evening."

He nodded, grinning down at her, his black hair falling across his forehead. "They do enjoy a party. And now that my sister is of age, it gives them even more reason to introduce her—"

"And to introduce you?" she interrupted, smiling.

He laughed. "Yes, and me, to other young people in a more personal setting."

"Lord Swanley, I do believe you must have no problem yourself in that regard."

He cleared his throat and looked abashed—she found him just adorable.

"I am not so much a fool that I believe my charming personality alone makes me attractive to young ladies," he said wryly. "I am heir to a marquisate, and there are some who care more for that than anything else."

"I understand," she murmured, taking another sip of champagne. "I am cousin to a duke. It is an inducement to some."

He nodded. "So I've decided to leave it up to my parents."

She coughed for a moment, covering her mouth. "Excuse me?"

"Since I can never fully trust a lady's motives, I've decided that they have my best interests at heart. I'm certain whoever they choose will make me perfectly happy—make both of our families happy. And until then, I'm free to enjoy my youth without the pressure of looking for a suitable match."

"How very wise," she murmured.

What he said was true of many people, of course, both men and women, who often had no choice in their marriage. But usually these beleaguered souls . . . struggled a bit against their fate. Not Lord Swanley, she thought ruefully. She couldn't imagine so blindly accepting another's choice. This was *her* life—she would have her say.

When he bowed and took his leave, promising another dance later, she watched him go, feeling melancholy. She wasn't sure that such a man actually had a will of his own.

Or perhaps he just hadn't met a woman worth fighting for, she told herself.

"Miss Leland, I trust you're enjoying yourself?"

Susanna turned to find Lord Greenwich standing beside her, offering another glass of champagne. Strangely, hers was empty, so she gladly accepted.

"The evening is lovely, my lord," she said, knowing it the truth even if she only meant the weather.

"I saw you speaking with Swanley. A good man," Lord Greenwich said.

"I didn't know him well before this house party, but I'd have to agree with you."

"Concentrate on someone like him—not Wade."

Jolted, Susanna took another sip of champagne and raised wide, innocent eyes to the earl. "Mr. Wade? Why would you mention—"

"Miss Leland, you are an innocent. Wade is paying too much attention to you."

"But . . . is that not what a young lady wants, a suitor?"

"Wade is no one's idea of a suitor," he said darkly.

"Why, my lord? I have heard rumors, of course, but that is gossip. How can one tell what is true or not?"

"What is true is that involvement with him can harm a young lady's reputation."

He must have seen something in her face because he quickly added, "Not that anyone believes so of you, Miss Leland."

She calmed her suddenly racing heart. It wouldn't do for people to think she and Mr. Wade were an item.

"I am speaking of another young lady altogether," Lord Greenwich insisted.

"Just one in particular? And you're saying this is not a rumor?"

He looked about as if for eavesdroppers, then lowered his voice. "One young lady was a flirtatious girl, given to dancing and socializing, but not in an inappropriate manner—until she was caught up with Mr. Wade. She spent too much time in his company. *Alone,*" he emphasized. "Soon she was regarded as fast, her reputation quite ruined. And once it was discovered that her dowry was insubstantial, she had nothing else to recommend her."

Susanna swallowed. "So she is unmarried still?" *A spinster like me,* she thought.

"Ahem," he said, looking down to his toes. "No, she was lucky enough to find a man who married her, regardless of her . . . situation."

"Oh."

"But not before she had to lower herself by working as a companion to an elderly lady," he added, frowning.

"Thank you so much for your words of caution,

Lord Greenwich," she said solemnly. "Have no fear. I know what kind of man Mr. Wade is."

"Excellent. I was worried that a woman of your . . ." He trailed off, his face reddening.

She tilted her head, tempted to make him explain. Her age? Her bluestocking proclivities? But she resisted the impulse, saying, "My unmarried situation?"

"Yes, yes, I was simply worried that an innocent woman such as yourself wouldn't understand a man like Wade."

"Thank you for your concern, my lord, since my own father is not here to advise me."

"Do give the professor my regards," he said, bowing before leaving her.

Susanna took another glass of champagne from a passing waiter. She was feeling warm and a bit giddy, and although she knew it was the alcohol, she didn't mind. Lord Greenwich wasn't telling her anything she hadn't heard whispered about, but the fact that he knew an actual woman so harmed by Mr. Wade was troubling. Did the man really care so little for whom he might hurt? Had he been lying when he told her he didn't harm debutantes? Or was this young woman older—and presumably wiser—and that was how he'd justified his behavior? Her gaze searched him out and saw him standing near Miss Norton, smiling down at her in that rakish way of his.

Just like he smiled at Susanna. But she would not be easily misled. They played a game between them, and she found herself too eager to win.

She turned away and went to the window. The moon was full, a small cloud scudding through the dark sky near its bright surface.

"Susanna?"

She turned to Caroline with a smile.

"You've been much in demand," Caroline said.

Susanna leaned her shoulder against the window frame. "It is an unusual feeling. I tend to prefer being the wallflower."

"I remember. But not anymore?"

"I promised my brother I would do my best to find a husband," she said quietly, then took another sip of champagne. "Oh, he is not insisting—he wants my happiness. I do as well, for I was never one to meekly obey my brother."

Caroline laughed.

Wearing a rueful smile, Susanna said, "It is much harder than I imagined, trying to be what a man might want, especially at my age."

Caroline nodded. "I think it's that way for most women."

"Some days I simply want to retreat into my art and think of nothing but light and shadow and how best to represent what I feel in my soul."

"Beautifully said," Caroline murmured, regarding her thoughtfully. Then she glanced over her shoulder at her parents, who were talking to the Randolphs. "What about tonight?"

Susanna straightened. "What do you mean?"

"You spoke to us about capturing a night scene when you sketch or paint—why not tonight?" Caroline hiccuped just as she tried to take a sip of champagne, then covered her mouth on a giggle.

Susanna found herself wanting to giggle, too. "You and I would sneak away?"

"No, no, we'll wait until everyone is abed, then you and I and the rest of the girls will meet in the . . . where would it be best to sketch at night?"

Susanna felt invigorated at the thought of being daring yet still doing what she loved. "The gallery! There are high windows there to let in the moonlight—although we'll still have candles, of course—and there are statues that we can draw."

"As if we're sketching people," Caroline breathed. "It always seemed so . . . intrusive to sketch actual people. I can't imagine how it must feel when an artist has a model—unclothed!" She laughed a bit too loudly, and some of her champagne splattered to the floor.

Susanna took the glass from her hand. "Don't drink any more, or you might fall asleep before we can meet. How should we tell the other girls?"

In the end, their secret was passed from lady to lady during the dance, and by the time the house seemed settled, Susanna's feelings of reckless daring were still running high. And the look on Marie's face when she hadn't wanted her gown unhooked—the maid thought Susanna had an exciting assignation with a man, and she'd regretted having to disabuse the woman of that notion. Marie had been disappointed.

Holding her sketching supplies under one arm and a candle with the other hand, Susanna crept toward the front of the house. She was right in front of Caroline's door when it opened, and both of them gasped and backed up, their candles flickering wildly. Covering their mouths against giggles, eyes shining in the soft light, they gestured with their heads toward the front of the house. Susanna followed in her friend's wake, pleasantly surprised at Caroline's daring. She'd been worried everyone might have second thoughts.

The gallery was above the ground floor, spanning the width of the house, and during the day, held a magnificent view of the countryside. At night, moonlight streamed through the tall windows, casting strange shadows among the sculptures and vases on display. Giant paintings were crowded together on almost every wall, but their subjects were vague in the darkness.

To Susanna's surprise, Miss Norton rushed forward from where she'd been perched on a sofa in the darkness.

Caroline gasped, and her candle went out. As she relit hers from Susanna's candle, she said, "Aurelia, there's no need to startle us!"

"You startled me!" her cousin cried, looking furtively over her shoulder. "I knew I should have met you in your bedroom. Mama's chamber connects with mine!"

"You're here now," Susanna said calmly. "Let us find a place to work while we await the others."

By the time Miss Randolph and Lady May joined them, they'd settled on several sofas grouped together near a statue prominent under moonlight.

"We'll pretend it is an actual person," Susanna said, walking about the white marble statue. It was of a young man, garbed in the loose, sleeveless tunic of ancient Rome, his well-muscled arms hanging fluidly at his side, his head turned as if he heard someone in the distance.

Miss Norton giggled. "I used to pretend he was real, Caroline. Did you know that?"

"You always were fanciful," Caroline said fondly.

Lady May, wearing a plain gown far different from her eveningwear, circled the statue right along with Susanna, then ran her hand down the arm. "If only he *were* real."

Susanna kept her amusement to herself. She'd spent many years sketching the real thing, but it was not something she could share with proper young ladies. Her own family didn't even like discussing her work. It wasn't as if the men were *alive* when she sketched them!

"Ladies, take up your sketchbooks. Let us see if you can make the white of this marble shine against a dark background, yet still with a softness, a paleness that seems to hover in the darkness."

"You're a poet, too," Caroline said.

The other three ladies laughed softly, and Susanna felt strangely included. It was a comfortable feeling, since only her family had ever been able to make her feel that way. She'd attended many house parties, of course, but had always spent her time with her sister or cousin. Perhaps she'd missed out on the chance for women friends not related to her.

Their silence was companionable for long minutes, except for the occasional question directed at Susanna. The darkness seemed to recede, the moonlight brighten, until the statue was the only beacon in the night.

"Ladies?"

The male voice made several of them gasp, and Miss Randolph even dropped her sketchbook with a clatter. Susanna wondered if Mr. Wade had been lingering in the dark watching them. It made her skin tingle just imagining it, and she found herself suddenly eager for the unfolding scene.

"Mr. Wade," Caroline said, rising as if she greeted him during a morning call. "Did we disturb you?"

He came forward out of the darkness, his hair gilded by the white moonlight. Susanna knew she was not the only one to notice that his cravat was tossed over his shoulder instead of tight about his neck, his collar buttons opened to see the smooth line of his throat, his Adam's apple, and even the faint depression at the base of his neck. Much more skin than a lady was used to seeing. Though his eyes gleamed, she thought there was a trace of weariness there.

"No, I have not yet retired," Mr. Wade said, grinning. "We gentlemen are in another wing playing cards and billiards, and wouldn't have heard you all escaping your rooms for the night."

"We are not escaping," Susanna said lightly. "We are sketching a night scene."

He walked closer until he stood even with the statue. He was taller by half a head, but the curling hair could have been the same.

"So you are sketching this?" he asked, eyeing it, then the ladies.

They clutched their sketchbooks to their chests in shared embarrassment, as if caught doing something indecent.

Lady May gave a drunken giggle. "We have been sketching statues our whole lives. I think we should use a living person as a model."

Every eye went wide. Susanna stared around her, looking for affront and instead seeing their intrigue. "Ladies, many of us sketch people."

"But not someone like Mr. Wade," Lady May continued. "Would you pose for us, sir?"

Susanna opened her mouth, uncertain what her duty was as the eldest—and most sensible—lady present, but Mr. Wade spoke first.

"Only if you truly believe I could help further your education," he said with sincerity.

Caroline's gaze collided with Susanna's. Perhaps she saw the double meaning in Mr. Wade's words as well.

He rested his forearm on the shoulder of the statue. "I do believe I can hold very still. It will be a lark, will it not?"

Lady May giggled again. "Let us have a new subject to draw, Miss Leland. There is no harm."

She could have reminded them what might befall them if their parents discovered this night lesson, but lately, she wasn't the sensible one at every occasion. And she liked the feeling. Their eyes were alive with excitement—and truly, what was the harm?

"Very well," she said.

Mr. Wade just watched her, that ever-present smile gleaming. She never forgot the wager—he never allowed her to forget, what with his constant presence. His deeper plan was to seduce her secrets from her, or so he'd boldly said. She lifted her chin in answering challenge as she watched him. How this helped him, she didn't know, but was curious to find out.

Mr. Wade rubbed his hands together. "What should I do?"

All four women stared at Susanna silently.

"Since we already began with the statue standing," she said, "we'll keep that for the theme tonight. Stand just at the edge of the window, partially in the light, partially out."

He did as she instructed. "I just stand here?"

"What a shame we don't have a book for you to read."

"There's a book on a lower shelf just past the fireplace," Caroline said. "The bookend is an antique. Otherwise, it would be in the library. Shall I fetch it?"

Soon Mr. Wade was holding the open book in one hand. "I'm reading in the moonlight?" he said with faint sarcasm he directed Susanna's way.

She gave a pleased smile. "It will give the ladies

more to draw, especially where your hands and arms are concerned. Shall we begin? Remember, we will not have time for a detailed study—not if we wish to arise before noon."

Miss Randolph snorted, then covered her mouth with embarrassment.

"This exercise is more about his form in darkness, how the shadows are different at night. Don't spend all your time on his face or hands; we simply want an impression of the lines of his body."

Lady May whispered something to Miss Norton, and they both started to giggle.

Susanna took her seat on the long sofa beside Caroline. "Ladies, begin. And no talking, Mr. Wade. I know that is difficult for you, but we need to concentrate."

There was more smothered laughter, but Mr. Wade genially shrugged, then focused on the book he held in one hand. Susanna didn't think he'd last long, but when she next glanced at the clock she'd brought from the mantel nearby, three-quarters of an hour had passed.

"Mr. Wade, I have been impressed with your silence," she said. "Have we made you regret your generous offer?"

"Not at all."

"We could give the poor man a few minutes' rest," Caroline said, smiling at Susanna.

"Excellent idea," Mr. Wade said quickly, lowering the book. "Ladies, let me see what you've done."

Susanna watched as he seated himself on the floor

before the sofa. For the next few minutes, he looked through their sketchbooks, praising and smiling and flirting. Caroline went to fetch him water, which he gratefully sipped.

How was this helping him? Or perhaps he simply enjoyed female adoration.

At last, Susanna said, "Let us do one more session, Mr. Wade, then we will allow you to escape us."

"I'm not trying to escape, Miss Leland. This has been most informative."

She called a halt not all that much later, seeing her students hiding the occasional yawn. Mr. Wade looked as if he could stand still, flexing his arm, all night. Looking down his body one last time, she had to admit to herself that he was in superb physical shape.

She helped the women gather up their pencils and sketchbooks, and all took their leave of Mr. Wade as a group. It wasn't until she reached the corridor of their bedrooms that she realized she hadn't picked up her own sketchbook.

She returned to the gallery alone, peered in—

And found him sprawled on the sofa, her open sketchbook in his hand. He waved at her as if he'd been waiting patiently.

She walked across the gallery and held out her hand. "My book, please, Mr. Wade."

He studied the rendition of himself. "You're talented, Susanna."

"Thank you," she said. "My book, please."

"It must have been easier for Roger Eastfield

to paint you," he said quietly. "He had oils at his command."

She looked over her shoulder, feeling a surge of uneasiness. "Everything begins with a sketch. Please hand me my book."

"But his black background looked so nuanced."

"Because the paint was a mixture of different colors, not just black." She stepped closer until she stood above him. "Mr. Wade, my book please. Do not make me take it from you."

His eyes widened with feigned innocence, the green gleaming catlike in the shadows. "Can you? I would be most impressed."

He slid it beneath his thigh, then shrugged out of his black evening coat. His shirt was light gray in the shadows, his waistcoat striped black and red. To her surprise, he turned and lay back on the sofa, crossing his legs at the ankle atop the far armrest.

He smoothed his hands along the fabric of the sofa. "When you *supposedly* posed for that painting, did you lie on something as exquisite as this, Susanna? What did it feel like against your bare skin?"

She pushed away the images his words evoked, knowing that they were too dangerous so late at night, with no one about.

"Show me how you posed," he said, not smiling, though the usual spark of amusement still touched his eyes. "I believe I should lift my arms—"

"I am surprised you dare tease me," she interrupted. "You know nothing about me or what I've done—"

"But I want to hear every detail."

It was one thing to play a game with him, another to take too many risks that would damage her reputation. She gripped his arm and tried to draw him upright. Suddenly he grasped her by the upper arms, pulling her off her feet until she sprawled across his chest, her knees brushing the carpeted floor.

She gaped at him, their faces so close she could feel his warmth—or was that the warmth of his torso, pressed against hers clear down to her waist? She could actually sense the quickened thump of his heart against her ribs and knew that her pulse pounded an answering rhythm.

She felt all hot and tingling and *aware*; she was so very aware of an ache in her breasts, a trembling in her limbs, and how her mouth seemed parched because her lips were parted with her frantic breathing. Without thinking, she licked them, and saw an answering flare of interest in his narrowed eyes.

"Ah, you know just what to do to a man, Susanna," he murmured.

He pulled her closer while she tried to lean away. "Mr. Wade, I only know that you need to release me. This is—"

He lifted his head to kiss her. She had only a brief impression of soft, warm lips, a moment to think, *A man is kissing me!* before common sense had her turning her head away.

"Mr. Wade!"

"Leo," he murmured.

She gasped as he nuzzled behind her ear, then

began a trail of kisses down her neck. His lips were softer than she'd imagined, moist, tempting.

"How is this seduction if I'm resisting?" she demanded, hearing the tremble in her voice.

He dropped his head back against the pillows and looked up at her. "Truly? You're resisting?"

"Yes, although you may be unused to the reaction."

When he released her arms, she rose to her feet and pulled her sketchbook out from under him.

With his usual smooth grace, he sat up and swung his legs to the floor, then patted his thighs. "Perhaps if you sit down in my lap, we can discuss our differences."

Shaking her head at his daring, she made for the door at a brisk pace.

"Coward," he called after her.

His laughter lingered in her mind until she reached her bedroom. Though she was still trembling at the unaccustomed sensations—and resolved to be more wary of her own reactions toward him—she felt a sense of triumph. He had thought such crude methods would work on her—and now he knew he was mistaken. Perhaps he would give up and return to London.

But she didn't want him to.

Chapter 6

The next day, as the men began an early-morning outing through the fog-dotted lanes of the estate, Leo managed to ride beside his host even as he fought the dull tension of a headache from another restless night's sleep.

He mentioned the Roman remains, surprised he was bringing them up, especially after he'd tried to convince Susanna his interest was only momentary. But he couldn't seem to stop thinking about them afterward. Bramfield didn't know much, only that his ancestors had always known about the wall although someone had only found the mosaic in his father's time.

"Have you let other archaeology societies have a crack at them," Leo asked, "since the Hertfordshire group is preoccupied?"

Bramfield's horse danced sideways as several other horses raced past with their riders and out into a pasture. "They've looked but are deferring to the local society. Right now they're focused on St. Albans, where there is much more for them to do.

They asked for my promise that they could work here eventually, and I gave it. No harm, eh? But if you're interested, I own a book written about the work they're doing nearby, and they included some sketches of my antiquities. I'll find it for you."

"That's not necess—"

"No trouble at all, Wade. Not too many men have an interest, but it's our past."

Bramfield sounded like Susanna. Leo kept his mouth shut, not knowing why he'd opened it in the first place. The Roman remains had made him feel . . . uneasy, and he didn't like it. He hoped simply mentioning it to Bramfield would get the thoughts out of his mind, but now his host believed him intrigued.

He was only interested in one thing here—and she was proving more of a challenge than he'd thought.

As he rode along, the faint mist coating his hat and shoulders, he found himself remembering the evening sketching lesson. He'd been inspired to hold on to her sketchbook, and been rewarded when she'd returned. He'd barely kissed her, hadn't even parted her lips. It should have made him laugh, his urgency to kiss a bluestocking like Susanna. But he wasn't laughing—he could still smell the lemon scent of her hair, feel the soft roundness of her breasts. And the way he'd fumbled the seduction! He should be more bothered at his own ineptitude, but he wasn't. Susanna was too different, nothing like the other women he'd seduced. His normal methods simply didn't work.

And she'd been just as affected, he remembered with satisfaction. He wanted to taste her, and his urgency had nothing to do with a painting.

It was . . . altogether strange.

But she wasn't so affected that she lingered with him—no, she'd fled from him and her passion as fast as she could. That was telling. She desired him, but she didn't want to.

After an early-morning walk—and pleasantly, Caroline had accompanied Susanna—the mist had turned to a steady rain, and the house party retreated indoors. As all the ladies gathered in the drawing room to write letters or read before luncheon, Susanna went off to the library. The men were changing after their morning ride—surely some of them might stop in the library for a rainy day's entertainment. And she would be waiting for them, writing her own letters.

She chose a desk near a window, for the overcast sky still let in enough light. After making herself comfortable in a leather chair, she began with her mother, who would want to know every detail of the guest list, the food, and the entertainment. Susanna obliged her like a good daughter.

With Elizabeth, Susanna could only be circumspect, in case one of their mothers asked to read it. She used some of the details of the house party, and asked subtle questions about who was still in London, and was anyone paying close attention to her. Rebecca's was an easier letter to write since she was visiting their aunt in the Lake District. Great-Aunt Rianette would hardly demand to read her niece's letter—her eyesight was bad enough that Rebecca might be asked to read aloud, and she could pick and choose what to say. Susanna was just about to quiz Rebecca about the Earl of Parkhurst's pursuit when she heard steps in the corridor.

She tried not to tense with excitement—more than one servant had walked past in the time she'd been there. But these were confident, masculine footfalls. Removing her spectacles, she made certain she wasn't hunched over the letter, that her head was gently tilted, that her expression was pleasant but not too intent—

And then Mr. Wade paused in the doorway and grinned at her.

She relaxed back in the chair. "Can you not leave me alone for even part of a day?" And what man would enter when he saw her already speaking with Mr. Wade?

He walked toward her, and she found herself watching the way his arms swung, the confidence in his step—but this was how she looked at the world, she reminded herself. She'd always been curious about how things moved, how she could capture that with her pen or brush.

Like she captured lips, she thought, staring at his.

"You ladies are the ones who set the deadline," Mr. Wade chided, sitting on the edge of the desk, his hip close to her arm.

She deliberately remained where she was. "You

have a month. Surely that gives me time to breathe."

"Ah, but is that by weeks? That means only twenty-eight days, and eight of them are already gone." He leaned over her. "Winning matters, Susanna. You want to win, after all."

"But not for the sake of winning, or for money."

"You have your prize; I have mine." His smile faded a bit as he leisurely studied her face. "You didn't give me a chance to talk with you last night after the dance."

"You didn't have talking on your mind," she whispered, glancing at the open doorway.

"True, but I'm talking now. When you weren't dancing, I thought you looked pensive, and now here you are, writing letters. Whom do you miss so much, Susanna? It's only been a few days since you left London."

He took the letter she was working on. Grabbing at it would only tear it. "Once again, I'm asking you to return to me what's mine," she said patiently. "That is private correspondence with my sister."

He lowered the letter to rest across his thigh. "So you miss her? I don't know her well at all. I do believe she did not socialize much until the last few years."

"She was ill much of her life."

"I'm sorry to hear that. That must have been difficult for you."

"For me?" she echoed in disbelief. "I'm not the one who almost died."

"But when one child is ill, surely parents fear that

others will succumb as well. Overprotectiveness would be understood."

"Speaking from experience?"

He smiled. "No, my mother let me do anything I wanted."

"I assumed that from your spoiled behavior."

"Did your mother watch over you even more closely because of your sister?"

He wasn't going to leave; she could see that now. She preferred not to be seen alone with him by a possible scholarly suitor. Rising to her feet, she gathered her papers and started to step around him. He took her elbow.

"I called you a coward last night," he said quietly. "And here you are, even in the light of day, retreating. I'm beginning to think I hold such an attraction for you that you fear losing control."

She met his gaze thoughtfully. "You may think I forget the wager, but I don't. I don't need to answer your questions, Mr. Wade."

"Leo," he said again.

"I cannot address you so familiarly. Please release my arm."

"If I do so, will you tell me about your sister and cousin and this bond you share? There are not many who would risk their own reputations for another."

"You believe the worst of people, Mr. Wade."

"In exchange, I'll tell you about my friendship with Julian and Peter."

She hesitated, then could see the growing triumph

in his gaze. If she might learn something that could help Rebecca and Elizabeth thwart the other two men, how could she refuse?

"I have you now," he said, letting go of her arm. "Go ahead, sit back down."

She did as he asked. Much as he was charming, she knew she could steer this conversation the way she wanted to.

"So if I answer questions, you answer questions," she said.

"Agreed. And since I asked first, you have to answer first. Tell me about your relationship with your sister."

"She is seven years younger than I. Naturally, I felt protective, especially when she began to take ill." Briefly, she looked toward the window, adding in a strained voice, "You have no idea what it feels like to watch a child strain to breathe, to wonder if she'll live to see the morning when you promised her you'd read to her again." She glanced at him, almost embarrassed by such a display of emotion.

He wasn't smiling now but nodded with understanding. "I know something of such helplessness, if only because I watched my brother suffer agonizing headaches before he went blind. But that's not the same as wondering if death is hovering that night."

Keeping her lips pressed together, she nodded, admitting reluctantly, "But this makes you understand my love for my sister."

"Men don't admit to love each other," he said, lightening his voice. "We offer admiration and respect."

She almost smiled at anyone offering him such but couldn't be so cruel. "So you admire and respect your brother?"

"Of course I do."

"No envy? There are many who would feel thus."

He shook his head. "The family title is in far better hands with Simon. He cares about each of us—even our mother—and makes our lives easier where he can."

With an allowance? she wondered, but would never ask. "He takes care of your sister, too. I have met her. She is . . . quite unlike you."

He grinned. "I believe you think that a compliment."

She grinned back. "Isn't it?"

"Not according to our mother." He seemed to regret the words, for his smile faded a bit, and he looked away.

She said nothing, amused to find herself hoping he'd continue, telling herself she was only curious because he'd made himself her opponent.

"You've said your mother allowed you free rein," she said at last. "But not your sister?"

"Georgiana is not like me or Simon. There is a . . . reserve to her, a fragileness. It took her a long time to maneuver among the shoals of Society. I did not help matters."

"You mean your reputation?"

"No, it started long before that. Once Simon was gone, I turned all of my pranks on Georgie."

Susanna winced.

"She was such an easy target."

She arched a brow.

"Do not believe I did anything terribly unkind," he insisted. "She hated spiders, and I made sure they found her. Little-boy pranks."

"And yet pranks turned into concern for her happiness."

He shrugged as if a discussion of feelings made him uncomfortable. He was like all men in that way. Yet . . . not all men cared about their siblings as he obviously did.

"I've always liked your sister," Susanna said.

He smiled. "Why am I not surprised?"

"I hear she is engaged."

His smile broadened. "She is, to a neighbor of ours who consorted with Simon and me and treated Georgie like his own sister. And when that stopped, no one was more surprised than I."

She found herself sharing laughter.

"So you, too, spent much of your childhood indoors amusing your sister," he said.

"An accurate deduction, Mr. Wade. Should I spell 'deduction' for you?" she asked sweetly.

Other men would take offense, but not he. He flashed his dimples at her. "No need. Your closeness to your sister is obvious, especially with what you do for each other. But your cousin?"

"Elizabeth is closer to my sister in age, more proper than either of us—and more popular, as well, being the daughter of a duke. She has always borne scandal well, as you must certainly know, since you love gossip."

"She has come under the knife of scandal?" he asked, frowning. "Before this painting?"

"No, but all of our parents have."

"How?"

"Now, now, Mr. Wade, the fact that you don't know such juicy details amazes me—and is not my concern. I promised to tell you of my sister and cousin, not our parents. Elizabeth had her childhood rebellions, but she matured into a wise and lovely lady."

"Before you mixed her up in this painting—according to you, that is."

"No longer believing that I'm the model?" she asked. "Even better."

He sank deeper into the wingback chair, crossing his legs leisurely before him. He was not a man given to proper etiquette, but then she knew that.

"But why would each of you say you were the model?" Mr. Wade asked, studying her closely.

"Because we swore a vow to protect each other," she said simply. "It's very simple, really. When we thought my brother dead—surely you've heard of my brother's miraculous return from India?"

"I have," he said.

"Well, when we thought he was dead, I felt . . . even more protective toward Rebecca and Elizabeth. We'd all been devastated by the tragedy. Family was important, and we only had each other, so we each swore we'd defend the others, no matter what."

"And so you're all the model since it has to be one of you," he said slowly.

"Brilliant, I know."

"It's a shame I can't remember who claimed it first."

"You were a drunkard that night—you even proposed the wager. I'm surprised you remember anything."

"I was barely inebriated."

She put her hand to her chest and fluttered her eyelashes. "Another big word! I am so impressed."

He laughed.

"So now it's your turn. How did you meet Lord Parkhurst and Peter?"

"Peter?" he echoed curiously. "I knew he grew up near the ducal seat, but you are on such personal terms as to use his Christian name?"

She willed herself not to blush. "Childhood friends usually are. But you were saying . . . ?"

He hesitated, and she steeled herself to lie if necessary. The foolish mistakes of her past were none of his business.

But he only smiled and shook his head. "I can find out your secrets when I want to, so I'll be fair and answer your questions. I went to school with Julian until his father withdrew him because they hadn't the money."

"I remember something of that," she murmured, frowning. "Lord Parkhurst resurrected the earldom."

"He did."

The pride in his voice showed that at least Mr.

Wade respected his friends' accomplishments and didn't only think about himself.

"But if he was tutored at home, how did you see him?" she continued.

"I invited him for holidays."

Though his words were simple, Susanna guessed that the young earl must have felt grateful to Mr. Wade to be a part of the world he could no longer afford. She knew most others would ignore such a family. Mr. Wade's kindness reluctantly impressed her.

"And Peter?" she asked. "I don't remember you visiting him in Cambridgeshire."

"No, our friendship is more recent, through Julian. Julian advised Peter on railway investing, and since many of their discussions occurred at our club, I became friends with Peter."

"What a shame their discussions surely went over your head."

He grinned at her. "What do I care about investing in railways? I have a man of business who handles everything for me."

At least he was smart enough to hire someone competent to be in charge. So many younger sons went through their money far too quickly. Or perhaps Lord Wade insisted that Mr. Wade have help.

"You're lucky they tolerate you," she said dryly.

"I'm handy to have around. I know all the women."

She knew she blushed because he laughed at her.

"Respectable women, of course," he amended. "You surely didn't think otherwise."

"You don't want to know what I think of you, Mr. Wade," she teased, rising to her feet.

He did the same, and she was disconcerted at how much taller than she he was. His shoulders seemed too wide for an indolent rake, and the distance she wanted to feel for him did not encompass the trembling sensation his nearness evoked.

He looked down at her, his smile lopsided. "But I know what you think of my kiss," he murmured.

"That I couldn't escape your advances fast enough?" She tilted her head, studying him.

"You can tell yourself that."

"Believe what you wish," she shot back.

Stepping around him, she came to a halt to see Mr. Tyler standing uncertainly in the doorway. She stiffened, dismayed that at last a man had come to the library, only to find her consorting with Mr. Wade.

And had Mr. Tyler heard them discuss the kiss? But he didn't look outraged or intrigued. Perhaps something could be salvaged. "Good morning, Mr. Tyler," she said cheerfully.

"Good morning, Miss Leland." He glanced at Mr. Wade, using his fingers to push back his unruly brown hair. "Am I interrupting?"

"Not at all," she said. "Mr. Wade was simply lost, and I was giving him directions to the conservatory."

Mr. Wade paused, then nodded. "Thank you, Miss Leland. I'll see you both at luncheon."

He left, and for all she knew, he lingered in the corridor to eavesdrop. She didn't care.

Mr. Tyler had stepped inside to allow Mr. Wade to pass, but now still seemed to hesitate.

Susanna spread her letters across the desk and sat down. "This is the quietest place to write. Did you come looking for a good book to pass the rainy day? Please don't let me stop you."

He nodded and turned to a wall of floor-to-ceiling shelves. She pretended to write as she watched him surreptitiously. He spent long minutes moving slowly from shelf to shelf.

"Looking for something in particular?" she asked. "I've already explored the library—one of my favorite places. Perhaps I could help?"

He smiled a bit nervously, showing one slightly crooked tooth that made him look sweet rather than overly amused. She could hardly let herself be so nervous if he was.

"Lord Bramfield said he had quite the collection of books on the naturalists' study of Hertfordshire," Mr. Tyler said. "Not very interesting, I know, but—"

"It sounds fascinating to me, but then I'm an artist." She took a deep breath, embarrassed by how eager she sounded. "I draw everything I can find, and nature has abundant subjects for my work." She smiled. "You must have enjoyed the antiquities yesterday."

He walked closer to her desk. "I did, but perhaps not for the reason you might think. I noticed a rare flower nearby, and I had to study it. The Latin classification would bore you, so I won't bother."

"I would never be bored by such a topic, Mr. Tyler. Do you conduct research?"

His eyes widened, and she noticed that they were as bright blue as a sunny sky.

"That is not a question a young lady ever asks me."

"My father is a professor at Cambridge, sir. I know much of research." But it would not do, at such an early moment in their acquaintance, for her to mention *how* much she knew.

"I had heard that and forgotten," he said, sitting down where Mr. Wade had just been.

It was refreshing to be treated as an intellectual equal. Mr. Tyler watched her as if he couldn't wait to hear what she said next.

Pleasure and happiness washed through her, as if the sun had parted the clouds. They discussed his passion for botany, the research he was doing, his laboratory. More and more, Susanna found herself thinking that at last she'd found a man she could respect and admire. Her library strategy had worked!

Leo stood in the deserted hall and listened with amusement to Susanna's breathless, eager responses to Tyler's description of his microscope. He knew she never spoke like that to him, but that was just fine. He wasn't interested in her mind anyway. If the way she looked at him was any indication, she wasn't interested in *his* mind either. All the better.

There was much he could do to encourage such carnal interest.

But not that night. He and the other young men rode to the nearby village tavern and enjoyed rousing company that included several young women who flirted shamelessly. Leo didn't take them up on their unsubtle offers, but more than one of the men did. Leo contented himself with winning at cards, which required only half of his concentration. All the while part of his mind dwelled on his plans for Susanna.

The next afternoon, it took some time for him to find her, for she'd left the main party, and he couldn't openly ask about her without encouraging the rumors Susanna abhorred. Luckily, a servant knew she'd packed a picnic lunch and gone off by herself to the Roman remains with her watercolors. When he saw her in the distance, she'd set up an easel, had a palette in one hand and a brush in the other. She was wearing yellow and white stripes, with tiny little yellow flowers embroidered down each white stripe. Who was this fashionable woman? he thought with amusement. His amusement faded as he studied her small waist, and the shoulders that so effortlessly moved as she worked her brush across the Bristol board.

Shoulders weren't usually what he thought about when he admired a woman's beauty, he reminded himself.

He moved silently through the grass and was able to see much of her painting before she even heard him. Once again, he was surprised to find the emotions her work could evoke in him, a yearning for the past that he knew he didn't really feel. Though there was no one in sight, she'd put a man in her painting, roughed out yet, but with an indolent posture. Even as he neared, she was working on the details of his blond curls.

"That's me," he said aloud, delighted.

She cried out, dropping the brush, and juggling her palette as she spun to face him. "Why would you sneak up on me that way?" she demanded.

"Why would you put me in your painting?"

She lifted her chin. "It is not you."

"That's my hair, and I do believe the posture mirrors my own. I had no idea you were studying me so well," he added, coming even closer and setting his hand on her waist.

She backed away from him. "No touching, Mr. Wade. Leave me be."

"I don't think you want me to, Susanna, not if you're putting me in your watercolors. Perhaps the kiss we shared has given you fanciful notions."

"Stay away—oh very well, go stand by the remains, then! Make yourself useful, unlike the other men at Bramfield Hall. They emerged from their bedrooms far too late this morn." She squinted at him. "You don't look the worse for wear as some of them do."

Grinning, he made a sweeping bow. "Dissipation is an acquired art." It wasn't until he neared the remains that once again, a faint coldness seemed to come over him, as if a dark shadow began a slow climb up his body.

He was being a fool. Taking a deep breath, he faced away from the old wall and concentrated on Susanna. "It is a warm day," he said, shrugging out of his coat and tossing it on a nearby boulder.

She eyed him with faint suspicion.

"I am decently clad in shirt and waistcoat," he protested. He put a hand on the rough stone wall and looked off into the distance. "Am I doing this correctly?"

"Yes. Be quiet."

"Then you need to talk to amuse me. Tell me why you posed for the painting."

She remained behind her easel, invisible as she briefly worked.

When she reappeared to study him, he said, "You didn't answer my question."

She looked at him over her spectacles, eyes twinkling. "It's none of your business."

"Come now, what harm can there be? You keep telling me you're the model, and you seem to want me to believe it true—though as you've already admitted, you're protecting Rebecca and Elizabeth."

"I am the model."

"Then talking about it isn't concrete proof, correct?"

With a heavy sigh, she said, "Very well," and disappeared behind her Bristol board again. Her voice was distant as he heard her say, "I had met the artist, of course, and he persuaded me to sit for him."

"Oh, please, it would take much more than that." With his forearm, he wiped his perspiring brow.

"Really?" she asked, ducking out from behind her work to stare at him. "And you know me so well?"

He paused, considering her words. "You're right.

Before this party, I only knew what I assumed you would be."

"Because I'm not your typical young lady."

"You can call yourself a bluestocking—I won't mind."

"Good of you," she said dryly, and disappeared again.

"I assumed you to be interested in knowledge for its own sake."

"Which I am."

"I'd deduced that from your breathless conversation with Tyler."

When her head reappeared, she was frowning at him. "I knew you'd have the discourtesy to eavesdrop. You'd do anything to win."

"Not quite anything. I didn't force a more passionate kiss on you last night. And don't hide yourself from me. You know it's true."

She looked away, her blush bright in the sunlight. He remembered that she'd blushed the same way when she talked about Peter. And if she'd posed nude for Eastfield . . . perhaps he was underestimating the time she spent alone with men. She said she wasn't a typical lady. Maybe he should believe her capable of much more. And there was that mole on the thigh of the model, high up, almost lost in the shadows. But he'd seen it. Did Susanna Leland have that same mole?

"So *how* did Eastfield persuade you to pose for him? He couldn't have easily imagined a proper Society miss would agree to remove all of her clothing, risking her own ruin."

"We were both artists; he assured me the painting would never be made public. I was taking risks—it appealed to me."

"Were you intimate with him?"

She gasped and stepped out from behind the easel, waving her brush as she spoke. "I would never be so foolish!"

"Perhaps Rebecca would. You said she'd never lived a normal life. Did she want adventure?"

"No, it was me. I was the one captivated by his interest."

"I don't think I believe you. After all, you pushed me away last night. I think you're very concerned with propriety."

"Do not imagine that my rejection of you implies I would reject all men. You know I'm here looking for a man who shares my interests—do you not think Roger Eastfield would be included in that group?"

"Then you take risks," he said slowly.

"I do." She put her nose in the air before disappearing behind her painting.

"I'll remember that."

Though he wanted to continue to confuse Susanna with his questions, the wall at his back radiated an ancient coldness. He found himself a bit too anxious to be done modeling for her and stopped distracting her.

When at last she began to pack away her supplies,

he approached her. "May I see what you've done?"

"If you'd like," she said.

He studied her work, impressed at how she'd captured the beauty of the countryside, the ancient exoticness of the Roman antiquities, even the lines of his body, giving the impression of lazy satisfaction.

But she hadn't given him a face.

He sent her a questioning look.

She shrugged. "I'll finish it someday."

"I'm in no hurry today."

"My hand is tired. Perhaps another time. I'd thank you, but since I didn't ask for your help . . ."

"You just don't want anyone to know I was your model."

"You may think that if you'd like."

But he wasn't really sure what to think.

Chapter 7

To Susanna's surprise, after the impromptu modeling session, Mr. Wade kept his distance for the rest of the day. She was able to go for a leisurely ride before dinner with Mr. Tyler, and although she knew Mr. Wade saw them leaving, he didn't insist on accompanying them.

It would have been an utterly pleasant late afternoon, full of good conversation—and Mr. Tyler was so eager to talk!—except for one thing: thoughts of Mr. Wade.

When he was near her, she had to be so alert, prepared to verbally duel with him. It wasn't the same as her easy conversations with Mr. Tyler; there was an element of danger, of triumph whenever she scored a clever riposte. And she and Mr. Wade were hardly debating intellectual theories!

But then she remembered his discussion of the antiquities with Lord Bramfield, and the way he knew about species classification though he'd turned her curiosity aside. Very puzzling that he seemed far more intelligent than he let on. Why would a man who cared so little what Society thought of him feel it necessary to hide part of himself? And then he'd even protected her reputation against the other men where that painting was concerned.

And Mr. Wade made her so very conscious of her womanhood. It was his lips she looked at, his boldness that moved her. She wanted to put her fingers in his hair as if she could sort all the many colors of dark and light. She liked the way the fabric of his shirt folded at his elbow, allowing a glimpse of the shape of his biceps.

She was weak, just like every other woman he flirted with—drawn to his rakish demeanor and handsome looks. Whatever woman he finally deigned to marry would have no peace of mind. He treated all women the same, and when he grew bored with the marriage . . .

She shuddered, and her horse gave a little dance sideways.

"Miss Leland?" Mr. Tyler said, watching her closely. "Are you catching a chill?"

She realized she'd let her mind drift away from him. Mortified, she smiled, and said, "I guess the sun is beginning to set."

"We should return to dress for dinner," he agreed companionably. "My mother says that one should always follow the host's rules."

He mentioned his mother often, but how could Susanna not respect a dutiful son? She experienced no wild flights of emotion, of yearning—and she liked that. It made her feel comfortable, secure, unlike how crazily her emotions careened when she was with Mr. Wade.

And Mr. Tyler must be interested in her, for that night, he watched her from across the drawing room as they played charades.

Mr. Wade did, too, and it felt totally unreal to have *two* men looking at her. Caroline kept sending her a wide-eyed gaze whenever she thought no one was looking, and Susanna could only shrug. She had both an introverted scientist and a handsome scoundrel following her about—but only one was welcome.

The rest of the men seemed to be discussing Mr. Wade's luck at cards the previous night. Apparently, he'd relieved everyone of their money, and she wondered how much practice such a feat took.

Lady Bramfield and Mrs. Norton kept their heads together as they talked and watched the interest in Susanna. Susanna told herself they were simply jealous their own daughters did not have two gentlemen vying for their attention. Although their daughters were welcome to Leo Wade.

Though Mr. Wade might have a reputation that led some to look down upon him, no one denied his charm or the pleasure of his company as he circled through the guests. While Susanna sat with Miss Norton, both working on their embroidery, Leo paused behind their sofa and bent to look over their shoulders.

Miss Norton poked her finger with a needle and quickly put it to her mouth, eyeing Mr. Wade with wide eyes.

He studied her embroidery with a critical eye. "Miss Norton, lovely colors you've chosen for a pastoral scene. I see you've just begun a rainbow."

While the young lady nodded, Susanna frowned, wondering at Mr. Wade's intent.

"Did you know you have the colors of the rainbow lined up incorrectly?" he asked. "The order is red, orange, yellow, green, blue, indigo, violet."

He had them memorized? Susanna thought in disbelief.

Miss Norton blinked up at him as if stunned. "How do you know this, sir?"

"Besides looking at one displayed across the sky, I've also seen one formed by passing light through a piece of shaped glass."

While Miss Norton made him explain this achievement, Susanna tried not to frown. He must have had a superb governess. Yet she wouldn't have imagined it would be easy to get Mr. Wade to memorize something so useless in a gentleman's daily life.

When the ladies began to sing, Susanna demurred, but she did play several selections for the guests. She did not have a terrible voice, but it had always seemed so uncomfortable to display one's talent before a group of people not one's family.

When she was accepting the applause of the guests, she noticed Mr. Wade step out into the corridor. She thought nothing of it until she saw Miss Randolph looking almost guilty as she left the room, following Mr. Wade.

A planned assignation? Miss Randolph was only

recently come out, and her innocence was a mask for—more innocence, regardless of the way she stared at Mr. Wade with awe when he wasn't looking.

But the girl didn't know what Mr. Wade was like; even her parents seemed to like him, as if they hadn't heard the stories. And somehow, because Miss Randolph was one of her students, Susanna felt a sense of responsibility. Susanna was older, and though far from experienced, she was learning quickly.

And Mr. Wade had insisted he did not harm innocents. She had to make certain that was true.

When Lady May began to sing in her pure, captivating soprano, Susanna was able to slip away from the rapt audience and down the corridor. She'd seen both Mr. Wade and Miss Randolph go left, toward the back of the house—toward the conservatory. Susanna marched there with purpose, determined to stop Mr. Wade from leading the girl on.

But when she stepped foot into the humid warmth of the indoor garden, she saw them almost immediately, on the far side of the fountain. And they were kissing.

Susanna wasn't surprised by his behavior, but by her own dismay. She knew he was hardly courting her—he wanted something from her, a wager, a good time. But it seemed . . . shameful to her to kiss two different women.

But not to him. Obviously, not to him. And he had no problem lying to her about his typical behavior either.

Angry at her own naïveté where he was concerned,

she turned on her heel and walked out. She hadn't gone more than a half dozen paces when she saw Mr. and Mrs. Randolph heading for the conservatory.

Susanna came to a stop, fraught with indecision.

Mr. Wade would be caught at last for his bad behavior.

And poor Miss Randolph might be stuck married to such a cad for life.

"Susanna!" Mrs. Randolph said in her open, friendly voice. "I must say again how talented you are on the piano."

"Thank you, ma'am," Susanna said, trying not to look over her shoulder into the conservatory.

What was she supposed to do? If the Randolphs saw what their daughter was doing, everyone's lives would change irrevocably.

"The creative arts must come easily to you," Mr. Randolph said. "Our daughter compliments your painting talents constantly. We greatly appreciate you taking her under your wing."

That made the decision easy. Susanna turned and walked with them toward the conservatory. As they entered the room, she spoke as loudly as she dared. "There is nothing to thank me for! Miss Randolph is a good girl, with sense and talents of her own."

"We're not certain where she went," Mrs. Randolph said, frowning.

They all looked out over the ferns and trees but saw no one. Susanna's tense shoulders bowed a bit in relief.

"She did say she'd meet us here, Mr. Randolph, didn't she?" his wife asked.

Meet them in the conservatory? Susanna thought, feeling a bit ill. Did that mean Miss Randolph *planned* to be caught in a compromising position with Mr. Wade? Or was she just carried away by his mere presence?

Once Susanna would have scoffed at such a notion, but she didn't feel so superior anymore.

"She wanted to show us something," Mr. Randolph said. He smiled beneath his bushy mustache at Susanna. "She spends hours in our gardens at home."

"Mama?" Miss Randolph appeared on a far path and followed it around the fountain. Brightly, she said, "Isn't it beautiful here?" She turned to Susanna. "Hello, Miss Leland. Are you joining my parents and me for a tour of this lovely garden?"

"No, I simply encountered your parents in the hall." Susanna resisted the urge to look past the girl. Where had Mr. Wade gone? Was he hiding, or was there another door to escape through? At least he hadn't allowed Miss Randolph to be shamed before her family, whatever fool notions the girl might have.

"I'll leave you to your tour," Susanna said. "Good night!"

In the heat and darkness of the summer night, Leo stood on the balcony and stared through the open French doors into Susanna's room. Although the moon spilled onto her carpet, it left her bed a murky shadow in the far corner.

He stepped inside and waited for his eyes to adjust. Susanna was a dim form in a white night-gown, sprawled across the sheets but without a counterpane or blankets in the heat.

She suddenly gasped and sat upright. "Who—Mr. Wade!"

He was used to sneaking into bedrooms and didn't startle easily. She was a blur in the darkness as she grabbed her dressing gown from the foot of the bed and hurriedly donned it. He watched in amusement though his smile faded as she cinched the garment at her waist. Her hips were rounder, more lush than he'd imagined, and he thought again of that painting. As she came into the moonlight, the long braid of her auburn hair fell over her shoulder.

Clutching the dressing gown at her neck, she whispered, "You must leave at once. Didn't your bachelor ways almost end tonight? Why would you risk that again?"

"Ah, so you did know that I was there. Then it's proper that I came to thank you."

"You could have done that tomorrow," she answered with a sigh.

"I couldn't sleep."

"Why—dreams of Miss Randolph?"

"Are you jealous?" he asked, his smile broadening into a grin. This was better than he'd thought.

"Jealous? Perhaps I was leading the Randolphs

right to you." She whirled away from him and went to the door, listening.

"It's long after midnight, Susanna. No one will hear us. And I *know* you weren't leading them to me. I could hear your conversation with them as if you'd shouted. You were warning me."

"I was warning Miss Randolph."

"Perhaps I'm the one who needed to be warned about the innocent Miss Randolph. *She* kissed *me*, not the other way around." He scratched his head. "I was truly stunned. I know you won't believe me . . ." His voice trailed off as he studied her.

She looked away from him, her gaze unfocused. "I—I must confess that I have to believe you."

"I beg your pardon? Why would you believe *me*, of all people?"

"Not used to people having confidence in you, Mr. Wade? How sad for you."

"You can stop the pity and explain how I have not sunk in your estimation."

She sighed. "Her parents told me she asked them to meet her there."

His eyebrows rose. "You don't say? And she told me she followed me because she had to speak to me. Not quite so innocent, is she?"

"Or perhaps she's innocent—and foolish all at the same time. After all, it seems she settled on *you* as a husband."

He smiled and reached to tuck a stray lock of hair behind her ear.

She froze, watching him intently. But she didn't run away.

"Some people think me a good catch," he said.

"Some people consider your relationship to a viscount rather than your own suitability."

He leaned over her. "What do you think, sweet Susanna?" He let his hands rest lightly on her shoulders.

"I think you need to leave."

Her voice sounded breathless, uncertain, and that alone was enough to bring a part of him to complete attention.

"Or perhaps you wish it had been you I was kissing in the conservatory."

Wrong words. She backed away.

"I have experienced your kiss, Mr. Wade, and I would not risk myself for it."

"No? And you are such an expert?" He let his hands run gently down her arms until he could lift both hands before him. Then he turned them over and pressed his mouth to the center of one palm.

He heard her intake of breath, but she didn't tug her hand away. He did the same to the other palm, then met her wide-eyed gaze as he let his tongue touch her.

"What are you doing?" she whispered.

"Tasting you." He trailed his mouth slowly up her arm to her elbow, closer and closer to her body.

"This is madness," she cried softly.

He sucked on the flesh of the inside of her elbow. "Madness," he echoed, his own voice husky.

"You don't want me—you don't want this."

He smiled, placing both her arms on his shoulders. "How do you know what I want? Are you so talented that you read minds?" His hands slid about her waist, using the smallest bit of pressure to see if he could draw her near.

She resisted. "You told me what you want. To defeat your friends."

"Why can we not enjoy ourselves at the same time?"

She opened her mouth, and he put a single finger upon her lips.

"You are no innocent maiden, Susanna—not if you're the woman in that painting."

She turned her head away from his finger. "My art and this—this—" She gestured with her head at the dark room, as if encompassing the intimate scene. "They're not the same."

Yet her arms still rested on his shoulders. He was not so foolish as to point that out. He was enjoying himself, enjoying the surprise of Susanna's boldness.

Maybe she really was the model in that painting. He glanced at the wardrobe, then her trunk in the corner. He wondered what sort of proof he might find. The jewel itself, the one that had nestled between her breasts in the painting?

She was staring up at him, her deep brown eyes mysterious in the darkness. Her smooth skin glowed, even down to the vee of her dressing gown, which had parted beneath her throat now that she wasn't holding it together. She was unbound, no longer any walls of stiff propriety between them. This was a side of her he didn't think she'd allowed any man to see.

Except perhaps Eastfield, he thought, and was surprised to feel the first touch of jealousy.

Had there been other men?

He leaned down toward her until their breaths mingled. She was still staring up at him wide-eyed. He gently pressed her toward him, and this time she came. The surrender of her body touching along the length of his made him inhale sharply. Without a corset, she was all woman, sweetly rounded breasts and a soft stomach made to cushion his erection.

With a soft moan, he captured her mouth. No demure kiss this time. She was willing, and he took advantage, seducing her to part her lips. His tongue swept her mouth, and he felt the trembling of her body. But he didn't stop—couldn't stop. He was hot for the taste of her, the feel of her. He pressed her even closer, urged on when her arms tightened about his neck.

And then she was kissing him back, and the shy touch of her tongue made his head reel. He couldn't tell whether she was inexperienced or only reluctant, but it didn't matter. Their tongues mated, and his hand came up to cup her head, to hold her close. His other hand dropped to her ass, and he cupped her there, feeling the fullness, the femininity. His fingertips brushed her cleft.

She dropped her head back with a gasp, whispering, "You shouldn't—"

Breathing hard, he answered, "Shouldn't . . . what?"

"Touch me like this."

Her trembling was worse, and now he suspected she clutched him so she wouldn't fall.

And although he longed to lift her thigh, to press deeper between her hips, this was not a game to be won by force.

It was harder than he'd imagined to release her, but he did so, stepping away. Her arms slid from about his neck, and she hugged herself.

He ran both hands through his disheveled hair. "You do things to me, Susanna. I'm not certain I like it."

He saw a wince of dismay cross her face.

"Let me make myself clear," he continued. "I'm not certain I like how easy it is for me to forget myself when you're in my arms."

"Now you're lying," she whispered.

"Lying? Did it feel like I was lying? Could you not tell how you aroused me?"

She looked away, and in the moonlit darkness, he swore he could see her blush.

"Just go, Mr. Wade."

"Mr. Wade?" he echoed in disbelief.

"Leo."

She only murmured his name, but he was content. "Thank you again for your help with Miss Randolph."

"Please don't thank me anymore," she insisted, following him to the balcony door.

When he stepped through, she closed and locked it behind him.

* * *

Susanna rested her back against the glass door, eyes closed, hands fisted at her sides. Her lips still tingled from Leo's kiss, and she raised trembling fingers to touch them, feeling their wetness.

Why couldn't she resist him? Why hadn't she insisted he leave immediately? Instead, she'd bantered with him, as if she could use words to change his mind.

Words were too subtle for him. He needed an obvious action to show him the truth.

And instead, she'd let him kiss her.

She groaned, and with a few steps, flung herself across the bed with a melodrama that felt briefly satisfying.

He'd even given her time to refuse—she couldn't blame him for her surrender. And he'd tasted . . . magical, wonderful. Hot and male.

And forbidden. Every young lady was brought up to avoid such intimacy, and she logically understood why. But she'd dismissed logic the moment Leo had touched her. He made her too curious about what he was hiding about himself and why. He'd been tall and shadowy, a dream lover. They'd been in their own world in that moment, as if no one and no concerns existed.

His body had felt so different from hers, hard to her soft. On a clinical level, she certainly knew all of that, knowing the human body as well as she did from the anatomy laboratory.

But . . . *feeling* him against her, alive and urgent,

hot with need, had overwhelmed even her good sense. This dismayed her, made her question her own resolve.

Could he really seduce the truth from her? Would she tell him anything he wanted?

No. She couldn't imagine it even though tonight had shown her a glimpse of her own vulnerability. She would not be carried away the next time.

Chapter 8

The night was hot and muggy, and though she had the windows open, Susanna slept poorly. Dawn had barely broken when she took some cheese and bread, along with her sketchbook, and escaped the house. The air still felt oppressively heavy, and perspiration soon coated her face and dampened her gown until it clung to her uncomfortably. She walked for some time down a country lane until she followed a less-trodden path that ended up on the banks of a tributary of the Colne River.

She was alone, and it looked so inviting. Dipping her hands in, she splashed her face and neck, even unbuttoned her collar to cool more of her skin. Soon, she was barefoot and holding up her skirts as she waded in the delightfully cold water.

After sitting on a log to eat her bread, she opened her sketchbook and began to capture the lovely scene as a memory to flesh out on another day. Trees overhung that spot on the river, sheltering her with peace.

"What a surprise."

She closed her eyes and inhaled deeply. Leo's

husky voice aroused the memories of her dark room, and his body beneath her hands.

"Following me again, are you?" she asked mildly.

She opened her eyes in curiosity as he passed by, his clothes brushing against her.

He was heading for the river, already discarding his coat in the grass. "I had to follow you," he said over his shoulder. "Who else would you draw?"

"The scenery is enough," she insisted.

He unbuttoned his waistcoat and tossed it onto his coat.

"What are you doing?" She felt a surge of curiosity and intrigue—and unwelcome excitement. She reminded herself of her resolve to resist him. They could play these games, and she would remain in control.

He removed his boots and stockings next. His bare feet in the grass looked shockingly intimate though she'd seen a man's feet an untold number of times.

"Other ladies could be out walking," she reminded him. "If you're discovered—"

"You know everyone is still asleep at this ungodly hour. The sun has barely risen."

"Why aren't *you* asleep?"

With his hands at his collar buttons, he paused and met her gaze at last, his smile gone, every line of his body tense. "I couldn't stop thinking about you and that kiss."

She should scoff, but she could only stare at him as he pulled his shirt over his head. He was nude from the waist up, and the beauty of his sculpted body made her mouth go strangely dry. Her fingers itched to capture the ridges of his abdomen on canvas and the shape of his torso as it narrowed to his waist. The hair on his chest was sparse, and his nipples seemed as bare and evocative as if she'd uncovered her own.

And then he turned to wade into the river. Gaping now, she watched the play of his back muscles as he moved into deeper water, then brought his arms above his head to dive beneath the surface. She came to her feet, sketchbook tumbling into the grass.

He broke the surface, tossing back his wet hair as he floated on his back to look at her. "Joining me?" he called.

"Of course not." She was proud that she could answer immediately, when her tongue felt like it might not work properly. "This would be considered indecent by our hosts."

"And you like it. You're dying to put me on paper. So go ahead and do it, I dare you."

But she only watched him swim back and forth, her hands fisted in her skirts, wishing she could join him. Her gown felt sticky with perspiration, and now he would be cool and damp to the touch.

As if she was going to touch him.

She should leave—but knew she wouldn't. With her determination to risk herself to find happiness, it had seemed to call forth a wildness inside her she'd never thought existed. Whenever someone in her family gave in to emotion, to temptation, bad things happened. But she remained still, as if modeling for someone.

At last, he rose to his feet, water sluicing down his

body as he waded toward shore. When he reached the grass, he raised his face to the rising sun and closed his eyes. He looked exotic and male and so very alien to everything she'd ever experienced. The sun sparkled on his wet skin.

Susanna slowly seated herself on the log and picked up her sketchbook. Leo lay down in the grass, crossed his arms behind his head, and closed his eyes. She didn't say a word, only bent her head and began to sketch quickly, longing to capture him before it was too late.

She didn't know how long she worked; time didn't matter. A drop of perspiration rolled between her breasts, a fly buzzed at her ear, but she ignored the distractions. She was obsessed with detailing the vitality of his superb body hidden behind the indolent pose. The whole scene was one of tranquility, but she had to show that he was only briefly at rest, that he might leap to his feet at any moment.

But she didn't work on his face. There were secrets hidden there, behind his mask of geniality.

"I wager Tyler wouldn't be so easy to sketch," Leo said.

She only heard him as if from a distance. At last she raised her head, realizing that her fingers trembled from gripping the pencil so hard.

She blinked at him. "Mr. Tyler?"

He laughed, coming up on one elbow.

She inhaled at the way his arm muscles slid beneath his skin. She was used to seeing muscles unmoving, but his . . .

"Yes, Mr. Tyler," he said, his voice smooth with amusement and satisfaction. "Have you forgotten him already?"

"Of course not. And everything I draw has some degree of difficulty to it. Sometimes it's simply capturing the light correctly. Other times it's an expression in the face. If drawing were easy, everyone would do it."

"So you'd sketch Tyler."

"If he wanted me to, of course I would."

"Then you want to spend more time with him."

She propped her elbow on her knee and her chin on her hand. "I do. We have so much in common. His temperament suits mine. And we have individual interests we enjoy pursuing, as well as sharing with each other. He's simply perfect for me."

"And that's it. In just a couple hours' conversation, your mind is made up."

"Well . . . it isn't that easy, of course. His preferences matter, but—"

"No question of his status in Society, his ability to support you?"

She blinked at him. "I have heard nothing negative. And he's an invited guest here; I'm certain they know his character well. And I find him so easy to talk to, now that he's gotten over his shyness with me."

Leo gave a low chuckle, and she couldn't help but watch the way his torso faintly shook. "That's how I feel with Miss Randolph."

Susanna felt something inside her tighten. "Pardon me? The woman you insist you did not kiss?"

"That's true; I didn't initiate the kiss. But I do enjoy her company."

"She speaks in this . . . breathless voice. Surely you find it annoying?"

"Not at all. I find it flattering, as if she's nervous to talk with me but is overriding her natural shyness."

"Shyness?" she retorted in disbelief. "This is the woman you insist kissed *you*."

"I know. But her eagerness flatters me."

Did Mr. Tyler think *her* eager? Susanna wondered, feeling the first hint of dismay.

"She doesn't demand I amuse her or intrigue her. She simply enjoys my company, a lighthearted story, a flattering exchange."

"So you're saying I demand too much of men?" she said, letting too much of her uneasiness show.

He lay back slowly, hands once again linked behind his head, body graceful in repose, even as he smiled. "I don't think I was discussing you at all."

She heard the satisfaction in his voice, knew she'd betrayed even more of her own insecurities. But he'd betrayed more of himself, too. She made a few half-hearted lines on the paper, then sighed. "We're losing the light and shadows of dawn. It is enough for now. Please dress."

They looked at each other for a long moment. In command of herself, she was able to turn her back and begin to gather her supplies.

Susanna approached the drawing room before luncheon, wondering if the other guests had begun

to gather. To her surprise, Leo was the lone gentleman, surrounded by all the older ladies. Lady Greenwich was laughing at something he said, trying to
hide her amusement behind her hand. Mrs. Norton
stared at him with open fascination. And Leo held
court, looking every inch the satisfied male. It could
reap him no young woman's attention although
it might soften their mothers' opinions. Yet he'd
amused them all, when most young men would flee.
His consideration was another piece of the puzzle
that was Mr. Wade.

At luncheon, Susanna was mollified when Mr.
Tyler arrived with a book he wanted to show her.
She spent a pleasant hour discussing the plants of
Hertfordshire and promised to accompany him to
paint the rare flower he'd mentioned before. She
basked in the glow of his admiration, in his pleasant
companionship.

Unlike the wild moments last night, when she'd
felt overwrought, unlike herself, eager for the embrace of a reckless man.

Mr. Tyler obviously appreciated every discussion they had; Leo didn't know what he was talking
about.

More than one older lady looked on her and Mr.
Tyler with approval, and Susanna knew her family
would feel the same. He was just what she'd been
looking for.

She never once looked at Leo throughout the luncheon. She knew he was taking in her cozy discussion with Mr. Tyler, and she barely stopped herself

from giving him a triumphant smile. She was more concerned about her future, she reminded herself, not this very temporary wager which pitted Leo and her against each other. It would not do to make Mr. Tyler think she shared a connection with a man like Leo.

"When will you next be in London, Mr. Tyler?" she asked. "Certainly there is a botanical demonstration at—"

"Oh, I seldom travel to London, Miss Leland," he interrupted.

"Don't you miss the excitement?" Leo asked, from his place near the end of the table.

To Susanna's dismay, heads turned as people began to pay attention to their discussion. Mr. Tyler looked baffled even as his face reddened with the attention.

"The Season is quite wonderful," Miss Randolph added, her expression worshipful from her place across from Leo.

"I receive all the publications from my peers and the scientists I respect," Mr. Tyler said, clearing his throat afterward as he met the interested gazes of the other guests. "I correspond with many of them to increase my knowledge. Life at my estate and in the nearby village are all that I need."

"I could not agree with you more, Mr. Tyler," Susanna said. "London is hectic and dirty, and rather than inspire my art, only makes me long for the clean air and open spaces of the country."

Leo shook his head. "Then your art is missing

grand inspiration, Miss Leland. How can you say
that the horses and carriages parading through Hyde
Park are not a spectacle worthy of your pencil? The
ladies sparkle like peacocks in their finery, the men
are elegant and attentive."

"Yes, but—"

"Have you been to the Thames on a foggy morning, where the mist hovers over the water and
through the bare yardarms of the ships like the ghost
of memories past?"

She blinked at him, trying not to stare.

"Why, you're a poet, Mr. Wade," Lady May said
with some surprise.

Susanna could almost agree. He spoke with actual
imagery.

He smiled at Lady May before continuing. "All of
you ladies like to draw—how can you not be inspired
by the most powerful city in all the world? Every sort
of person lives there, from the freckled country girl
calling out her fresh strawberries to the man light-
ing gas lamps at dusk. Mudlarks scrounge through
the muck of the Thames at low tide looking for treasures." He looked about at the surprised or curious
faces all around him. "All of them are images, both
good and bad, of our London. Is it not the best place
to experience life?"

"But the air in London isn't fit for some plants, Mr.
Wade," Mr. Tyler said with hesitation and regret in
his voice. "I cannot conduct my experiments there."

Leo glanced at Susanna. She still felt surprised at
his descriptions and experienced a playful need to

contradict him. "And I prefer to paint landscapes and the people who live in the country, from the farmers guiding their oxen through freshly plowed fields, to the miller who grinds our corn, to the girl who works at my village bookshop. I will never run out of things to capture my imagination in the country, Mr. Wade."

He shrugged. "Then I guess we have a difference of opinion, Miss Leland."

"Ah, but you crave excitement," she countered, knowing she should keep her opinions to herself but unable to stop. "Much as you are trying to convince us all of the beauty of London, I think its entertainment is what you need."

She saw Caroline's eyes go wide but didn't think she'd said anything wrong—or untrue.

Leo lounged back in his chair with a laziness that would be slovenly on other men but made her think of energy banked and waiting to erupt.

"We all like to be entertained, Miss Leland," he said, smiling with roguish charm.

"But you especially," she countered. "Are you not content with a peaceful countryside, alone with your thoughts? Or perhaps having no one to talk to makes you nervous."

Out of the corner of her eye, she saw Lord and Lady Bramfield exchange an unreadable look.

"I like to swim," Leo answered, "and throw myself down on the bank to dry off in the sun. Then I enjoy being alone with my thoughts."

There was a murmur among the young ladies as

they twittered and blushed. Though Susanna tensed, she found she didn't fear that he'd reveal what they'd done by the river. He'd gradually revealed to her more honor than she'd guessed he possessed. But he liked to tease, and she could respond in kind.

"Alone with your thoughts? Then that is a rare moment for you, Mr. Wade," she continued amicably. "But it must not satisfy you, for as you say, you prefer the excitement of London. From what I hear, you are a man who is usually in the company of others. I wonder if you truly can be content with a simpler life, where you'd have to find something that would satisfy your intellect. Like Mr. Tyler."

Mr. Tyler reddened even as he gave her a nod.

Leo leaned his forearms on the table. "We cannot all be like Mr. Tyler. If every gentleman were alike, you ladies would be bored."

She leaned toward him as well. "I hope you find comfort in that sentiment, Mr. Wade."

"Well!" Caroline said brightly. "What a lively conversation. I do hope such spirit will carry on to the competition I have planned."

Susanna's eyes still sparked with Leo's, and she had to force herself to look at her friend. It was then she noticed more than one appraising glance her way and realized she had stepped over an invisible boundary. She'd done something unexpected, perhaps even given the other guests something to talk about. She hated being talked about. But she'd done nothing inappropriate.

"Lady Caroline, do not keep us in suspense," Lord

Keane drawled, even as he eyed Leo and Susanna. "What can be more entertaining than this?"

A chill passed through her. She had not meant to entertain the likes of Lord Keane. Had she calculated incorrectly? Leo was still watching her, without the smug smile he might have offered for the benefit of the men, leaving her feeling confused.

"An archery competition!" Caroline exclaimed. "Even as we were eating, the servants were setting up targets in the park. Yes, it is an entertainment," she added slyly, "but one of the best available when one visits the country."

If Susanna expected Mr. Tyler to demur, she found herself surprised.

"I enjoy archery," he said, smiling.

The glimpse of that crooked tooth once again tugged at her. He was such a nice man. Of course he liked the sporting country pursuits. After all, he rode well, didn't he?

"And I enjoy a good competition," Leo said, waiting until Lady Bramfield rose to come to his feet.

The afternoon sun hung hazily in the humid air. Leo felt that he couldn't take a deep enough breath in the unusual early-summer heat. Even the grass seemed wilted, and the trees bowed as if their branches were too heavy to support. After choosing his bow, he removed his coat, knowing he scandalized the London-bred young ladies. He usually enjoyed this ability of his, but today he felt . . . distracted.

He liked Susanna's verbal challenge, the way she'd spoken her mind before all the guests. There weren't many souls brave enough to risk either condemnation or intense regard from the *ton*—except himself, of course. She'd generated the latter and hadn't batted an eye.

But something she'd said had pricked him. How had she known that lately he'd been bored?

Satisfy his intellect indeed, he thought. Was that it, what he'd begun to miss?

For his usual haunts had seemed somehow stale of late, his club full of men drinking and gambling to excess. Much as he was good at both, his opponents had begun to seem . . . aged by the behavior, the men with red, veined noses and paunches growing larger as the years passed. Boxing matches had lately bored him, and racing his carriage in the park had begun to seem pointless. What did such competition matter?

And each new crop of debutantes seemed younger and sillier—when he'd always liked them best young and silly.

He'd been bored in the country, too. When he visited his family, he could only attempt to defeat his brother in rowing competitions so many times. And then his brother would retreat to consult his secretary about his estate business, leaving Leo idle and restless. He didn't care about business and thought his money best spent hiring competent people to look after that sort of thing.

He found himself watching Tyler, who tested his own bow and gathered a handful of arrows. The man's interest was botany—Leo couldn't see the appeal.

And then Tyler looked at Susanna, who shielded herself with a parasol as she watched the beginning of the competition. Leo bristled at the man's regard. She looked cool and composed, even regal. But the faint dewiness on the narrow swathe of skin visible below her neck made him think of vigorous sex in the heat, with that auburn hair spread gloriously around her.

He turned away before his trousers became too uncomfortable. He couldn't remember the last time he'd battled arousal as much as he had recently. The challenge of the wager and besting Susanna had interested him as nothing had in a long time.

She'd even agreed to try her own hand at archery, and he wondered if she'd be good at it. If she put her mind to it, she would. Unlike his normal conquests, she was that sort of woman, one who had talent and drive, and the ability to use both.

Leo had always had things to master, too, though they would not impress a woman like Susanna. And they no longer seemed to impress him.

But he was good at archery. If a competitive skill could earn him money and a victory, he attempted to master it.

But there was little left in life to master, and that left him searching for . . . something.

He glanced at Miss Randolph, who waved at him when she saw him looking. He waved back. Perhaps this restless feeling was how men knew it was time to marry.

The thought startled him, for although he'd told
Susanna what sort of woman appealed to him, he
had meant in the far-off future. But perhaps the
future had snuck up on him when he hadn't realized it.

Miss Randolph certainly wanted him—and her
parents actually liked him. He needed to look more
into her family before his reputation caught up and
made the decision more difficult. But money could
smooth that over.

Miss Randolph wasn't the only choice, he thought,
letting his gaze wander lazily over the other eligible
women. And then the archery competition began,
and he focused on the challenge.

Susanna did not know what to make of Leo's quiet
concentration. He'd seemed introspective—and she'd
never seen that side of him. What had he been thinking behind that faint frown?

Winning, of course. She admired his drive to
master whatever he attempted—even the wrong
things. She conceded that perhaps he wasn't a man
to float through life, buffeted by currents taking him
where they might. He seemed to choose his path
even if it was not one she could admire. That was
one thing she'd learned about him that surprised her.

But that made him even more of a curiosity to
her—why hadn't he chosen more productive pursuits to focus on, especially since he'd betrayed hints
of a hidden intelligence?

She watched the other ladies practically swoon
over the sight of him in fluttering white shirtsleeves.

His waistcoat hugged his torso, showing his flat stomach and lean hips. She had to fight to keep her small sketchbook in her pocket.

Mr. Tyler had excellent form as well, she thought, when he took his own turn. And his arrow hit the center of the target, unlike Leo's. She considered the difference in her reaction to the two men. Mr. Tyler did not make her heart race, or her knees tremble. She was in control, with a quiet feeling of warm friendship because of their shared interests and an outlook on life that she could respect. This was what she wanted to experience for the rest of her life.

And then she looked at Leo, who rested his shoulder against a tree as he talked to Miss Randolph. She found herself wanting to warn him that he was leading the girl on again, that she'd only try her plan to entrap him another time.

She didn't need to protect him, Susanna reminded herself. She didn't need to feel all tangled up inside, as if she were a mix of pigments that muddied into a confused brown instead of a vivid, confident color.

When all the men had taken a turn, the ladies stepped forward. To Susanna's surprise, Mrs. Norton had quite the keen eye. When Susanna took her own turn, she was dismayed to find herself trembling as she sighted down the arrow. She was used to fading into the wallpaper, being unseen, living her own life. She was suddenly very conscious of the bold choices she'd been making, her obsession with Leo, the risks she was taking to find happiness.

It would be worth it, she told herself, even as she

felt Leo's amused regard. She let loose her arrow, and breathed a sigh of relief that she at least hit the target.

"Well done, Miss Leland," Leo called.

She nodded her thanks, wishing it had been Mr. Tyler who'd thought to compliment her. She looked at the scientist, and he was smiling and nodding at her, and the tension in her stomach eased as she smiled back.

Mr. Tyler was standing with the other men, who were congratulating his marksmanship. Susanna moved behind them to the refreshment table, looking for something to drink. To her surprise, she heard the men quite clearly.

"Tyler," Leo said, "I am impressed with your archery skills."

"Thank you, Mr. Wade. It was a boyhood diversion I enjoyed, a gentleman's competition of skill."

"Well, you easily ignored my attempts to distract you."

The gentlemen all chuckled. Susanna wondered what she'd missed.

"You read me too well," Mr. Tyler said agreeably. "Mentioning the specimens Mr. Darwin sent back from his trip around the world was almost a low blow. Cambridge is lucky to have them."

She could no longer be surprised that Leo might know about scientific specimens at Cambridge University. She remembered that his brother had attended—had Leo? When she next saw her father, she would have to ask if he remembered the Wade brothers.

"At least you naturalists now have confirmation that the platypus wasn't a fraud," Leo continued.

"Do not put me among those cynics, Mr. Wade," Mr. Tyler quickly said. "To believe someone could sew a duck's beak onto the pelt of a beaver—balderdash."

"I'm certain that Miss Leland will be relieved that you weren't taken in. I saw that she admired your talent at archery."

Susanna tensed, but Mr. Tyler only awkwardly cleared his throat. For what purpose did Leo bring up her name?

"Though we'll have to differ about the true gentlemen's competition," Leo added. "I always thought it was fencing."

To her surprise, Mr. Tyler answered in a confident voice.

"I, too, enjoy that ancient art. Perhaps you would honor me with a match?"

The fork Susanna had picked up tumbled from her fingers onto the table.

"Tyler, it would give me great pleasure to cross swords with you."

Were they—were they going to fight . . . over her? She felt flattered and dismayed and far too excited.

Would she be able to watch?

Chapter 9

The heat proved too much, so Susanna took her students back to the gallery late that afternoon, where their assignment was to choose a portrait and paint a watercolor of it, particularly emphasizing matching paint colors. She wandered from lady to lady, giving her thoughts on which colors to mix to create the right result. The room seemed to hum with their quiet voices, and Susanna tried to dwell on her usual feeling of contentment where sharing her art was concerned.

But thoughts of Leo and Mr. Tyler kept intruding.

"Susanna?"

She gave a little start at Caroline's call, then approached her. Caroline was working at the far end of the gallery, away from the other young ladies.

Susanna studied her Bristol board, seeing that she'd roughly sketched in the hounds and horses from the fox hunting painting. "You've chosen a difficult subject," Susanna said. "But I admire how you've—"

"While I have you alone," Caroline interrupted in

a low voice, "it's not the painting I wish to discuss."

Susanna's eyebrows lifted. "Oh?"

"Your . . . discussion with Mr. Wade at luncheon was most illuminating." Caroline bit her lip, as if she was holding back a smile.

Susanna sighed. "You can tease me—I will not be offended."

Caroline chuckled, even as she continued to study her painting. "When you practically told him of his intellectual failings, I could have fallen out of my chair!"

"I did not say it quite so boldly . . ." Now it was Susanna's turn to bite her lip. "I hadn't meant to offend, only to inspire reflection."

"On Mr. Wade's part?" Caroline asked. "I do not imagine many women have ever demanded such a thing of him."

"And he has been the poorer for it."

Caroline laughed again, causing both Miss Norton and Lady May to glance at them with curiosity.

"Oh, dear, I must control myself," Caroline murmured. "I simply never knew how amusing you are! Or should I say I was so preoccupied with Rebecca that I never took the time. I apologize for that failing."

Blinking in surprise, Susanna said, "You have no need to apologize to me. You are a wonderful friend to Rebecca, and I'm incredibly grateful to you."

Caroline smiled and glanced over her shoulder. "Then forgive my boldness for asking an even more personal question. Are you interested in Mr. Wade as a suitor?"

Susanna spoke firmly. "Most certainly not."

"Other guests have noticed his preference for your company."

"Is there . . . much talk?"

"Only the usual. We are all confined together in one house for many days. You know how gossip spreads."

Susanna sat down heavily on the sofa closest to Caroline's chair. After everything her family had gone through from her grandfather's scandals through her parents' near divorce, the last thing she wanted was to bring her parents censure. They had only recently mended their own disagreements, growing deeper in love than they'd ever been before. She had hoped her search for a husband would keep them from being disappointed in her, keep them from worrying.

"I know Mr. Wade has an . . . interesting reputation," Caroline continued, "but I have seen him behave compassionately. I cannot help but think him kind because of it."

"Kind? How so?" Susanna asked, trying not to sound too intrigued.

"Toward his sister, at least."

Susanna remembered the conversation about siblings she'd shared with Leo and knew that he was fond of Miss Wade. But he'd mentioned pranks rather than any kind deeds.

"You know the terrible first Season Miss Wade had, do you not?"

"How could I forget? I was there when she

sprawled onto the floor when she was presented to Queen Victoria."

Caroline winced. "I remember the hush, then the awful whispers, and the look on the poor girl's face . . ."

Susanna sighed. "If only that were all. Didn't she trip a duke's son? And spill her drink on . . ."

As if sharing a simultaneous memory, they both turned to stare at Lady May, who was biting her lip as she studied her painting.

"Does Lady May remember?" Susanna whispered. "I do believe she complained for months afterward."

"If she does, she doesn't associate it with Mr. Wade. It was several years ago, after all."

"What kindness did Mr. Wade display in all of this?" Susanna couldn't help her curiosity.

"I do believe that after Miss Wade tripped the ducal heir—whichever one it was, for I forget—Mr. Wade made it a point, when all the other men were laughing about it—to defend his sister's honor and remind them all how young she was. Or so my brother told me. Mr. Wade didn't have to speak up; he could have laughed with all the others."

Susanna knew he had a fondness for his siblings, and she felt pleased that he had no qualms about showing it in public. She had always enjoyed a good relationship with her own brother, and was glad that whatever trials Miss Wade had suffered, at least she had the support of her brother.

Caroline leaned toward her and lowered her voice. "Though there is no talk of what I'm about to say,

I cannot help feeling that perhaps you prefer Mr. Tyler."

Susanna nodded. "Yes, we are quite well matched in interests and temperament."

"Are you?" Caroline pressed, watching her.

"How can you be surprised?" Susanna asked, her tension returning. "His love of botany and the country life?"

"Yes, I know, but . . ." Caroline trailed off, then shook her head.

"You cannot believe I favor Mr. Wade."

"Perhaps not *consciously* . . ."

Susanna felt flushed and flustered all at the same time. "There is no doubt that his ability to live on the edge of Society's good regards might appeal to some, Miss Randolph in particular," she added, lowering her voice.

"I have noticed her adoration." Caroline glanced at the other young lady.

"Oh, believe me, Mr. Wade has noticed it, too."

"And how do you know that?" Caroline asked, eyeing her with curiosity.

"Because—" Susanna broke off, knowing she could not in good conscience mention the kiss she'd seen in the conservatory. "Forgive me, but I cannot betray a confidence."

Caroline didn't press for an answer, for which Susanna was grateful.

In the end, finding the men's fencing match proved far easier than Susanna had imagined. After an evening of cards among the ladies and gentlemen—in which Leo was by far the biggest winner—she waited to be the last lady to retire. But instead of heading to her rooms, she hurried around the corner to a small parlor and, blowing out her candle, stepped into the darkness within. Perched on the edge of a sofa, it was easy enough to overhear the men laughing and drinking. That seemed to go on forever though she couldn't judge the time in the dark. Every time her head would bob drowsily, a roar of laughter would awaken her. Was this what they did every night? How did they get up early and start the day? Perhaps a house party wasn't all that relaxing for men.

One by one, she heard the older gentlemen take their leave, and confirmed it with a quick peek. Surely now the younger men would fence. When she heard the scrape of furniture being moved across wood floors, she tried not to get too excited, for after all, it might just be—

"My father keeps blades in his study," Lord Swanley called with gusto. "Come take your pick!"

Her mouth fell open. They were actually going to fence. Had Leo talked the rest of them into it?

Susanna dared to peek out into the corridor and saw the men, many now in shirtsleeves, trooping down the main corridor, laughing and jostling each other. Without giving it careful thought—for if she thought it through, she'd never be brave enough—she hurried to the drawing room and peered inside. It was empty, with all of the furniture and rolled carpets pushed against the walls.

Where could she hide?

As she considered and discarded several chairs and tables, she heard the rising sound of male voices. Feeling a shot of wild fear and thrilling excitement, she ran to the nearest sofa beneath the windows. Pushing it until she made a space for herself, she ducked behind it.

Just in time, too, for she next heard the sound of steel meeting steel.

"Not yet, gentlemen," Leo drawled.

Mr. Frobisher gave a nervous laugh. Was he actually going to fence, too?

As they decided who would fight whom, their words were more ribald and masculine than they ever used in the presence of a lady. She did have a brother and male cousins, of course, so it wasn't as if she were shocked.

But she didn't hear Mr. Tyler being crude. It wasn't until Leo said, "Tyler?" that she heard his voice at all.

"Any blade will do," Mr. Tyler said simply.

"A man should choose his weapon," Leo said to many chuckles. "It must feel as if it were made for you, as if it's an extension of your arm."

She swallowed. Sometimes she felt that way about her brush. It was a part of her when she touched it to canvas, as if it did her bidding.

"That sounds quite . . . dedicated," Mr. Tyler said. "Then I'll choose this one. I see the safety tip is already buttoned on."

Susanna couldn't wait anymore. On her knees behind the sofa—and she'd done her best to make

certain the draperies were also hanging nearby—
she slowly leaned forward until she could see the
scene. Several more candles had been lit, and every
man was in shirtsleeves now. The competitors were
Mr. Evans, Lord Keane, Mr. Tyler, Lord Swanley, Mr.
Frobisher, and Leo. An even number of men for three
matches.

But the room wasn't large enough to accommodate them all, so four of them hung back, lounging
across sofas or leaning against walls, as the first two
met. Leo and Mr. Tyler faced each other. Leo had
already removed his waistcoat, but Mr. Tyler kept
his on, properly buttoned up. They studied each
other for a moment, and Susanna felt a strange feeling come over her. They looked . . . intent, focused.
It was not Leo's usual expression, and if Mr. Tyler
wore such when he was in his laboratory, she still
hadn't seen it.

Could it be about . . . her?

No, no, she was making too much of this. Leo had
practically boasted that he was a superior swords-
man, and Mr. Tyler, fresh from his archery victory,
was surely only humoring him.

She was belittling herself again, believing that
no one could possibly desire her as a woman. She'd
sworn to stop that, to portray confidence in herself.

She felt the most confident with a sketchbook in
her hands. She pulled the small one from her pocket,
along with the pencil, and clutched it tight, even as
the first clash of steel made her shudder.

Quickly looking out, she saw Leo and Mr. Tyler,

crossed swords held before them, eyeing each other, Leo grinning, Mr. Tyler serious.

And then Leo started to move, lightning slashes that Mr. Tyler parried, falling back step by step as he did so. Susanna gasped, and heard several of the men murmur their approval. Leo was quite skilled at something besides cards.

Next Mr. Tyler took the offensive, more deliberate with the placement of his blade, until he slashed low. Leo jumped with grace, and Mr. Tyler's sword swung wildly beneath, throwing him off balance. Leo waited without pressing his advantage.

Mr. Tyler straightened. "Well done, sir."

Leo attacked again. For several minutes, Susanna forgot to breathe, watching his skill and grace. And then in a momentary pause, he stripped off his shirt, and she was treated to an awe-inspiring display of his torso in motion. His muscles moved with health and vitality, unlike the ones she was used to looking at, the blood pounding through them, highlighting the miracle of life.

This vision of Leo, shining with the low candle-light, full of taut, deliberate purpose, was even more overwhelming. She was caught up in the spell of how he made her feel, and she barely realized she'd begun to draw him. Faster and faster she sketched, glancing up occasionally, but letting the emotions burst forth from her pencil and spill all over the page.

Only vaguely did she hear the applause and realize that Leo had been declared the winner. The victory didn't matter to her when compared to the beauty of the scene. She continued to work as the other gentlemen took their turns against different opponents. Leo gave simple instructions, even as she'd been giving art instructions to the women. The irony escaped her, all concentration riveted to her sketchbook.

His body was coming to life on the page, sword extended, left arm behind him, hair damp with perspiration. She couldn't stop, didn't want to stop, could only be grateful that several candles burned on the table nearest to her, providing just enough light.

She didn't notice the growing silence, or that her pencil provided a faint scratch along the paper. Her knees ached from having her legs folded beneath her, her back was bowed over her lap uncomfortably, but she didn't care.

And then a shadow came between her and the candles. She looked up and found Leo standing above her, one hand on his hip, the other holding his sword with the tip pricking the floor, perspiration sliding down his damp chest.

"I was waiting for everyone to go," Leo said softly. "I saw you quite a while back and knew there was only one reason you could be here."

Unable to form words, she gestured to her sketchbook.

"Once again, you haven't drawn my face."

She licked her lips. "I'm—I'm not finished yet."

With his foot, he kicked the sofa farther away, and she gasped. He caught her up by the shoulders, and her sketchbook tumbled to the floor. Her feet, numb with disuse, had trouble finding the ground. She fell against him, and he took her weight.

Her palms rested on his bare chest, rising and falling with his breath. His skin was hot and damp, twisting something deep inside her tighter and tighter. She slowly looked up his neck, and past his square jaw into his face. Those jungle green eyes were narrowed as he watched her, all humor gone, and suddenly she felt a sense of smoldering danger.

She pushed away from his chest and freed herself. "My sketchbook."

As she knelt, searching in the shadows for it, he said, "Perhaps you should draw yourself into the picture. You could be standing behind me, a maiden of ancient times, as I defend your honor."

She didn't look at him, her face so hot she felt burned. "I could never do that."

As she slid her sketchbook out from beneath the sofa, she heard movement behind her, then turned to find him squatting until they were almost at eye level.

"Never draw yourself?" he asked. "You've never looked in a mirror and drawn what you see?"

"I—I—"

He reached for her spectacles and slid them off her nose, blindly setting them on a table behind him. "There's nothing wrong with this face. You could capture those high cheekbones." He slid his fingers along her cheek.

He was too close, his thighs spread, his upper body gleaming in the candlelight. She tried to scuttle backward, and ended up falling onto her backside beyond the sofa, staring up at him, feeling a sinful heat work its way deep into her belly and spread outward, taking over her body, until her hands itched to touch him, her mouth burned to taste his damp skin.

He knelt on either side of her legs. With a mortifying gasp, she sank back on her elbows.

"Your mouth is wide and full," he continued, staring down at her.

"Too big."

His smile seemed fraught with tension. "No man would think that."

She could not keep her eyes on his face though she tried her best. She was so used to examining and evaluating, determining line and shadow and form, that her gaze naturally slid with sinful slowness down his body—or so she told herself. He let her look, saying nothing. How had she not seen this morning that the hair scattered across his chest narrowed as it went down his stomach?

And she followed it helplessly, past his waistline until she saw the proof of his desire, straining against his trousers. She was no ignorant girl; her anatomy sketching had given her knowledge many young women didn't have.

Leo wanted her, and he wasn't trying to hide it from her.

And then he lowered himself over her, dropping onto his hands and knees. She sank back, holding her breath beneath his smoky regard. His hands were on either side of her hips, lost in her skirts. She found herself mesmerized by the way he studied her.

"This isn't fair," he murmured. "You get to see much of me by candlelight, or in sunlight, and I never get to see you."

"But—but—"

"I want to see the candlelight glimmering on the bare curve of your hip."

She gaped, barely able to breathe, as he lowered his head and pressed his mouth to the edge of her hip. Though she wore layers of clothing, it felt scandalous to have his face so close to her thighs. Every limb was shaking, not with fear, but with the most incredible sensations of . . . pleasure. Bone-melting, skin-heating pleasure that seeped throughout her body. She'd never felt this before—never imagined that Leo could inspire such feelings.

"As you lie on your back," he continued, his voice deep and husky, "your stomach dips inward." He slid his cheek from her hip and along her body until he reached the center of her. "There's a shadow cast by candles deep in your navel, but were you naked, I would slip my tongue there anyway."

She'd lost control of her limbs, quivered and shook beneath him as he continued his slow climb up her body.

"And then we reach your breasts." His voice was filled with hoarse satisfaction. "Creamy globes to fill my hands, my mouth."

Breathing quickly, frantically, she pressed her thighs together, but that didn't help the ache that was building. She felt a desperation for his touch, a feeling that only he could quiet her body.

He lowered his head just above her left breast, then met her eyes. "Should I?" he whispered, his lips faintly grazing her bodice.

Her lips parted but couldn't form words.

"I'll take that as assent." And then he opened his mouth and covered her breast right through her garments.

The pressure, so new and intense, made her jerk beneath him. "Leo!" She breathed his name, even moaned it.

After nipping at her breast, gently biting at her nipple, he took her hands and pulled them up over her head. "Like the painting," he said.

She didn't care about the wager at all. She was caught in a world of new sensations, new feelings, her body alive in a way she'd never imagined. She arched beneath him, and for the first time wished she were wearing nothing at all. It was scandalous and wicked—and so very, very tempting.

His face rose just above hers, and she almost begged him to return to her breasts.

He smiled, as if he knew everything she was thinking, and delighted in it. Slowly, so slowly he lowered his mouth over hers, hesitating just above her lips. She couldn't get enough air—and then she had to admit it—she couldn't get enough of his kisses. She lifted her head, straining toward him, their lips touched—

And then Leo was shoved off her.

She gasped as Leo rolled until he was on his knees again. Above her, she saw the red, angry face of Lord Bramfield, stout in his dressing gown over trousers and shirt.

Hands on his hips, Lord Bramfield said, "Mr. Wade! How dare you abuse a female guest in my home!"

Susanna felt shocked into speechlessness, as weak as a doll when Lord Bramfield helped her sit up.

"There, there, Miss Leland, you've had a terrible shock," he said, patting her shoulder awkwardly.

For a moment, she stared up at him, feeling as dizzy as she must look, if his concern were any indication. Hovering just behind him, she saw Lady Bramfield, eyes brimming with tears beneath the wispy, gray curls on her forehead.

The shame of what Susanna had done suddenly swept over her, and she wished she could sink beneath the wood floor. They had seen her . . . *beneath* Leo, like a common—

And then she realized what Lord Bramfield had said, what he'd implied—that Leo had forced her.

Though she'd avoided looking at him, now she slowly turned her head. Leo had risen to his feet, his arms folded across his bare chest, watching her impassively. He made no protest, no excuses.

Would he be just as silent if she let Lord Bramfield believe a lie? Part of her knew that Leo courted censure, that his behavior made everyone think the worst of him. If she lied, no one would know—Lord Bramfield would never tell anyone what happened here tonight, she knew. They were close friends of her parents, would protect her.

But they'd think far worse of Leo, might even make certain he was no longer accepted in the *ton*, even if they never said why. The marquess had that sort of power.

And Leo would accept it, she realized. In his own way, he had proven an honorable man. She felt nauseated at the thought of such lies. There was even a chance that Lord Bramfield would call Leo out as a point of honor. She couldn't let that happen.

She struggled to her feet, glad that Lord Bramfield kept his arm about her. The world tilted at the thought of what her own stupidity had cost her, how her future was now warped and ruined. But she wouldn't add cruelty and lies to her sins.

"Lord Bramfield," she began hoarsely, "I cannot let you think that Mr. Wade would—would deliberately harm me."

Leo's eyes narrowed, and he opened his mouth.

She rushed on. "He did nothing I didn't ask for in my foolishness."

Lord Bramfield stiffened.

His wife gasped, covering her face with both hands. "Oh, Miss Leland, no!"

Lord Bramfield took her upper arms and gently shook her until she was forced to stare into his face. The first tears trickled down her cheeks, and she felt mortified and heart-broken and weary all at the same time.

"Miss Leland, you must speak honestly. Are you

certain you were a willing participant in . . . whatever was going on here this night?" He glared at Leo. "Make yourself decent, Wade."

Leo suddenly looked furious, an emotion almost shocking on his usually amused face. "Susanna, don't—"

"I'll have no intimidation from you," Lord Bramfield interrupted with anger. "Let her speak freely."

Leo meant to protect her. She could see his jaw clench as he pulled his shirt over his head.

"I've spoken the truth, my lord," Susanna said, then forced herself to glance at Lady Bramfield. "And I'm so sorry for my behavior."

"I have heard rumors these last few days about the two of you," Lord Bramfield said, his demeanor growing impassive.

She could not hide her wince, could feel herself lessening in his eyes. She, who'd never wanted to be at the center of attention, had brought a terrible focus upon herself.

"And now this," he continued. "Miss Leland, you have brought the risk of ruination upon yourself."

She nodded, but could not help speaking with faint hope. "But only you and Lady Bramfield know about my stupidity. I'll leave here, and if you would say nothing—"

"No, it is too late, my girl," he said heavily. "As my wife and I were coming down the stairs, we both saw someone running away from the doorway to this very room. It was too dark to discern who it was."

Susanna closed her eyes and bowed her head. "Then I should leave."

"You'll leave, but only to marry Mr. Wade."

Her mouth fell open. Marry Leo Wade? Lord Bramfield didn't know what he was asking, how opposed she was to the very idea. He was nothing like the man she wanted for her husband, and any woman married to him might soon be a laughing-stock because of his reckless behavior.

She looked frantically at Leo, needing him to protest and stop this foolishness.

But he spoke softly, unemotionally. "Of course, Lord Bramfield. I will make this situation right."

"Leo!" she cried, aghast, but using his Christian name was the wrong thing to do, as Lord and Lady Bramfield looked at her in dismay and disappointment.

Chapter 10

"She is in shock," Leo heard himself saying. "And that is my fault, too, my lord."

Bramfield nodded, and Leo glanced at Susanna once more. Her face was bloodless, although a moment ago she'd been red with shame.

She could have let him take the blame—and he would have deserved it. He'd played this game more than once and had almost been caught. He'd even vowed to stop, knowing the risks he was taking with a woman's reputation. Any other woman would have gladly let Bramfield assume the worst about him.

But not Susanna, and he respected her for it, even though his own frustration felt like a simmering volcano. He knew the kind of wife he wanted, the simple, easily pleased woman he needed, who wouldn't ask too much of him, wouldn't demand to know him down to his soul.

Susanna wasn't anything like that.

Whether she'd posed for that painting or not didn't matter—she'd been a part of the challenge, had started this whole craziness, and now they both were going to pay the price.

"Mr. Wade," said Lord Bramfield, visibly relaxing, "I am not certain you can wait to make things right."

"I won't, my lord. I'll purchase a Special License."

"No!" Susanna interrupted.

"Be quiet, child," Lady Bramfield said, putting her arm about Susanna's shoulders. "You are not in your right mind. This is for the best."

"But I don't want to marry him," she whispered.

Leo was surprised to feel a faint sting at her words but shrugged it off.

"Think of your family, my dear," Lady Bramfield continued. "They want what's best for you. They don't want you to be shamed. Nor should you shame them."

Susanna bit her lip but remained silent, to Leo's weary gratitude. He wanted this evening over with, and her futile protests weren't helping.

"Let me tuck you into bed," Lady Bramfield said in a soothing, motherly voice.

Susanna didn't look at him as she was led away. Leo had his waistcoat and coat on by the time Bramfield frowned at him.

"I can trust your word, Wade?"

He stiffened but answered evenly. "On the life of my brother, my lord. I will make this right."

But he knew Susanna might be her own worst enemy. After a final discussion with Bramfield, Leo went up to his room, then crept down the balcony of Susanna's wing to her room. Through the French door, he could see Lady Bramfield tucking her into bed. Although he should perhaps pity Susanna for the stark sadness he could see on her face, he didn't feel quite in the mood for that. They'd both have to live with what was being forced upon them.

Marriage. Together forever, two people who didn't suit.

He rubbed both hands down his face, then stared through the window as Lady Bramfield departed. If Susanna cried into her pillow, he wasn't certain what he would do.

But instead, she flung back the counterpane, sending the candle flame fluttering, as she began to furiously pace.

He opened the door, and she came to a halt, glaring, then advanced on him. She hadn't taken the time to braid her hair, and it flew behind her like a cloud of red fury, rippling erotically down her shoulders and back. She looked even more appealing, which was a good thing, since they would be stuck with each other throughout eternity.

He held out his upraised palm, where her spectacles lay. "You left these behind."

She snatched them away and pointed her finger at him. "I'm not going to marry you."

"You don't have a choice. After all, you could have let them believe the worst about me, and you'd have been safe. Why didn't you?"

She opened her mouth, then groaned and whirled away from him. "Much as you are a rake and a scoundrel, you tried to absorb the blame all yourself, so I would never condemn you with a lie."

"You would have saved yourself and done little harm to me. What do I care if they don't receive me anymore?"

"Oh, you'd care if all of Society didn't receive you," she shot over her shoulder, "or if your brother suffered because of our stupidity. Just as I'd care if my family found out."

"You're being overly dramatic."

"Am I? Did you not see Lord Bramfield's fury? He is a good friend of my father—he would have felt obligated to call you out on my behalf."

"So you were also protecting the old man," he said.

"I was. But once I leave here, he will think differently, perhaps wash his hands of me, or leave me to my family when I don't marry you."

"Of course you're marrying me."

"Keep your voice down!"

They glared at each other, and he was shocked to realize she meant exactly what she'd said.

"I guess what I took for intelligence on your part," he said, "doesn't include common sense."

"Someone has to consider the future. We do not suit. You don't want to marry me, and I certainly don't want to marry you."

"Our feelings don't matter," he said. "I almost ruined another woman's life, and I vowed I would never let that happen again."

"You think showing a hint of honorability will alter my opinion? I know the kind of man I want to marry, and you aren't he."

"Don't believe yourself my ideal wife, either," he said dryly.

Now she flinched, and he almost regretted his honesty.

But she needed to hear the truth. "You know if we don't marry, this night's events will quickly spread. We don't know who saw us, or who might gleefully do us harm. We owe it to our families—"

"If you truly cared about your family, you wouldn't have behaved the way you have for so long. And the way you were flirting with every young lady here, you could have randomly been trapped with any of them and been facing any of their families."

"Jealous?" he taunted.

"Why would I be jealous?"

"Perhaps it would have been better had you left me to Miss Randolph's manipulations."

"You'd probably have been happier."

"Or perhaps you were saving me for yourself."

"Don't be a fool. You have provoked me beyond measure, taken advantage of my innocence—"

"You are not nineteen, Susanna. According to you, you've posed nude. You damn well knew what you were doing. And you never pushed me away."

They both had their hands on their hips, leaning into each other's faces.

"My family will save me from a terrible marriage," she said in a furious voice.

"Your family will want you safely married, so that when word gets out about how we were found—and it will get out—at least it will look like foolish love, rectified by a proper ceremony."

"You don't love me," she said indignantly, "and I could never love you."

Though her words were true, he was surprised to find they made him uncomfortable. "So you planned to fall in love with Tyler?"

She blinked at him before looking away as if to hide from the truth.

"You cannot deny that your plan was to marry someone like Tyler, someone who was safe—someone you didn't passionately love."

She drew herself up, eyes flashing. "I would have learned to love him because I respect him. I wanted that above all."

"You don't have to respect me," he said between his teeth. "But you will marry me."

She opened her mouth, but he turned his back and returned to the balcony. Though he wanted to slam the door hard, he closed it with such gentle control it didn't make a sound.

Susanna was so furious as she stormed about the room, she found herself wondering why she hadn't let them pin all the blame on that foolish, arrogant man. Marry Leo Wade? The mere thought frightened her. However he made her body feel, that was nothing upon which to base a marriage.

So what if he admitted he'd almost ruined another

woman's life. Susanna was not about to suffer because of his past mistakes. She'd rather live with the shame.

When she heard a soft knock on the main door, she almost locked it, thinking it must be Leo again. But he wouldn't come through that way.

"Susanna, may I come in?" Caroline called softly.

Had Lady Bramfield spoken to her already? How many other people would find out? Susanna decided she would be gone before breakfast, even if she had to walk. She never wanted to see Leo Wade's face again.

She opened the door, and Caroline stood there, watching her with such compassion that Susanna felt the first sting of tears she'd been controlling since her foolishness had been discovered.

Caroline stepped through the door and closed it. "My mother told me you will soon be married."

With a groan, Susanna whirled away and covered her hot face. "Oh, how many more people will she tell?"

If Caroline thought Susanna was slandering her mother, she didn't betray her thoughts, only laid her hands lightly on Susanna's shoulders.

"I am the only one, and only because she knew I might be of comfort to you."

Shuddering at the sweet concern in her friend's voice, Susanna sagged onto the chest at the end of the bed, and Caroline joined her. "I am not getting married," she said in a low voice that broke, revealing her foolish vulnerability. If she was embarrassed that

Caroline knew the truth, imagine how she would feel when Mr. Tyler . . . She couldn't even swallow because of the lump of shame in her throat.

"My mother says you and Mr. Wade were kissing."

Susanna wondered if Lady Bramfield had said *how* they were kissing: she'd been lying on the floor, and he'd been crawling up her body, putting his mouth—

Oh, even now she could hardly think about what she'd let him do. Away from his influence, it seemed crazy, delusional. But when she'd been with him, he'd taken away her every inhibition, had altered her very will. If only she could take it all back.

"And there was someone else in the hall watching you?" Caroline continued.

Susanna could only shrug, staring at the carpet muted with shadows.

"Then you must marry him," Caroline said with easy conviction. "It is not such a terrible thing."

Susanna gave a very unladylike snort.

"When I questioned you about Mr. Wade, I suspected you might feel more for him than you wished to let on."

"I feel nothing for him," she countered in a low voice. "This has all been . . . a terrible mistake."

"But you were kissing him, Susanna, and Mama swore to me that Mr. Wade was not forcing you."

How could she say that he'd been seducing her, had *told* her he'd attempt to seduce her? Caroline would demand to know why Susanna hadn't confided in someone, so that Mr. Wade could have been sent away.

No, she thought, *I was convinced I could control him, that I had the superior mind. I enjoyed the game and trying to best him.* But it seemed she had a lot to learn about her body's superior will.

"No, he wasn't forcing me," she admitted at last. "Don't ever be alone with a man, Caroline, for you don't know what you'll do in the heat of the moment."

Her friend sighed. "I wouldn't have believed it, but if *you* could so easily . . . succumb to a man's charm, then anyone can."

"Me?" Susanna said, stiffening. "What do you mean?"

"You are so intelligent, so confident in yourself."

Susanna's chuckle was bitter. "I have never been confident where men are concerned, and if I gave you that impression, I should have been on the stage. I'm obviously not intelligent either, as I'm sure you've realized."

"No," Caroline said, taking her hand. "I'm thinking that you are not the only woman taken in by a man. But he wants to marry you, and that is promising for his character. From what I heard before I knocked, you're resisting."

Susanna stared up at her taller friend. "What did you hear?"

"I could not make out the words, but I knew he'd come to see you, and I heard your refusal."

"Would *you* want to marry such a man, with his terrible reputation?"

"Many men enjoy themselves far too much before

marriage. My mother once hinted that my father was quite the scoundrel."

The thought of old Lord Bramfield as a rake at last made Susanna's lips quirk in a faint smile.

"And he made a very good husband and father," Caroline added.

"I am glad for your sake, but Leo—Mr. Wade is not the same sort of man."

"Whatever sort of man he is, you've been very drawn to him. I could not mistake the tension between you, and I know others felt the same."

Susanna could only groan.

"It is a good start, my dear, far better than indifference."

"He has only been using me." Susanna allowed her bitterness free rein, without thinking of the words.

"Using you?" Caroline echoed, frowning.

Susanna could not tell her about the wager.

"If you mean for your dowry, you must be practical, Susanna."

Her dowry. She hadn't even thought of that motive. Her insides seemed to sink within her body as another flood of shame suffused her. Of course it was her dowry—how had she not seen that? Had that been his real motive all along? No wonder he'd felt free to seduce someone like her! Had he given her glimpses of his intelligence as a method to lure a spinster like her? It wasn't as if she had a great inheritance, so he must truly be desperate, or in such a hurry he couldn't wait for the usual courtship of the daughter of a peer.

"He is a second son," Caroline continued, "as are many men. They all have to marry to better their situation. You must not think too poorly of him because of that."

Susan could only squeeze her eyes shut.

"It is done now," Caroline finished in a quiet voice. "You can make the best of this. He's a handsome young man. Don't forget our friend Lady Blanche, who had to marry a man old enough to be her father—or grandfather!"

"My parents never asked such a thing of me," Susanna said quietly. "In return, they expected me to honor them with my behavior. And I haven't."

"They'll think it a love match, my dear. Everyone will, after what has happened this week, I promise."

"And what am I supposed to tell Mr. Tyler?" Susanna demanded.

Caroline squeezed her hand. "You will find the words. I know you will. You and Mr. Wade were drawn together—surely that can be the beginning of a good marriage."

"We are both furious with each other. That would be a bad start to any union."

"Don't think on it. Time will heal both of you."

Susanna nodded, but didn't say the words that would make her even more a liar. She wasn't going to marry Leo Wade.

Chapter 11

Susanna's trunk was packed before dawn, and she wore a traveling dress that buttoned up the front, to make it easier for her to dress and undress herself. She'd debated leaving a note for Caroline and Mr. Tyler but did not know how to express herself. She would write to Caroline later, knowing she might never be permitted to associate with her again. As for Mr. Tyler—what was the point? He would be glad he'd escaped her unscathed. Leo would come to believe the same. She'd taken all the risks she was going to, and she'd failed. It was time to return to Cambridgeshire, to the ducal palace Madingley Court, where she could assist her father and remain in the country forever.

After the servants brought her baggage down to the luggage entrance, she asked the butler about borrowing a carriage for the drive back to London. He went off to take care of it while she went to the front portico to wait. The guests were surely beginning to stir, and she didn't want to risk meeting any of them.

The sun was just beginning to emerge from the crest of a far-off hill. It was a peaceful sight, with a flock of sheep in the distance, and the first gardener trudging toward a row of bushes on the grounds of Bramfield Hall.

She was doing the right thing, she told herself, taking a deep breath. Mr. Tyler might be hurt, but he was better off. Her parents would be disappointed, but they would understand. They'd always supported her. And although she'd considered having children, she had always thought to content herself with those of her sister and brother. It turned out, she'd been right.

She heard the rumbling of carriage wheels before she saw the vehicle itself take the turn from the rear of the house. The marquess's coat of arms was not on display, for which she was thankful. She wanted to disappear back into anonymity, hoping that someday she would live down the shame of her foolish impulses.

From behind her, a footman strode past her to open the carriage door and lower the stairs.

The coachman, bundled up in long black coat even in summer, touched the brim of his hat to her. "Good day, miss," he said, his grin displaying a missing front tooth. "I'm John Coachman."

A smile felt strange on her face. "I'm pleased to meet you, sir, but surely you have a name."

He ducked his head shyly. "Bradley, miss."

"Thank you for the ride, Mr. Bradley."

The footman took her hand and helped her up

into the gloom. She wasn't certain why the windows were shut and the blinds lowered, but perhaps the coachman was leaving her the choice. Once she slid onto the bench, and her body no longer blocked the light from outside, the shadows in the far corner dissipated, leaving her to start with fright at the man who lounged there.

"Hello, Susanna."

Shocked by Leo's presence, she turned in panic, only to see the door close in her face.

As she touched the handle, Leo said, "Too late. Lord Bramfield knows all about my plan and agrees completely that you're being a foolish female."

She glared at him. "I cannot be forced to marry you, Leo Wade." The coach jerked into motion, and she fell back onto the front facing bench. "You still have to purchase a Special License. I'll have plenty of opportunity to escape in London."

"We aren't going to London," he said.

She kept waiting for his smile of triumph or satisfaction, but he wasn't offering one. In fact, he looked downright grim, dimples banked, eyes narrowed. She flung up the blinds on both windows, the better to see him, but his expression was unmoved, nothing like she'd ever seen from Leo before. Her fear ratcheted up another notch.

"I told the coachman . . ." she began, but trailed off.

He raised one eyebrow. "Lord Bramfield and I gave the coachman different instructions. I won't expose you to the gossips of London without a wedding ring. We are eloping to Gretna Green."

Though she was dazed, the efficient part of her brain remembered that Scotland allowed any couple to marry as long as they had witnesses. No banns had to be read, no expensive Special License needed to be procured.

"No!" She put her hand on the door handle again, but this time he didn't protest. Through the window she saw the scenery flying by her. It was too late to jump. "Then I'll stop Mr. Bradley. He'll respond to a knock." If she had to crawl across Leo to knock on the ceiling of the carriage beneath the coachbox, she would.

"Go ahead, delay us all you want, but the coachman knows what's at stake, and he has his orders. We are romantics, Susanna," he said, not bothering to hide his sarcasm. "Young lovers running off to marry, knowing no one can stop us because we are both old enough—or should I say mature enough?"

Ignoring the gibe, she slowly sat back, although her stiff shoulders never touched the back of the bench. "I won't say the vows."

"Then you're a fool. Already the guests must know we've run off to be married."

She flinched, eyes narrowed, saying in a low voice, "You dare much, sir."

"I dare because it's necessary." He never leaned forward, but even his lazy elegance hinted at tension. "By the end of the day, whoever saw us last night will have spread the scandalous rumors of what we did. At least this way, the rumors are tempered by the knowledge that marriage followed that kiss."

"It was more than a kiss," she shot back. "If they saw what you did to me—"

"We were partially hidden by the sofa. And it's not just what I did but how you reacted, let's not forget."

She blushed; she couldn't help it. The night now seemed so far away, a bizarre moment out of a very sensible life.

"The party will break up today," Leo continued firmly. "They'll all flee back to London to see who can be the first to tell *both* our families what we've done."

With bitterness, she said, "And yours will be relieved, for the scandalous black sheep can now take care of himself. It was the dowry all along, Mr. Wade, wasn't it? I was so foolish not to see the truth for what it was. The wager, the painting, meant little, except as an opportunity for you to exploit." He must have needed money quickly, for after all, why else would he attempt to seduce someone as plain and old as Susanna when he had all the beautiful young debutantes fluttering around him in London?

Leo clenched his jaw, holding back an outburst. He'd never shown much emotion beyond pleasure and happiness and amusement—there hadn't been a need. And an outburst implied lack of control, and that had never been a problem. He'd always enjoyed his life, especially once he'd escaped his parents' endless arguments. Even in the dark days of his brother's pain and gradual blindness, the grief had remained hidden inside him for Simon's benefit.

He felt a momentary stillness, a memory he

couldn't quite reach, but as he considered it with confusion, it fled.

Now he found his stomach roiling with outrage and anger, and was appalled by these emotions he didn't want to feel. But he didn't protest her conclusions. She would not believe him regardless, and he felt a surge of rusty pride; groveling was beneath him.

"Believe what you will," he said. "It still doesn't change what must be done."

"I now realize that my dowry has been a sizable lure all along, or else you would let me go."

"Your dowry? As if I couldn't have had my pick of dowries anytime I chose."

"I didn't see fathers dangling their daughters like prizes in your face."

"The fact that I don't wish you ruined doesn't matter to you?"

"You said you almost ruined a woman before— I certainly don't matter, since if left alone, I would simply retire to the country and leave you to your outrageous life in the city. So now you're trying to tie me to you, to make me bear the snickers of the *ton*, as you take mistress after mistress?"

"Whatever you think of my motives, give me some credit. I hardly wish your brother or cousins to be forced to come to your aid because of my behavior."

"Fine, you'll do your shameful deeds in secret, as you've done with me." She paused. "I know many women are supposed to turn away from a husband's infidelities. But—"

And then her voice broke, and she turned her head and looked blindly toward the closed window. To his surprise, self-righteous anger didn't stop him from feeling a momentary sympathy for her.

"But I'd wanted a different sort of marriage," she whispered, fisting her hand against her mouth.

"Respect and shared interests," he said with sarcasm. "So you told me. I wanted a different marriage as well, to a woman willing to make a comfortable, peaceful home I wished to return to each night, to be at my side in Society, to come to my bed gladly and give me children."

"You won't get that from me," she said in a low voice that sounded as hollow and grim as a brutal winter morn. "None of it."

He knew—he hoped—she was speaking out of anger. "These protests will achieve nothing. Society believes us to have eloped. We will answer their expectations."

And then she retreated into icy silence, looking out the window, but he imagined her eyes saw little.

It took a day and a half to reach Scotland at a fast pace, changing horses constantly through the night. At their first break for a meal, Leo watched over Susanna closely, but she seemed resigned at last to her fate—their fate, he reminded himself. It was one thing for her to return home having disgraced herself by kissing a man, and another to have supposedly married, then not. Her family's standing might never recover from such a scandal. She was a sensible woman. At last he let himself doze now and then, but he had to time it for when she was sleeping. He felt . . . self-conscious sleeping when she was awake. He couldn't know how he looked when he had those dreams of darkness and dread. The last thing he wanted to do was answer her questions about them.

During the last few miles before crossing over the River Sark, the border between England and Scotland, the barren land suited his mood. Meager huts were scattered near copses of fir trees, and even scruffy children worked the land. Leo's head pounded from the stress and rough travel as the roads worsened this far north and west. Susanna's face looked white and pinched, and she only spoke to him when necessary. Which wasn't often. She dozed most of the time, so ladylike that her lips didn't even part.

The dust on their boots covered the mud from the downpour that had hit as they'd ascended the Yorkshire dales. His garments felt stuck to his body after two days occasionally sweltering in the carriage. He was used to the freedom of traveling by horse, and felt confined and restless with this silent woman he would soon marry. He imagined she felt filthy as well, but she would have to share his suffering.

They arrived at the gate just over the river, and Leo listened to the coachman pay and insist to the toll collector they did not need to stop for a libation. Leo had heard that anyone could marry a couple in this place, and the man probably did good business persuading eager couples to come inside and do the marriage now, in case they were being followed by angry fathers.

That wasn't the case with them—his father was dead, and Susanna's father . . . This wasn't the way he would have wanted to present himself to a father-in-law, but the deed was done.

He glanced out the window, knowing he needed his own distraction about now. As they entered Gretna Green, they passed thatched-roof cottages, a church, then the green itself that the village must have been named for. Beyond it rose a two-story mansion, with a long drive cut through a green lawn. This had to be Gretna Hall, where the majority of marriages took place, or so he'd been told at their last rest in Carlisle. Although he could have stopped at any number of marriage shops, he wanted Susanna to realize by the solemnity of the occasion that they were truly married—even if it was a blacksmith who performed the ceremony, as rumor had it.

But the rumor was wrong. No sooner had they entered the hall and been shown to a parlor for refreshments than the owner, Mr. Linton, on hearing they wished to marry today, offered to send for the Gretna priest—not a real priest, but one of their own, a man to whom the marriage duty had been passed down from father to son.

"I would like to refresh myself," Susanna murmured to Leo as she removed her gloves listlessly.

He shook his head. He was not about to rent two rooms and give her a chance to escape him before the wedding. She glared at him but did not ask again.

The "priest" arrived soon enough, and Leo wished for the ceremony to be over. He was still worried that Susanna would foolishly risk her very reputation simply to deny him.

Quietly, with sad resignation that made him grit his teeth, she answered yes to the question of her willingness to marry, and glanced at him briefly in surprise when he produced a ring. She didn't ask him where he'd bought it, so he didn't bother to tell her. The priest himself put it on Susanna's finger, and it was a close fit, Leo saw with brief satisfaction. The priest produced a marriage certificate, and Susanna filled out her name and place of residence without speaking, and Leo did the same. Their witnesses— the coachman and Linton, owner of the Hall—signed their names. With a smile, the priest declared them man and wife, and the simple ceremony was over.

Susanna blinked in surprise, looking around at all the men. "Nothing about God?" she asked with faint sarcasm.

Linton and Bradley exchanged an uncertain glance.

The priest smiled. " 'Tis up to you, lass, and I'd be happy to put your mind at ease. Whom God has joined together, let no man put asunder."

Susanna nodded, then glanced at Leo. "It's done, then."

He wished he could find words of reassurance, but he didn't even have them for himself, so all he could do was nod. He took both her hands in his, and though she tensed, she didn't pull away.

He leaned down slowly, giving her time to reject him if she would, but all she did was offer her cheek, which he briefly kissed. "Mrs. Wade."

Those brown eyes, so cold and composed for the last two days, gleamed briefly with gold near the center, as if hinting at emotions she wouldn't name.

Linton and Bradley clapped, and Leo forced a grin. He held up a glass of champagne. "To my wife," he said.

The priest and the witnesses toasted her as well, and Susanna bowed her head with formal graciousness and took a sip of her own.

"You must be tired after the journey," Leo said.

"Your lodgings are prepared, sir." Linton rubbed his hands together. "Will you be eating dinner here in the parlor?"

"No, have it sent to the room, please."

If anyone thought him eager to be alone with his bride, there were no smirks of laughter that he could see. He offered thirty pounds for the marriage certificate, which the priest accepted graciously. The man bowed, saying, "I will fill out the register, Mr. Wade, have no fear."

Leo nodded, put a hand low on Susanna's back, and guided her back to the entrance hall. Linton himself showed them up to the first floor, to a cheery room with a large four-poster bed. Their trunks had already been placed alongside a table and two chairs.

Susanna came to a stop beside the four-poster bed, glanced at it only briefly, then with no expression turned to face him. Before he could speak, a young maid bustled in behind them with a tray, a lace cap perched upon her black curls. She was cheerful as she placed a sprig of flowers in a vase upon the table, then soup, a meat pie, a bottle of wine, and two glasses.

"If ye don't wish to be disturbed, Mr. Wade," she said to Leo, "just place the tray in the hall, and I'll leave ye be. Mrs. Wade, can I take a gown to be pressed for the morn?"

"Thank you," Susanna said.

Leo added his own clothing to the pile, giving the maid a coin that earned him a pleased smile. And then she closed the door behind her.

Leo stared at Susanna. The air between them crackled.

"I'm not hungry," Susanna said, turning away to go to the window.

"I'm starving." He seated himself, poured a healthy draught of wine and drank with a sigh. The mutton pie proved delicious, especially after the food they'd eaten from meager taverns that could no longer count on travelers since the railways were far to the east.

He glanced occasionally at Susanna, who only hugged herself and stared out the window. She couldn't possibly be frightened, he thought in disbelief. Did she think he would force her into bed? He knew he would have to find a way to earn such intimacies.

When another knock rattled the door, she didn't look away from whatever captivated her view. A procession of servants brought in a tub and buckets of hot bathwater.

When the servants had gone for more water, Susanna glanced at him dispassionately. "There is no changing screen here. I will not bathe."

"Suit yourself."

Her frown increased. "You plan to bathe here in front of me?"

"You're my wife."

She flinched.

"You can see me naked. Perhaps you'd even care to draw me that way," he added with faint sarcasm.

She didn't respond, only turned away again. Her gown was covered in dust, her hemline spackled with mud—but she resisted. As he began to remove his clothing, he had a few fantasies about dunking her in the tub and bathing her himself.

Chapter 12

Susanna stared blindly out the window, and although it was only dinnertime, with several hours of summer daylight left, her eyes took in nothing. It was as if she were still in the parlor downstairs, signing away her life to a man she didn't love.

Married. She was Mrs. Leo Wade. The name alone would bring her curiosity or pity—good Lord, she hated pity, had been suffering under its burden for much of her life.

And disappointment, from everyone in her family. Her parents had never demanded anything of her except that she find her own happiness, and she couldn't even give them that. She'd squandered her future for a momentary pleasure and was almost as disappointed with herself as she was with Leo.

And now he was behind her, brazenly removing his clothing for a bath. Did he think the sight of his body would change her mind, make her pliant to his will?

Why *shouldn't* he think that? she thought. Time

after time, she'd mindlessly responded to just that. She couldn't even tell herself it was because she was an artist, and he had a particularly fine form. No, she'd been led astray by a passion she should never have let herself experience.

But she was finished showing weakness every time Leo touched her.

Behind her, she heard a splash and a ripple of water, and realized Leo was in the bathtub—naked. She wanted to groan but held it inside. She would be traveling south with him, and this would become a frequent occurrence. Surely she could find occasions, when he was out playing cards with strangers or flirting with women, when she could bathe in peace.

She had no illusions that he would leave other women alone. Her days and evenings would be solitary, when all she'd wanted was a companion to share her life with. Her throat felt so tight that swallowing was difficult.

"The bath is refreshing after days of travel," Leo said, his voice stiff but not unkind.

She wanted to ignore him but found the thought of endless silence too much. "I am glad to know it. Enjoy yourself."

"We both could enjoy ourselves tonight." His voice had gotten quieter, deeper.

"Then you must have a plan I know nothing about, for it will not be with me." The force of her rising anger could no longer be denied. She whirled about, hands on her hips. "Regardless of whether we share that bed, you will not have my body tonight."

Water gleamed on his skin and dripped from the waves of his hair. The bathwater just reached his waist, and she was grateful for the soapiness that obscured the rest of his body. His bent knees pointed to the ceiling. She reminded herself that she'd seen plenty of nude bodies before.

"I understand your anger, and I am content to wait," he said solemnly. "But you are my wife, Susanna, and pretending it's not so won't make it go away."

"You maneuvered me into this marriage—"

"You know I didn't plant someone in the corridor at Bramfield Hall to spy on us."

"Perhaps not, but I would have gladly retired to the country for good. The scandal of a kiss would have died down."

"You cannot believe that."

"Yes, I can. There was no reason for you to kidnap me except to finish a plan you must have started weeks ago."

He leaned back in the tub, impressive arms spread wide. "Now you're inventing stories that aren't true. Do they make you feel better, the righteous spinster done wrong?"

"You wouldn't be the first man to force a marriage for money. And though I can no longer control my own dowry, I can deny you the only thing left that's mine to give." She blinked damp eyes. "Don't confuse the naïve woman I was before with the wronged wife I am now. Believe me, you made certain I changed."

She stalked to the table and sat down to eat the

still-warm food. This marriage was a battlefield, and she would need all her strength and wiles. She wouldn't underestimate Leo's abilities at guile and persuasion, or her own weaknesses.

He finished his bath in silence. She could not miss the way he rose, dripping, from the water, since he was right next to her, but she kept her eyes on her plate. Let him think his nudity would sway her—*he* could be the fool for a change.

She heard him dressing, and then was surprised when he opened the door and looked out into the hall.

"You there, boy, can you bring more servants to replace the bathwater for my wife? And a bottle of champagne. We're celebrating."

My wife. The words made her tremble. She'd told him she wouldn't bathe in front of him, but apparently he didn't care.

When the servants had finished with the tub, they took away her tray of food and left behind the bottle Leo had requested. He poured himself a glass and sat down.

"So what is paying for that—my money or yours?" she asked coolly.

"Everything is now 'ours,' my dear. You signed your name to that."

She sighed. "You don't need to keep me company. The evening is yet early. Perhaps you'd find drunken compatriots in the nearest taproom. Isn't that your usual habit every night?"

"Not on my wedding night. One of us needs to

remember that rumors can reach London even from the wild north." He took another long drink of champagne.

Susanna could not watch him. She pulled a large sketchbook from her trunk, then sat near the open window to draw. Behind her, he drank in silence, and when at last even the sound of the glass hitting the table was gone, she peered over her shoulder. He was asleep in his chair, head lolling forward. The first snore passed his lips.

He *snored*, she thought with exasperation. That would prove difficult when they could not have separate accommodations, but once they were home, she'd be certain to have her own chambers.

Home, she thought bleakly. Where would that be? They hadn't discussed it, of course—they hadn't discussed anything. For all she knew, creditors were on his trail or a furious father with a pistol. But she would have to take each day as it came.

Would he insist they live in London with his brother the viscount? There was plenty of room at the ducal residences she'd grown up in, but she didn't imagine Leo wanted to be so closely watched by her relatives. And certainly he couldn't afford his own town house—even her dowry would only go so far, especially if he went through it at a quick pace.

She'd agreed to the marriage to avoid shaming her family—she was not going to shame them by living apart from her husband unless his behavior forced her to.

The gentle snoring continued.

"Leo?" she said softly.

He made no answer, didn't even move. She ducked out of the room to find the necessary. When she returned, he hadn't changed position. She took the glass from his hand and set it on the table, wondering sadly if she would be doing this often as his wife. Straightening her back, which still ached from the journey, she looked again at the tub—and made her decision.

Quickly, she began to unbutton her gown.

Leo kept his eyes closed and his breathing even. The snore required more conscious effort, but he'd needed it to convince her that he was truly asleep. And it had worked. From beneath his lashes, he watched her disrobe, feeling not one bit of guilt. She was his wife, after all.

He'd hatched this plan to allow her to bathe after their journey since she was too proud to give in to his suggestion, and he wasn't quite ready to risk leaving her alone. Now he wondered if he hadn't subconsciously planned this for his own benefit—or his own torture.

Susanna began to remove the pins from her hair, until the auburn locks fell one by one around her shoulders and down her back. He'd never imagined a woman's hair could be so sensual, but then he'd always been able to touch as much as he wanted, and being forbidden was a new sensation for him. She kept her back to him as she stepped out of the gown, laying it across the bed. Several petticoats soon contributed to the stack. To his surprise, her corset unhooked at the front, something he'd seldom seen in his vast experience. But then a relative of a duke would have the latest fashion conveniences. With her back to him, she managed to unlace her boots, remove her garters and stockings, and untie her drawers. Each feminine step had his attention, as more and more of her willowy shape was revealed. He swallowed heavily.

At last, she was wearing only a chemise. She turned from the tub and glanced at him, but he'd been careful not to move, and to continue snoring. She crept to her trunk and brought forth another small pile of clean clothing to set beside the tub. She gave him a last glance, then unbuttoned the delicate fastenings of her chemise, and, turning her back, pulled the garment over her head.

Leo could have choked on a snore, but he forced it down. In the candlelight, her warm skin glowed like soft, creamy satin, so pale and flawless. Her back curved down to a slender waist, and her hips flared with womanly grace. Her legs were long and supple for a woman who spent much time sitting as she painted. When she bent over the tub, his eyes widened at the erotic display. Was this the body in the painting? He wanted—needed—her to turn around. If he couldn't enjoy her passion this night, at least she could satisfy his curiosity. There was a little mole on her thigh that would convince him once and for all.

He swept his lashes almost all the way down again. He was unhappily married because of that damned painting—why was he dwelling on it? If winning the wager was the only satisfaction he was to get, his life would be bleak.

She stepped into the tub and sank down with a sigh that made him think of a moan of pleasure. It skittered along his nerves until he needed to adjust himself, but couldn't move—didn't want to move. He'd tolerate much to watch Susanna's bath.

She wasted no time using the facecloth to wash her body. Though her back was to him, every time she reached for the soap on a stool beside her, he could see the glistening roundness of her breast. He wanted to see if her nipples were as dark as the woman's in the painting, but was having no luck.

Since the tub wasn't deep, she used an empty bucket to dampen her hair, then soaped it, catching up every tendril. He liked the lean limberness of her arms and imagined them about his body, holding him to her.

But perhaps she'd already done such things with a man if her intimate "friendship" with Roger Eastfield held any clue. He couldn't imagine a man spending hours with a naked woman and not trying to bed her. Unless artists were a different breed of men—or perhaps Eastfield even preferred men. But the hand that had painted that gorgeous nude had envisioned his creation with a deft touch, a means of worship of the female body—perhaps a body he'd worshipped.

Was Susanna no longer a virgin? And did it matter to Leo? Logically, he knew his own past was quite stained, and he should not care about hers, but a primitive part of him wanted to be the first, the only man in her bed.

She rinsed her hair with the last bucket of fresh water, and he expected her to scurry out in case he should awaken. Instead, she sat still, her shoulders hunched, not even as if she were enjoying the bath.

And then she covered her face, and he realized she was crying. Her body trembled with it, though she made no sound. He didn't know what he was supposed to feel, but his jumbled emotions were mixed up with a bleak sensation of loss. This was the only wedding night he would ever have, and his new bride was crying as if the worst thing imaginable had happened to her.

He wasn't a monster out to destroy her life. He wouldn't keep her from her art or her family. He would give her children to love if she ever offered him the chance.

The fact that he'd brought such a strong woman to grief made him feel sad and empty inside. He'd played a game of seduction, and it had led to this moment of despair. His marriage was already as bad as his own parents' had been, and it was only hours old.

That thought made a sick feeling of disbelief twist inside him. He didn't want to be like them, making Susanna and their children miserable. Somehow, he had to earn her trust, to prove to her—and himself— that he could change.

When at last with a sigh she rose to dry off, she donned a nightgown, then the dressing gown he remembered. At the window, she took a comb and began to work it through her hair, letting the cool evening breeze help dry it. But this wasn't southern England, and she soon shivered and moved away, fastening a quick braid.

He watched her turn down the bed and debated what to do. Should he wait for her to fall asleep, then crawl into bed when she couldn't refuse him entrance? That seemed cowardly, and not an example he wanted to set for the rest of their marriage.

He gave a little start, then opened his eyes in a bleary manner and looked around. She was watching him warily from her place near the bed, and once again, she gripped her dressing gown closed at the neck.

Feeling sad and guilty, he said quietly. "I have never had to force a lady into my bed, and I certainly won't start now. Trust in that, if nothing else."

"I don't intend to sleep on a wooden chair, but that's not the same thing as giving myself to you."

"No, you did that earlier today."

He rose up and saw the way her eyes widened as he towered above her. He suspected she was more afraid of herself than him. A woman like Susanna prided herself on control, something he'd grown to admire. But since being compromised, she no longer had it. He was tempted to use the chamber pot, but decided it wasn't the best way to romance his wife, so he went to the public privy.

When he returned, he pulled off his shirt and trousers.

"You can stop right there," she said.

He arched a brow. "Wear drawers to bed? What a novel concept. I haven't worn nightclothes since my childhood."

"Then you can start learning to be civil now."

She climbed up into bed, sliding to the far side.

"Not going to remove your dressing gown?" he asked.

"No."

He came up on the bed and was surprised when she didn't shrink away from him. She flounced onto her side, giving him her back, and pulled the counterpane up to her chin.

He blew out the candle and lay back in bed, arms clasped behind his head. He was not a man to dwell over regrets now that he'd made up his mind to change things for the better. Yes, his wedding night was nothing like he'd ever imagined, but he would never be able to accuse Susanna of being boring. She'd been a challenge from the moment he saw her dressed as a boy, trying to steal that painting. Never had he imagined finding a challenging woman interesting, but from that moment, she'd been all he could think of. He'd told himself it was about the wager, but now he couldn't help wondering . . .

To his surprise, she fell asleep quickly. He could almost feel the relaxation steal languidly through her. Though he wanted to sleep up against her, it was too soon. He would need to slowly seduce her all over again, her mind and heart, as well as her body. And this time, there was more at stake than a wager.

The rest of their life together pivoted on a point, and it could go either way.

She followed him into sleep—or at least the painting did. Her golden curves beckoned him, and he kept expecting it to come to life. Instead, the paint seemed to fade, to dry. Faint cracks began to alter the surface, brittle little spiderwebs that marred its beauty. The paint flaked, the canvas crumbled, and Leo awoke in the night with an even deeper feeling of dread.

Chapter 13

Susanna slowly emerged from sleep, feeling so very warm, as if she floated in a cocoon that kept out not only the cold, but even the most unpleasant thoughts. She'd been so exhausted that emerging from her deep sleep seemed . . . confusing. She didn't want to leave the safety, didn't want to remember—

Her marriage.

Her new husband was flush against her back, his thighs against hers, his hips cradling her backside.

"Good morning, Mrs. Wade," he murmured against her neck.

The soft press of his lips took her by surprise, as did the very obvious erection against her backside. Her first impulse was to jump up and flee, but that would only either amuse or anger him. Either way, he would feel like he had the upper hand.

And right now, his hand was moving slowly up her rib cage.

She gripped him by the wrist and lifted it away from her. "Excuse me. I thought I might have embarrassed myself by moving toward your warmth in the night, but since I'm still on my side of the bed, I can see what happened."

She sat up, betraying no urgency, no dismay. Because some deep part of her had responded to his warmth, to his very maleness. She'd wanted to roll over, press against him, and learn everything—*everything*—about him. Even after all he'd done, how he'd trapped her for eternity. He had some kind of control over her body that bewildered her.

Looking over her shoulder, she said, "I do believe it's time to depart Scotland."

He sank onto his back and stretched, eyes closed, which allowed her to take in the stubble of his beard, the intimidating width of his chest, the way his spine arched, and how his muscles stretched over bone. Fascinating. She gave a little start, even as her fingers itched for a pencil.

But he was . . . different this morning, his expression one of peace. She could only conclude he was satisfied that he'd gotten everything he wanted from this marriage.

Well, not everything, she reminded herself. And he hadn't insisted on his husbandly rights. Much as she'd been angry when she'd denied him—she was *still* angry—she was rational enough to realize that he was being patient with her. He'd always been able to have any woman he wanted, and now his own wife had denied him. That could have sent many men into a towering rage. But not Leo.

"We aren't leaving today, Mrs. Wade," he said, as

his eyes half opened to take in her disheveled state.

"Staying here won't change anything."

"But it will rest our coachman, who stayed awake through the night to see us love-struck fools safely married. I think he deserves another day of rest."

She pressed her lips together, a bit embarrassed that she hadn't considered the poor man and reluctantly grateful that Leo had. "Of course."

"No need to amuse yourself. I can give you all the attention you need."

As he reached his hand toward her hip, she stood up. "Unlike a young debutante you might have married, I need little of your attention. I am used to being on my own."

He shrugged. "Have it your way, Mrs. Wade."

She stiffened, wondering if he would find other amusements, feeling another stab of self-pity at what her married life would be like. "Will you please stop calling me that?"

"Mrs. Wade? But it's your name."

"I've been Susanna to you from the beginning."

"It was far too familiar for me to use, or so you constantly reminded me. Now you've changed your mind?"

She didn't need to answer as they heard a knock on the door. "It must be the maid. I'll send her away until we're dressed."

Leo sat up and tucked the counterpane around his waist. "No need. I'm starving. Come in!" he called.

The little maid paused on the threshold and couldn't miss Leo's display. The girl turned away to hide an obvious grin, then brought in a breakfast tray.

"Ye'll be stayin' another day, Mrs. Wade?" she asked.

Susanna nodded, speaking through clenched teeth. "We shall."

"Let me take the rest of your garments and have them cleaned."

"Thank you," she answered. "I don't think I heard your name."

"Bess, ma'am."

She was a ma'am now, Susanna thought despondently.

They busied themselves over the domestic chore, and she would have sent Bess away, but the girl said, "Would not the master want his clothes cleaned?"

Leo, arms folded over his chest, grinned wickedly at the girl. "Mrs. Wade can't quite think straight this morn, Bess. I'll have to remind her again that she's married now."

Susanna's face burned as Bess giggled, but she forced herself to open Leo's trunk and remove several garments. She handed over another coin and saw the girl out.

She stared at the laden tray, her eyes unfocused, fighting melancholy. She didn't hear Leo approach until he put his big hand on her waist to lean over her shoulder and sniff appreciatively.

"Ah, shall we eat?"

She stepped away from his touch and the very heat of all that naked skin. "It cannot be decent to eat in your underclothes." Now she sounded like a prude, and she certainly had never considered herself one. But he was wearing so little, and it was affecting her regardless of how angry she was.

"It's our marriage; we can decide what's decent." He sat down and uncovered a plate of boiled eggs and fried fish. "Won't you join me, Mrs. Wade?"

He knew how irritated she was by her new name, but he would keep using it. She could not continue to let him know how easily he annoyed her. Sitting down, she began to work at her own plate, trying not to look at him and his fascinating nude chest.

"Then we leave tomorrow?" she asked.

"If you wish. Or we could stay as long as you like. It is our honeymoon."

She gave him a bewildered stare. "A honeymoon?"

He only grinned and lifted an eyebrow suggestively.

"We must return the carriage to Lord Bramfield," she insisted.

"He has others. I'm in no rush. Do you have somewhere to be?"

"It no longer matters, does it?"

His smile faded. "It does to me. I do not plan to take over your very life, you know."

"But you already have."

"I won't keep you locked up in your room or force you out of London. Oh, that's right, you prefer the countryside, do you not?"

"Then where will we live?"

He put down his fork. "I admit, I've had no time

to give it thought. Though you insist on believing otherwise, I had no dark plans to force a marriage between us."

She didn't believe him.

He inhaled, then let his breath out slowly. "My brother and his wife will only be too happy to accommodate us until we decide."

She nodded, wondering what Viscount Wade would think of their quick wedding. Would he be ashamed or appalled, or was he used to his brother's behavior? Surely Lady Wade would be reluctant to associate with her.

"But we will be taking our time journeying to London," Leo continued. "I have people in the north I haven't seen for a long time. I'll introduce you."

What could she do but nod? Even if they reached a town with a railway station, she could hardly flee her own husband. She was trapped, she thought bleakly, until the end of her days.

"And I have other reasons to delay our homecoming," he said in a huskier voice.

She couldn't help but meet his eyes and found them half-closed, his face a picture of languid indolence. She should be affronted or angry; instead, his regard made her feel both uneasy and nervous.

"I want to learn everything about you, Mrs. Wade," he murmured, "every place on your body that's sensitive, every secret those dark eyes are hiding from me."

She trembled although it wasn't out of fear or anger. Hoping her voice didn't betray her, she managed, "Then you'll be waiting a long time."

"I have a lifetime." He gave her a wicked, sensual smile.

A lifetime, her mind echoed with dismay. She busied herself with the newspaper as he finished breakfast. He didn't ask for a section, nor did he even glance at the headlines, which made her frown. Was he interested in nothing but his own amusements? But she knew there was an intelligence inside his brain that he kept hidden. Whatever the reason, he didn't like anyone to know about it, not even her. Would she never have an intellectual conversation again except with friends? If she had any friends after this scandal . . .

When he rose to dress, she averted her gaze. He shaved his beard without the services of a valet, even as she ate her food slowly, wondering how she was supposed to see to her own toilette with him in the room. That feeling of being trapped was creeping up her throat again, as if a hand slowly squeezed. Last night proved he wasn't the sort of man who would force her to do anything, even dress in front of him. At least she hadn't been wrong about some of the honor she'd begun to associate with him before this farce. But what did she know of him after all, except every wicked, whispered rumor?

She jumped when he said, "Mrs. Wade? Shouldn't you be dressing? Or will you remain in the room all day waiting for me?"

"I'll send for Bess to help me. You may leave and

do as you wish. Find a card game or someone to drink with."

He laughed. "I assure you I do not imbibe so early in the morning. But very well, I will give you time to yourself."

And then he took himself off, and it was as if the very room deflated with his absence. The silence echoed hollowly, and she couldn't decide if she should be glad of it or see it as a preview of her life to come. Eventually, she would give in to him and do her marital duty; eventually—quickly?—he would grow bored with her, and stay away longer and longer. She would be alone all of the time.

Unless he gambled away all of her money, leaving them so poor as to remain beholden to his family for a place to stay. Then she'd never have her own home.

She put her face in her hands, but her eyes remained dry. Thankfully, Bess knocked and came in, allowing Susanna to briefly put her troubles aside.

The village of Gretna Green had a bookshop, according to their host, Mr. Linton, so Susanna donned her spectacles, gathered her colorbox and sketchbook, and walked down through Gretna Hall. She paused in the entrance hall, certain she could hear Leo's laughter. Walking quietly, she followed the sound to the parlor. She leaned against the wall and listened in dismay to his smooth voice, and the girlish laughter of a young woman. She told herself she could expect no better, that he was a rake born to flirt, and marriage wouldn't stop such a man.

She pushed away from the wall and out the door, following Mr. Linton's directions to the bookshop. It was difficult to keep her thoughts under control when her head buzzed with questions and worries. What was happening with Rebecca and Elizabeth, and were the pursuing men as dangerous to their lives as Leo had turned out to be? Would Susanna's reckless marriage affect them in some terrible way?

Gripping the handle of her colorbox, she berated herself for her stupidity. She'd foolishly thought to find happiness the same way her brother had, by taking a daunting risk. He'd returned from India, where he'd been thought dead, only to find Emily pretending to be his wife. They'd each taken a risk to learn to trust each other, to fall in love. Susanna should have known that such luck was rare, that her own risk-taking would make her miserable.

She glanced up at the overcast sky, thinking it matched her very mood. She'd tried to change herself, to find a husband who would suit her, and it had exploded in her face. She was tired of changing herself for others, and she wasn't going to do it anymore. Leo had wanted a conventional wife, so she would show him that he'd made a mistake—she would be the most unconventional wife imaginable, a bluestocking through and through.

She felt as if she could breathe again. She would be herself and let Leo reap his reward for compromising her. She entered the bookshop and took a lungful of musty air. It smelled so good to her! She greeted the hunched proprietor, Mr. Stanfield, who scratched his gray beard and smiled at her. With only a question or two, she discovered that he, too, shared a love of art, and soon they had their heads buried in dusty old shelves as he found her book after book.

When they returned to the front of the store, Mr. Stanfield wrapped the books she'd purchased in paper and tied it with a string. She said a cheery good day and left the store, only to come up short on seeing Leo leaning indolently against the building, his smile slow and knowing. She tossed the stack of books toward him, and he juggled the package against his chest. When he eyed her doubtfully, she felt almost serene as she began to walk away.

"Go on ahead to the hotel," she said, motioning across the green. "I'm going to paint by the church. I promised Mr. Tyler that I would send him a watercolor anytime I discovered an interesting flower."

If the thought of her doing something for another man disconcerted him, he didn't show it.

"I will allow your consideration," he said lightly.

"Allow?" she answered over her shoulder as she marched. "You misunderstand me. I am not asking for your permission. For the first time in my life, I can do what I want and have no one to please but myself."

She saw his arched brow but pretended she didn't.

"If you think to stop me," she continued, "I'll make certain your family knows exactly how our marriage began—and what you did."

"You make it sound as if such things can be kept secret," he mused.

She only shrugged. "So you don't mind that your brother learns of *another* poor decision on your part?"

"There are so many. What is one more?"

Fine, then she didn't have anything to threaten him with. Short of locking her up, he couldn't stop her—and even then, she would scream enough to wake the dead. And *she* ought to know how impossible that was!

To her surprise, he returned from depositing her books at the hotel with a blanket to sit on. No, not sit, lounge. While she sat on the church stairs, trying to concentrate on the light pencil sketch she was making before using her watercolors, he rested his head back on his bent arms and closed his eyes. Concentration was difficult with such an . . . improper man.

Her husband.

Glancing at him again, she spoke with disapproval. "It's only midmorning. Are you tired already?"

"It was difficult to sleep. You insisted on being in my arms all night, arousing me and leaving me frustrated."

She flushed with embarrassment, looking quickly around, but no one was near them. She opened her mouth to retort, but now he was watching her, and for a brief moment, she saw something unreadable flash in his eyes.

Was he lying? She didn't know the signs, after all, since every word he uttered was so smoothly spoken.

"Nothing to say?" he countered, his voice laced with amusement.

She leaned to examine the veins in the leaves. "You brought your travails on yourself," she said, then determined to ignore him.

That night, Susanna stared at the bathing tub that had been placed in their room while they had dinner in the public parlor. Steam rose from it, and she watched it longingly.

"Excellent service," Leo said from behind her.

She gave a little start, not having realized how close he was to her. He shut the door.

"You might as well bathe, Mrs. Wade. I watched you do so last evening, after all."

She whirled to face him. "But you were asleep!"

His grin reminded her of a pirate.

"You *weren't* asleep—or drunk?" she said.

"No. I am simply your husband, and I knew how much you desperately longed for a bath after our journey."

As words failed her, he gave a hearty sigh.

"You have no need to worry. I could only see your back."

All of her back—and below, she realized, swallowing. And yet he still hadn't pressed for his marital rights. One thing to admire, and perhaps she should hold on to that. Unless he'd only pretended to be attracted to her. But she could not believe so of him.

"It's sad when one can't trust one's own husband," she said. "But I cannot say I wasn't warned. I did hear the rumors. There was another young lady you nearly ruined."

His lips seemed to tighten though the smile remained. "So now you believe all gossip to be fact?"

"Isn't most of it?"

When he said nothing, she had her answer. But she refused to ask for all the details if that's what he wanted. Gossip was salacious—and when it was about one's own husband? Even worse.

The two of them had added even more gossip to London's seething stew. What must Society be saying? She didn't want to think about their pity—or their ugly curiosity.

Leo shrugged off his coat. "I can keep my back turned."

"What?"

"If you need that condition in order to bathe."

When she was silent, he added, "Must I put a vow into words?"

"No, I accept your offer."

"Do you need my assistance with the hooks of your gown?"

She shook her head, knowing she only had a few gowns that fastened up the front. Soon enough she'd have to don another, and then he'd be regularly volunteering to help.

But as she began to disrobe, Leo lazily undid the buttons of his waistcoat, watching her. There was almost a darkness in his eyes that still seemed heated, as if even his thoughts were burning. Certainly, his regard made her skin flame in response, confusing her. If he was putting on a pretense, her body was falling for it. She could not refuse him for long; she was his wife, after all. She well remembered the way he made her feel, stretched out beneath him on the drawing-room floor at Bramfield Hall. Eager and desperate and uncertain all at the same time. She closed her eyes, for she no longer knew what was real and what wasn't.

"Then please turn around," she said.

He dragged a chair to the window.

"You could read one of the books I purchased."

"No, thank you," he said dryly.

He hadn't even looked at the titles, she thought. Probably the last book he read had been at university—had he even attended? Though after his conversation about Darwin's specimens, she'd debated if he had. She would have given her life to attend Cambridge. But women weren't permitted.

Her clothing seemed loud as it slithered down her body, silk against silk. Glancing at him, she saw him turning her sketching pencil in little circles on the table.

She froze for a moment, naked, knowing he could insist she climb into their bed. What would she do then? Not scream even though she was still angry enough. Someone would send for the constable, and what would she say: *Constable, I don't wish to sleep with my new husband.* She bit her lip, surprised to find even a spark of amusement in the whole situation.

She stepped into the water and quickly sat, deciding that she needed to distract him. "Much as we are now married, I haven't forgotten the wager."

"Believe me, neither have I. One would think a wife would help her husband win."

Her snort was far from ladylike. "Not if it harms the wife's position. Besides, I have even more reason for not wanting you to win."

"Revenge?" he said over his shoulder. "Not difficult to figure out."

She tried to make as little noise as possible as she rinsed the facecloth and soaped her arms. But the sound of dripping water seemed loud in the small bedchamber. He continued to twirl her pencil, as if he couldn't sit still and had to do something with his hands. The hands that had touched her through her clothing, had felt so sinfully good that she lost all her sense, allowing him to do—

"We need to write to our parents," she said, wincing at the breathless sound of her voice. She quickly scrubbed her legs.

"Why? They'll hear our news soon enough."

"You cannot keep me a secret forever, much as you might wish to do so."

"And why would I want to keep my lovely bride a secret?"

"True. Your family will rejoice that you have your own money now."

"Sleep in peace, Mrs. Wade. My brother does not take care of me. And I'm not keeping any secrets from him. But as for my mother, we don't often correspond."

She paused, lifting her damp face from the cloth. "That is truly sad."

"Have you met my mother?"

"No."

"Believe me, you needn't be in a hurry."

"So you don't get along," she said, feeling a twinge of sympathy.

He laughed. "Far from it. I can do no wrong in my mother's eyes."

She frowned. "Then I don't understand."

"It was uncomfortable to watch how my mother fawned over my brother and me, while practically ignoring our sister Georgiana." He half turned his head so that she could almost see his profile. "You and my sister will be the best of friends."

"Much as your mother's behavior toward your sister is poor, it could not be bad that she loved you," she said.

"Love? Was it love when Simon went blind, and my mother couldn't be with him because he made her too uncomfortable? He was no longer capable of being the darling of Society, so she left as soon as she convinced herself he was healthy enough."

She winced. "That is . . . sad." So their mother paid attention to her sons when they were popular among the *ton*. It was as if another crack in the wall of his childhood secrets was revealed to her, giving her a glimpse of some of the reasons he'd made choices in his life.

"Luckily, he had my grandmother."

"And you and Georgiana?"

"Yes, although I briefly felt helpless myself. What does one say to a brother newly blind—everything will be all right?" His hand came down hard on the pencil, stopping its spinning. "And now it's all about me," he continued with faint sarcasm. "I've become my mother's golden child. And if one of my sins reaches her ears, she defends me as if I've graced her by floating to the earth wearing angel's wings."

Though she didn't laugh, there was a deep part of her that saw humor in that. Until she began to wonder how his mother would accept a daughter-in-law not blissfully in love with her son, one long past the blush of innocent youth.

She hoped they wouldn't have to live with Lady Wade.

"Do not worry about your parents," he said. "We'll visit them first. Are they in London?"

"They were going to Cambridgeshire, I believe."

"Then that's where we'll go. Will you still write a letter with our momentous announcement?"

She hesitated. "No. The news would be best delivered in person."

She dried off and quickly dressed in her nightgown, watching Leo the whole time. He cocked his head just as she was donning her dressing gown, then turned about before she could even offer permission. She didn't want to know how he so perfectly timed it, or if his hearing was that sensitive.

Leo slowly rose to his feet, his smile fading as he continued to undress. She wanted to look away, but his gaze seemed to challenge her, and the spell was only broken when he lifted his shirt over his head. She went to study the flower she'd painted and left to dry near the window.

"I won't be ready to leave tomorrow," she found herself saying, testing his insistence that he wouldn't be a tyrant.

"Very well."

"You don't even want to know why?"

"I assume there are more flowers Tyler needs to see?"

Drat. It was hardly as if he would care about another man. As her husband, he had no competition.

Maybe she could make him think she'd be unfaithful . . . but no, she could not be that sort of person, or even pretend to be. She wouldn't be like Leo.

Chapter 14

After a sleep-tossed night, where Leo alternated between lusty wakefulness and dreams of rats in the dark, he sat alone in their chambers. He was only too glad to let Susanna have her rebellion of painting pictures for Tyler. She needed to understand by more than his words that he wanted her to feel the freedom to enjoy her life.

She still slept peacefully. As the sun came up, he'd found himself watching her. Several locks of auburn hair had escaped her braid to spread over the pillow and even cup her cheek. With the warmer summer night, she'd tossed off the counterpane, and he could see her bare feet.

He must be crazed to think her feet captivating, but they were, especially since they were parted, implying the same of her thighs. His heart had stuttered momentarily. When she lay on her back, he could see the slope of her breasts, not so rounded as some, but an easy mouthful.

But she'd ignored or been blissfully unaware of his unrequited passion, and had taken her painting supplies and left their chamber. Now he sipped his coffee and considered what else had kept him awake. Surely his mind was muddled at her nearness. Rats in the dark? He'd never had such dreams before. And the more he considered it, the easier it was to go find something else to amuse him.

But what was there to do in this Scottish village?

In the carriage two days later, as they crossed the border back into England, Susanna stared out the window, feeling the tension in her neck like a band.

"Should I explain myself to you?" Leo asked mildly.

She heard something fall and turned her head to see a pile of her recently acquired books topple into his lap. As the dust rose, he sneezed.

"You don't need to," she said.

"They were boxing matches, Mrs. Wade. A tournament."

Once again, she winced the slightest bit at her new title. "It is a barbaric sport—no, it cannot even be called a sport."

"Of course it's a sport."

"It's an ugly amusement for bored men who only want to see blood."

"It is a competition of strategy with an element of risk involved. Scots are known for their hardiness. I wanted to see it in action. And remember, my new bride did not wish to spend her honeymoon with me."

She picked up a book that had fallen to the floor. "This was recommended by the proprietor. It's a biography of Giles Cobbett, a famous Yorkshire artist. I would like to visit his home when we're in York."

"Then you'd like York to be a stop on our journey." He leaned back in the corner of the carriage, eyes at half-mast.

"You don't need to accompany me to his studio."

He closed his eyes all the way and didn't answer.

But if he did accompany her, she would make certain he heard every detail of her new fascination.

"Is that a smile on my wife's pretty lips?" Leo suddenly asked.

With a start, she glanced at him. "Excuse me?"

"I have not seen your real smile since . . ." His words trailed off as he continued to watch her with speculation.

She picked up a book and opened it. Dust rose in a cloud. He sneezed again, and she pressed her lips together to hide a real smile.

By late afternoon, they arrived at a lovely estate nestled in the valley between two high ranges in Westmorland. The Edgecumbes were an older couple with a son away at Oxford, and three grown daughters at home, including one, a widow, who'd newly emerged from mourning. They all greeted Leo with easy familiarity, no hesitation in anyone's manner. Leo had already told Susanna he had first met them through his brother, but still, they didn't seem to care about his reputation at all, even around their daughters.

What they didn't hide was their shock when he introduced her as his wife. Lady Edgecumbe, dimpled and plump beneath her lace cap, glanced briefly at her daughters in dismay, as if she'd harbored hopes that Leo would make one of them his bride. Susanna wondered if they were surprised he actually married or at his choice in wife. The two of them must look so very odd: Leo so handsome, and she, so plain. To outsiders, it must seem either a love match or a need for wealth.

The clothing the family wore to dinner that night was of the smartest styles. Perhaps they looked at Susanna as if *she* were the country maiden, with her several-year-old gowns.

At dinner, Leo was seated between Susanna and Lady Edgecumbe, who gushed, "I still cannot believe you are here, dear Leo."

Christian names, yet, Susanna mused. She smiled at the sisters, who all studied her without making it obvious.

"You've always told me to call, my lady," Leo said, taking up her hand to kiss it.

She giggled and batted him away playfully. One thing about Leo—he flirted with young and old alike, and all seemed to appreciate it. Leo briefly told them about Simon's marriage and Georgiana's engagement, which seemed to lead right into—

"And how did you meet your lovely wife?" Lord Edgecumbe asked. He was tall and thin to his wife's short and plump, with thinning blond hair that was going white.

Susanna realized they'd never discussed in advance how they would explain their marriage to the world. She donned her spectacles and peered at him, daring him to explain his bluestocking wife.

Leo smiled at her with all the infatuation of a new bridegroom. "My wife moved in the same London circles, and I knew her brother. We share an interest in art that brought us together."

Art? She thought, amused. Her art? Or that painting in his club she'd tried to steal? But at least this story was tame and skirted the truth. She could not help being grateful at his tact, even as she realized she already trusted his discretion. But then Leo suddenly leaned forward, as if he were about to impart a great secret, and Susanna felt the knots in her stomach begin to tighten once again.

"At a house party at Bramfield Hall, we realized at last that we were experiencing the same love and longing."

The two younger daughters, both with blond ringlets, looked at each other and giggled. Their older sister, calmer with the experience of widowhood, only narrowed her eyes with consideration.

"I convinced Susanna that we need not wait to be happy," Leo continued, "that we were both old enough to know our own minds."

Every female pair of eyes landed on Susanna, and she knew her advanced age had not gone unnoticed. But she could only stare at Leo as she realized how honest he was about to be.

"So we drove to Gretna Green and were married," he said, grinning with open delight.

There was a brief moment of silence, during which

Susanna smiled at him with indulgence. She could never deliberately embarrass her husband.

Lady Edgecumbe clapped her hands together. "So this is your wedding journey," she cried. "We feel so fortunate."

Mrs. Appleby, the widowed daughter, didn't look as if she shared her mother's sentiments. She stared at Leo, blinking eyes full of questions and doubts. Leo had to know most people would think there was much more to their elopement.

They all retired to the drawing room together, where Leo took over the conversation, as if to set everyone at ease and make his story of a happy marriage even more plausible.

When Lady Edgecumbe offered Susanna an embroidery sampler, she declined, patiently watching Leo question his lordship about his crops. She wouldn't have thought he was interested in farming, but he gave that very impression. Much as it was gibberish to her, Lord Edgecumbe listened and nodded to everything Leo said.

Leo seemed to relax as the center of entertainment, questioning the younger daughters about their legions of suitors, even though he knew one girl was still in the schoolroom and the other freshly out. He made them giggle and blush, and Lady Edgecumbe watched the display with a touch of regret, as if he could have been her son-in-law.

Susanna adjusted her spectacles, picked up the book she'd brought, and pretended to read it. She was an unconventional wife, after all.

But somewhere during the evening, Leo seemed to forget his new status. Susanna listened with growing dismay as he actually seemed to flirt, behaving as a roguish bachelor rather than a newly married man. Had he forgotten about her already? The lovely Widow Appleby had begun to blossom under his attention, and soon was even persuaded to sing.

Susanna anticipated how it would be in London, under the *ton's* piercing regard. If they weren't careful, there would be no respect between them, perhaps even no cordiality after a while. She'd seen more than one husband and wife flee to separate sides of the ballroom the moment they arrived, as if they couldn't wait to be apart.

She didn't want her life to be like that. Leo wasn't the only one to blame for this marriage, for he hadn't forced her response to his seduction. They would be together for the rest of their lives, and somehow they had to find a way to suit, to make the best of their marriage.

But she was a bluestocking, and she couldn't let her husband think she would change her very nature for him. She pushed her spectacles higher on her nose, turned to Lady Edgecumbe, and began a long conversation about the famous artists of England, and the names of some she'd like to visit as they traveled south. She didn't look at Leo as he leafed through sheet music with Mrs. Appleby though she did give him a nod of soft approval when he danced with each of the young daughters. His answering smile was almost tender, and it made her feel flustered.

Susanna retired for the evening before any of the household. She had her own room in their little suite, but Leo never tried her door. She didn't even know what time he came to bed. Her thoughts veered back quickly into worry and dismay. Was he with Mrs. Appleby? Would Susanna's life now be an endless parade of widows and mistresses sympathetic to Leo's plight?

She could not wonder and worry every night; somehow she had to find peace, to become a wife Leo wouldn't want to ignore.

The next morning, Leo didn't even hesitate as he entered his wife's room. He knew she'd already be awake, for he guessed she was an early riser. He did not usually see the dawn unless it was just as he was going to bed, but he'd made certain not to stay up too late. He needed a clear head to match wits with Susanna. He used to prefer women with typical feminine interests, like shopping and gossiping, and witty wordplay was his contribution. But with Susanna, he constantly had to think, to come up with the right challenging phrase. He was still surprised at how much he looked forward to it.

He paused on the threshold, knowing she hadn't seen him yet. She was bent over a table, studying her latest drawing for Tyler—damn, it was getting harder and harder to hide his irritation, but hide it he must, lest she misunderstand his motives. He wasn't concerned about the man himself; Susanna would have grown bored with him if she'd spent any more time with him. Peaceful companionship? What was that next to desire and the delights of being in bed together? But of course, she didn't know that yet, and he was impatient to show her.

He imagined backing her toward their bed, leaning over her when she tumbled into the pillows, knowing she wouldn't resist for long.

But what kind of seduction was that? He wanted to see her weak with anticipation, unable to form even words of pleading, so suffused with desire would she be.

Patience, he said again, mastering himself. She would come to know him, would see that she could trust him. Trust came from knowing each other well, and he thought he was on the way to understanding her. Though she believed otherwise, she was not a woman to retire placidly to the country, with nothing to spark her curiosity but more pastoral scenes and a husband who put his scientific experiments above her. She hadn't ventured far into life, didn't know what he knew—that she was a woman of passion, and not just for the physical.

Since she still hadn't seen him, he called, "Good morning, Mrs. Wade."

Rather than give a start, she calmly turned her head to face him. He'd never met a woman with such control of her emotions. He knew she might very well be furious with his behavior last night—even he was surprised and chagrined at how easy it was to slip back into old habits, to flirt with every lady in the room, young and old.

And Susanna had responded with her own arsenal of tricks, becoming the bluestocking as she bored them to tears with her artistic obsessions. He'd almost applauded the show.

He approached her to look over her shoulder at the watercolors, murmuring, "Such talents you have, Mrs. Wade."

"But not of the singing variety, I fear," she said. "I hope it doesn't disturb you that you can't put me on display before your friends."

"Who says I can't?" he asked brightly. "We have another two days before we continue our journey. There's an archery competition this morn, neighborhood guests for luncheon, and horseback riding into the foothills. There might even be flowers to paint."

She studied him, her expression serene, unlike the disappointment and sadness that had suffused her the last few days. He felt relieved, even though he couldn't know if it would last.

"You heard the schedule at breakfast?" she asked.

"Lady Edgecumbe was making plans last night. I would never go down to breakfast without asking if you wished to accompany me." He held out his elbow. "Allow me to escort you, Mrs. Wade, so I can boast about your artistic talents. I'm sure the ladies will enjoy seeing what you're working on."

To Susanna's surprise, Leo proved correct. They spent a tolerable two days with the Edgecumbes, who seemed quite enthralled with her talents. She ended up sketching the daughters in a group por-

trait, and Lady Edgecumbe vowed to have it framed.
She never did win over Mrs. Appleby, though, and
she suspected there might be other women among
Leo's acquaintances who would feel just as annoyed
with his marriage.

He dozed the entire day on the journey to York.
He jerked awake regularly, as if he was trying not to
sleep in front of her, which seemed silly. She either
read or looked out the window at the breathtaking
beauty of green hillsides and the occasional water-
falls of Wensleydale. In York, they took lodgings at
a crowded hotel with only one bedroom and a small
parlor. During a late meal, Leo watched her too
closely and said surprisingly little. After several evenings with the Edgecumbes, and her private vow to
make a better marriage, she felt a heightened sense of
anticipation and nervousness being alone with him,
with only a single bed visible through the open door.
She waited for him to touch her, trembling over what
she might do. Her feelings were still so confusing,
especially the lingering sadness at how the decision
of her future was taken from her by her own foolishness and his.

When they were finished eating, he offered her
the bedroom and said he would sleep on the sofa,
bowing in a gentlemanly fashion as he left her
alone—and disappointed, to her surprise.

At breakfast, Susanna picked at her food even as
Leo lounged in his chair and watched her.

"You dozed yesterday, slept last night, but still

have shadows under your eyes," she said into the silence.

He arched a brow. "Concerned for me?"

"You need a sharp mind. How else will you earn your living at cards?"

"And your arrow strikes true," he said, his smile charming. "It's a good thing I always have money tucked away. The overhaul of your wardrobe will have need of it."

She set down her fork. "Excuse me?" Money tucked away? Enough for a *tonnish* wardrobe? That certainly gave her pause.

"York gives me the perfect opportunity. I know a dressmaker here."

"You do," she said, her creative mind filling in all the reasons he might have had need of a dressmaker.

His smile widened into an open grin. "I do. Give me free rein with my creativity—I already allow you the same. You must admit I have been the most patient of men with Tyler's paintings."

"I know you are not thinking of a wardrobe as some kind of enticement to me. You compromised the wrong woman if you believe so."

"No, I am not so blinded by lust."

Apparently not, since he hadn't even attempted to kiss her last night. She sighed, surprised that it was proving difficult to make the best of this marriage. "And how long did you plan to remain here if we order a wardrobe?"

"I can persuade the woman to work quickly."

She knew he could persuade a woman to do . . .

anything. After all, he'd persuaded her, when she'd known better.

But now he waited, watching her.

Free rein with his creativity, eh? And he claimed to have money put away? He had found the way to interest her. "Very well. I shall accompany you."

He rubbed his hands together. "Then let us begin."

Madame Chambord had a small shop on North Street. Beautiful gowns were displayed in the windows, and inside, glass cabinets showcased expensive lace and imported fabrics and ribbon. The dressmaker was only a decade or so older than Susanna, but with hair as dark as midnight.

Madame Chambord clasped her hands with delight upon seeing Leo. "Monsieur Wade, how good it is to see you again," she cried, rushing toward him as if she would throw herself into his arms.

A former paramour? Susanna couldn't help wondering. She had to stop assuming that, for every woman's eyes lightened with delight on seeing Leo. He was that sort of man, handsome and charming, with an edge of recklessness that made a woman wonder just how far he'd go to be wicked.

At the last moment, Madame Chambord dropped into a deep curtsy. "Monsieur Wade, what brings you to my humble shop?"

He stepped aside and gestured. "Madame, allow me to introduce my wife."

Susanna's own curtsy was a bit more circumspect. Madame Chambord was far more adept at mastering her surprise than the Edgecumbes had been, for obvious financial reasons, but Susanna knew it was there nonetheless.

"Ah, and you bring such a delightful woman to see me!" the dressmaker cried, her voice oozing delight and pride and humbleness all at the same time.

"We only recently married," Leo explained, "and I'd like my wife to look as grand as any Society lady upon our return to London."

"And how long will you be in York, monsieur?" she asked, narrowing her eyes as she studied Susanna's figure.

"As little time as possible, madame." Susanna spoke up for the first time. "I'm an artist, and have much work to do as we travel."

"Ah, I should have guessed your talents," Madame Chambord said, leaning down to peer at Susanna's dark red skirt. "I see a spot of paint."

Susanna could not find what the dressmaker referred to. "Then you see how little regard I have for my clothing."

The woman drew in a breath, and her skeptical gaze met Leo's amused one.

"My wife is a rare flower, madame, which is why I've come to you to bring forth her bloom."

Susanna smothered a laugh, saw Leo's surprised gaze and relieved grin.

"*Oui, oui,* then come with me, monsieur. We will discuss in private and let my assistants deal with the other customers."

The less-important customers, Susanna thought. Leo must surely have spent money here. Gambling winnings thrown away on women's clothing—on a whim? He was doing it again—and she was allowing it, wanting to take her measure of him. Did he really have a supply of his own money?

In a small parlor with comfortable chairs grouped around a large mirror, Madame Chambord brought forth dozens of sketches, which she proceeded to spread out before them. Leo sat at Susanna's side, and she thought for certain he would allow her to make at least some choices. She adjusted her spectacles, opened her mouth, but he took the first sketch away from her.

"Madame, surely this color would not suit my wife's auburn hair."

"*Non, non,* monsieur, as usual, you have the eyes for such important details."

Susanna tried to intercede. "Perhaps a dark green would—"

"Blue," Leo interrupted. "Deep night blue, with silver embroidery."

And then Leo and the dressmaker rapidly went through a dozen sketches, choosing an evening gown, several day dresses, and a riding habit. He had the fashion sense of a London dandy, and the need to see cleavage, by the way he insisted on displaying her less-than-abundant attributes. But the truly interesting fact that she took away from the afternoon was his memory. Every time he and the dressmaker disagreed about something, he would pull forth a previous sketch and refer to the exact alterations they'd discussed, without looking at Madame Chambord's copious notes.

When he wanted to concentrate on something, he could do so with amazing accuracy. Hence his success at cards. Then he merely glanced at the order slip on the dressmaker's counter, and added it up in his head long before she had finished the sum on paper.

And during it all, he tactfully explained his choices to Susanna, educating her without giving offense, leaving her impressed.

As he talked Madame Chambord into having the gowns basted together to be tried on in two days' time, Susanna found herself listening closely to the final arrangements. He knew just what to say to negotiate the price to his own favor. The price was not inconsequential, yet he didn't even blink at the expense, and Madame Chambord seemed perfectly confident in his ability to pay. Then he must have his own money, which made her feel so relieved. He hadn't wanted her simply for her dowry.

His abilities continued to impress her, hinting at more beneath the shallow mask he showed the world.

Chapter 15

For the next two days in York, Leo and his new wife danced about each other. She accompanied him on visits to friends as long as he also gave her plenty of time to concentrate on the hobbies so important to her. And she talked about her pursuits—to everyone—making him laugh.

She went to church while he slept in, what with his difficulty falling—or remaining—asleep. Walking the grounds of St. Peter's School led to more sketches for herself or watercolors for Tyler. Leo found the man's name grating more and more on his ears. What kind of man cared so much about flowers? If he hadn't met Tyler, he would have assumed it all a ploy for a lovely woman's attention.

But ever since the dressmaker's shop, Leo felt himself the object of her scrutiny in a way he hadn't been before. He wasn't sure what he'd done at Madame Chambord's except play a *tonnish* man of fashion and subtly begin to teach her his knowledge. And he'd liked it, for she grasped everything the first time he said it, and asked succinct questions.

Ignoring her newly sharp regard, he blithely went about doing what he did best—enjoying himself, as he patiently bided his time to earn her trust. He went to another boxing match, and thought perhaps she was enough of a rebel to accompany him, but no. She seemed content with his company at the late Cobbett's art studio though she'd earlier warned him she wanted to be alone. More and more dusty books piled up in the carriage, along with art supplies, and Leo had to endure the coachman's sympathetic smiles. Leo knew he looked like a groom willing to tolerate anything to please his new wife.

If only they were pleasing each other in bed.

But he didn't want to frighten her by insisting she give herself to him when she wasn't ready. He had thought his many years of sexual escapades would tide him over, but watching Susanna move calmly, elegantly through their two small rooms was playing havoc with his nerves. Even her spectacles aroused him, catching the gleam of candlelight and bringing his attention back to the mysterious depths of her brown eyes. He found himself prowling about, drinking more than he would have as he watched her, all to keep up his merry façade.

She started wearing gowns that hooked in the back, and calmly accepted his help, then remained perfectly still as each open hook revealed more and more of her corset and chemise. And her corset was pale blue, not the plain puritan white of a spinster. His fingers trembled, and his parched mouth longed to touch the slim column of her neck. Was she quivering, too? He couldn't tell. But when he placed his hand on the bare slope of her shoulder, she thanked him and stepped away instead of flinging herself into his arms, his fervent wish.

He accompanied her to the dressmaker's shop to look at her adorned in the basted gowns he'd purchased. She set her spectacles aside and emerged from behind the changing screen as Madame Chambord insisted she do. The sight of her breasts, now molded to perfection with the correct garments, was enough to make him wish he'd bound her up in a nun's habit.

At night, when she let down her auburn hair, gleaming like fire in the candlelight, he couldn't look away as she brushed it. He was daring himself, taunting himself, and at last this drove him away from their hotel. He felt . . . lost, not knowing what to do to win her trust, desperate to find the secret to unlocking Susanna's heart.

He hadn't returned, Susanna thought, awakening at dawn on top of the counterpane in her empty bed. She'd meant to wait up to tell him something, but she couldn't remember it now.

He hadn't returned.

Her corset had dug a groove into her side, her skirts were wrinkled—she hadn't even changed into her nightgown, for she'd waited too long to send for the maid, then been too foolishly proud to let the woman see that her husband had left her alone.

She wandered dispiritedly into the parlor, looking

at the new paintings she'd wrapped, ready to send to Mr. Tyler. Surely *he* wouldn't have deserted her so soon after their wedding.

Then again, Susanna had wreaked her subtle revenge on Leo but had never imagined she'd be hurting herself as well, she realized, rubbing her fist into her breastbone, where the ache seemed focused. He made her feel alive and breathless, as if every moment in his presence could be exciting and pleasurable.

And to think she'd once imagined marriage to Mr. Tyler preferable. She'd come to Bramfield Hall to take risks—and had originally settled for Mr. Tyler, the least risky man in attendance. She hadn't been the bravest woman then. She wanted to be brave now.

Someone knocked on the door, and she stiffened, then deflated as she realized Leo would never knock. The maid came in, a different girl than before, and Susanna asked for her help with the gown, making it appear as if she'd changed her mind already that morn. She requested a bath, and unlike the tub in Gretna Green, this one allowed the water to almost cover her breasts. She sank against the back, closed her eyes, and steamed, hoping for relaxation.

Where was Leo? It was well past dawn already. Had he come to mischief? Met a thief? Or fought a drunken duel? Her realization that she was worried about him seemed to have changed something inside her.

But when the door opened, and he swept in, smelling of the rain that beaded on the shoulders of his greatcoat, she could only stare at him in shock and relief, her body barely covered by soapy water.

He froze only momentarily, his gaze taking her in. And then he closed the door and leaned back against it.

She couldn't read his expression; he wasn't grinning in triumph. Without covering herself in maidenly modesty, she only tilted her head and waited.

"I should have sent a note last night," he said, slowly walking toward her. "I hope you didn't wait up."

"I didn't," she lied. She swallowed, too proud to look down and see how much of her body was visible beneath the water.

He emptied his pockets, producing vouchers. "I won."

She eyed his display and tried to smile. "I guess it's better than canceling my order with the dressmaker."

She felt consumed by his slow approach, and the way he looked at her as if she were a tasty morsel for his personal devouring.

He walked slowly about the tub until he was behind her. She was trembling so much that the water rippled. He bent over her, and she gasped, inhaling the scent of alcohol, smoke, and the night, but not a woman's perfume, as she once might have feared.

"Let me wash your back," he murmured.

She remained silent. He picked up the facecloth from the stool nearby and was rubbing it in the soft, fragrant soap. Her very flesh seemed to melt at the thought of such dangerous touches. He took her shoulder to push her forward, and she felt the warm cloth begin to soap her back.

And it was heavenly. She held her knees tightly, her face buried against them, and barely resisted the urge to moan.

"Breathe," he murmured, laughter beneath the word.

She did so, in far too shaky a fashion.

"I like to touch you," he said.

And she liked hearing that.

The cloth moved slowly beneath his open hand, and it was as if there were no barrier between his skin and her own. He added more soap, then began to move the cloth over her shoulders, making her ease back against the tub. He picked up her arm and ran the cloth down it.

When he touched her . . . it was as if he could turn down her brain like an oil lamp, letting it glow in the background while her body enjoyed the carnality. He worked soap between her fingers and around her wrists, making her feel utterly fragile next to his large hands. He took her other arm and did the same, until she felt like a warm, wet blanket, slumped with abandonment in the tub.

He moved behind her again, and she breathed a shaky sigh. But then he began to soap her shoulders, his longer fingers touching her collarbones with each movement, occasionally reaching beyond to her upper chest. She stared at the glimpses of his hands, feeling unable to breathe.

His fingers moved lower, sliding down to the

sides of her rib cage, brushing the outer curves of her breasts. She felt her back arching, the water lapping, knew her breasts were visible. With a simple movement, he could cup them and give her the pleasure she remembered.

She took a deep breath and words tumbled out at last. "I heard you having a nightmare the other night." She cursed her nervousness.

He didn't say anything, his upper body above her head, his hands still on her wet skin.

"It was nothing," he said hoarsely.

"It's not the first time. What were you dreaming about?"

And then he stood up, his hands sliding away from her as he turned his back. She let out a shuddering breath of disappointment.

"You've looked tired, so it must be affecting your sleep," she continued. "And did you stay out last night to avoid experiencing it again?"

He tried to toss her an amused look, but she thought it seemed a bit . . . forced. Intrigued, she picked up the discarded facecloth and washed her legs.

"So tell me, Leo," she urged.

He stared out the window, hands clasped on the back of a chair. At last, he said, "I don't know what it is. I'm in a dark place, and there are rats."

She shuddered. "That would disturb my sleep, too."

"And now there's a corpse."

She straightened. "A corpse? Do you know who it is?"

He shook his head, not facing her. "No idea. Foolish, isn't it?"

"Are you prone to dreams?"

He shrugged. "It's all because of your painting, you know."

"I don't understand." She washed her private areas while his back was turned, then reached for the bucket of clean water, stood up, and quickly washed off the soap. Her hair could wait another day.

"The most vivid dream was of your painting," he said, "and then it . . . changed. Until now, it was the only way to see you naked, of course."

"Perhaps seeing me naked gave you nightmares," she said dryly.

He turned about and regarded the towel hiding her body soberly. "I've never heard anything more foolish. That painting would haunt any man's dreams in the most provocative way."

"That is Roger's gift, of course, his incredible talent. And I can say that even though I'm still furious with him."

"He certainly had magic over you."

"It was not quite so easy to persuade me to pose," she told him, knowing that continuing such a discussion doubled her risk of making a mistake.

"How often did you have to do so?"

She hesitated, remembering the story she, Rebecca, and Elizabeth had agreed upon. "The sessions were twice a week for several weeks. We didn't talk much. I'd become his model, and his concentration was legendary."

"So you lay there"—his voice turned husky—"naked. For hours. Why, Susanna? Why would a properly raised girl do such a thing? For the sheer adventure of it?"

She looked away from him. "I originally thought the scarves would be able to conceal most of me, but then gradually he made me feel . . . beautiful." She flushed, still unable to meet his gaze. "You will think that ridiculous, of course."

"Ridiculous? Good God, Susanna, I've been able to think of little else since I saw it. You *are* beautiful."

She tightened the towel at her breasts, feeling far too aroused, as if she couldn't control her own body. "Thank you, but this discussion cannot help your curiosity. In fact, perhaps the painting is making you feel guilty, hence the dreams."

"Guilty? Over the wager? No. Over the marriage?"

She stood still beside the tub, waiting, wondering.

"Some guilt, yes," he admitted. "But no regrets. You'll be my true wife soon, and you'll want that." His eyes suddenly twinkled. "You may think you can hold out until the end of the wager, so I can't see your body in the light, but you're wrong."

She laughed. "You shouldn't bring up the wager. You only remind me how important it is that I protect my sister and cousin."

Leo watched her disappear behind the changing screen, his grin slowly fading away. He'd fled last night, hoping to enjoy his old haunts and forget about her, but it hadn't worked. He'd felt . . . bored, restless, when his thoughts weren't occupied with her. He'd never felt protective of anyone before, not counting his relatives, of course. He was responsible for Susanna now. He was used to expecting nothing of himself since no one else did. But now he had a wife.

Irritated with his own tumbling feelings, he stripped, washed quickly in the tub, then with only a towel around his waist, flung himself across the bed to nap.

"Wake me when it's time to leave for Madame Chambord's," he called.

But sleep didn't offer much refreshment.

The final trip to the dressmaker's was uneventful, although he caught Susanna studying him when he was insisting that the madame had altered the trim on a bodice without his permission. Susanna only smiled and turned away.

She had plans to visit a museum, and he remained in the background, watching as she copied the masters to study their technique. He was fascinated at how she saw curved, well-placed lines where he only saw a flow of movement. Her gifts at perception were impressive, and he knew she was turning those powers on him. Trust in a marriage had to go both ways. Did he want her to see so deeply into him? And she was capable of it, capable of upsetting all the equilibrium he'd worked so hard at.

He drew the line at traipsing up the hill to see the crumbling Clifford's Tower, part of the original York

Castle. She was hoping to find a dungeon, and he made the mistake of declining too quickly.

She frowned at him, standing in the middle of the pavement. "Leo?"

"After my strange dreams, I hardly want to be below ground. I know of a fencing academy. You go on and enjoy your freedom."

He walked away from his wife, knowing he'd left her far too curious.

When they departed York the next day, new gowns stowed in her trunks, Susanna passed the time by sketching Leo as he slept. It was easier to think about the relaxed posture of his body than about their strange marriage. But when it came time to draw his face, it now felt too . . . intimate, too revealing that she might know the lines of his face, experience them flowing out her fingertips. She closed the book with a snap and looked out the window.

They stopped for the night at an estate in Nottinghamshire, and this time there were children for Leo to amuse. The parents, Mr. and Mrs. Wyndham, had once been neighbors of Leo's family estate, childhood sweethearts. But the romance must have fled, for there was a chilly distance between them that caught even Leo's attention, for she saw him look between them with a frown more than once.

But it became an interesting evening, at least for her, and when they returned to their single room, she questioned him about it.

"Mrs. Wyndham has fond memories of playing

with you as a child," Susanna said, sitting down on the chaise at the end of the bed.

Leo was washing his face at the washstand and only grunted.

"She said you destroyed every clock in the house, taking them apart."

"Hardly destroyed," he said over his shoulder.

"That's right—you put them back together again." She hadn't even been surprised, having guessed early in their relationship that he had intelligence he didn't use. "How old had you been?"

"I don't remember."

But she suspected he did and was deliberating trying to avoid the subject. Why had he allowed his natural curiosity to disappear? No, that was wrong, the focus of his curiosity had changed, to things like cards and women. But once he'd cared about other things.

She sensed she would get no more out of him, that perhaps his carefree façade was his way of protecting a part of himself. That was understandable; she'd spent much of her life protecting herself from getting hurt. But his motive seemed . . . different.

He turned to face her, even as he pulled off his shirt. "I liked your new bluestocking conversation."

She blinked at him with wide, innocent eyes. "I was so excited when I found the book on the study of lepidoptera. I've always wanted to examine butterflies. They would make an excellent painting subject, even if I had to pin them to a wall to get them to hold still."

"And moths," he added, grinning. "Don't forget about them. I thought Wyndham's eyes would cross in boredom."

"But not you?" she challenged. He acted as if he'd forgotten his wish to have a normal wife.

"Oh, you never bore me, Susanna."

Her relief at his response still had a flicker of worry about the edges. Could she continue to intrigue him? Or would he someday roll his eyes in boredom?

"Did you win again at cards?" she asked, to change the subject.

"I always win," he said with a grin.

Because he was smart, she thought in triumph. "Even when you're drunk?"

"I'm not drunk. And did I tell you how lovely you looked at dinner in your new gown?"

"Thank you." She looked away, blushing at the compliment. He had turned her into a woman who cared about his opinion, who laughed at his jokes. The more he drew her closer, the more difficult it would be if he grew bored with her. She shouldn't let herself become too attached.

"I'll need to post those paintings to Mr. Tyler," she said. Her eyes wandered down his body. She'd seen many different male specimens, and Leo was one of the best. Of course, she usually saw only the corpses of old men . . .

She felt a little shiver of exhilaration, a perfectly natural response when one person admired the . . . physicality of another.

"We'll see if we can find the time—or Tyler can

wait," Leo said, tossing his shirt across a bench.

She slowly smiled. Was he actually jealous of Mr. Tyler? How had she managed such a feat? The ripple of excitement in her belly almost came out as a chuckle, but she held it in. She would hold her small victory close and savor it.

"Painting for Tyler is such a solitary pursuit," Leo continued, searching the washstand for his toothbrush and powder.

"Why, Leo, are you trying to find something we have in common? Something we could do together? How very marital of you."

"I like cards. Surely you have been raised to play them, like every other proper young lady. Perhaps tomorrow night you can play with the Wyndhams and me."

"So if I'm to play cards, what will you do for me?" Oh, she was being very daring.

His smile was slow and wicked. "I could do so much for you, Susanna."

"And how do you know you'd be showing me anything I haven't already seen?" she countered.

He laughed, then leaned back against the wardrobe. "What else could we share, Mrs. Wade? I certainly don't have any interest in bugs—"

"Lepidoptera."

"—or the studios of famous artists. But art . . . yes, I did say it's what brought us together. Let's discuss your art—your modeling career, to be exact."

It took all her control not to remain unruffled. "I did not have a career. Just that one project."

"What about the jewel?"

"Excuse me?"

"The one in the painting. I've never seen it before, and you are hardly the type to display your family wealth in such a way."

"Very crass."

"Is it a family heirloom?"

"Would I wear a family heirloom in a public painting?"

"You never thought it would be on display."

She forced a smile. "Must you remind me of Roger's deceit? He was false on all fronts, for the jewel was paste. He tossed it back in a drawer with others when we were done."

He continued to study her. "I was very tempted to search your trunk."

"You would not be so vulgar."

He gave an exaggerated sigh. "True, I've never needed such subterfuge."

"You've had to resort to outright questions." Instead of touching her. Words emerged from her mouth that were more daring than she could have planned. "I guess seduction isn't working out for you. Have you at last realized your charm has its limits?"

"Since you haven't offered yourself to me, you must be afraid to find out."

It must be the night, or the rising feeling of wildness that practically made her blood sing. She felt she was winning their little battle over the wager, and it made her say, "Go ahead and try. I dare you."

Chapter 16

Susanna never dared people—never accepted dares. She was too sensible for that.

But she wanted to change.

Leo straightened, eyes glittering with intrigue in the low light. "What are you saying?"

"I won't take off my clothing—that would be too easy. And when I stop you, out of boredom, I'm certain, you *have* to stop."

He came toward her swiftly. "You won't be able to stop."

She shrugged and leaned back on the bench. "Overestimating yourself again, Leo? The last time that happened, we were caught and sentenced to a lifetime of . . ." She let her words fade.

"Of what, Mrs. Wade?"

He was leaning over her, his bare arms on either side of her shoulders as she fell back. She was on the wrong end of the chaise, and her head tilted off, exposing her throat. She felt vulnerable and excited all at the same time, so very aware of his warmth above her. She could feel intimidated, dominated, but he'd never inspired that in her.

"Sentenced to what, Mrs. Wade?" he repeated.

She lifted her head to meet his intense green eyes. In that frozen moment, their game seemed distant, and real emotion trapped within her, bursting to be free.

She actually *liked* this—this crazy marriage, this battlefield. Was she becoming one of those women Leo seduced with his eyes and his charm, then left drifting behind him as he looked for a new challenge in a swift current?

Misery, sentenced to a lifetime of misery. She'd once thought that, but now couldn't say the words. She didn't want that kind of marriage. Would they ever trust each other enough to be content?

Right here, right now, he desired her—the challenge of her, anyway. She would use it for as long as she could.

At last he seemed to forget his questions, and she dropped her head back, waiting, daring him to test himself against her control.

"Not like this," he said. Gripping her waist, he slid her down the chaise until her head rested on the cushioned seat, and their eyes met. He lowered his head, their mouths but a breath apart. "I want to see your response when I touch you."

And then he kissed her, soft kisses, top lip, then bottom, suckling her flesh, touching her briefly with the tip of his tongue, until she could barely hold back a moan. His chin was rough with whiskers, his breath a hint of brandy. It was exotic and erotic, everything a spinster's fantasy should be.

Only she wasn't a spinster anymore.

He was her husband, and he said he'd stop when she told him to.

"Touch me," he whispered.

She let her hands slide up the bent columns of his arms. His skin was so very hot and hard, tight over muscle. She felt like she was memorizing every line of him for a future project, as she let her hands linger over the muscles of his chest.

And then he groaned and deepened the kiss when her fingertips brushed his nipples. Did he like that, too? His tongue swept her mouth, over and over again, and she met it with her own, tasting him. Then she clutched him, and he came down on top of her. The pressure of his body made her squirm and rub herself against him, but all the sensations were muted behind corset and petticoats and voluminous fabric.

And then his mouth swept over her jaw and down her throat, suckling, tasting, licking a path to her chest and to the neckline he'd approved. She'd made a rule that he couldn't remove her clothing—why had she made that rule, she wondered wildly, as her body seemed afire from his kisses and his touch.

She caught hold of her restraint just in time, even as his body sank between her parting thighs. Layers of fabric still separated them, but the wickedness of his position called to her.

"Hold on," he murmured.

With a yank, her corset slid down an inch, and her breasts seemed to pop free, overflowing as if she were far more endowed than she really was.

"This new one is a much better corset," he said with deep satisfaction.

And then he pressed his mouth between her breasts, and she hugged his head to her. She'd stop him soon, she told herself, but her panting was loud in her ears, and her body couldn't seem to remain still, arching and squirming, a soundless form of begging she should be embarrassed about—

But his mouth was so close to the peak of her very naked breast. He waited so long, looking at her nudity, that she almost shoved herself into his face.

And then he licked her, and her back seemed to come off the chaise, bucking him hard.

"You're strong. I like it."

The words were whispered against her erect nipple, and even that movement felt incredible. His tongue played with her, little touches, long licks. Then at last he gathered her into his mouth and suckled, and she clutched him as if she'd never let him stop.

The pleasure seemed to intensify, spreading through her body, sinking hard into that warm wet-ness between her thighs. His hip was there, push-ing against her, but the sensation was lost in all her clothing.

Until she felt the hotness of his bare hand on lower leg.

"Yes," she heard herself cry, and somewhere distant inside her, the first pitiful warning flag was raised. She needed to stop him, to draw out his intrigue with her. *But not yet, no, not yet.*

His mouth teased her other breast, his hand learned the feel of her skin behind her knee, then the tender flesh of her inner thigh through her drawers.

She didn't even remember the rules until he whispered against her flesh, "No removing clothing."

She almost moaned her disappointment. But he was watching her now, splitting his attention between one breast and the other, his fingers sliding over her drawers, his body lifting just a bit so his hand could cup her.

"Ohhh," she breathed, closing her eyes.

"Open those eyes, sweetheart, look at me."

She obeyed him as if vows made her do so. She stared at him, lips parted, taking in the sight of him at her breasts, feeling the gentle exploration of his fingers. And when he found the slit in her drawers, faint triumph lit his eyes.

His fingers slid along her cleft—oh God, she was so wet—and then delved within. She whimpered at the sharpened focus of pleasure, at the desperation that rose even higher, like a swollen stream needing to overflow its banks.

"Don't stop me," he said urgently, "you need to know all the pleasure we can give each other."

His fingers increased their tempo, his mouth found hers, even as his other hand cupped her breast.

And then something inside her simply came

apart, blasting away her last innocence, shuddering through her with sublime waves of bliss.

She came to herself in his arms. He'd watched her through all of it, as he'd given her pleasure, as she'd been unable to control the low sounds she made that now echoed in her ears.

How many women had he watched that way? Did he calculate the differences, keep track of who pleased him more or less? And she, with so little experience, could only be a novelty to someone like him.

"Stop, stop," she whispered, trying to get out from beneath, now feeling so pinned by the heaviness of his body.

He slid to the side, and she sat up. Her thighs touching made her wince at the memory of passion.

"It's just like before, on the floor of the Bramfield drawing room," she murmured, too dazed to pretend any longer. "I could have stopped you—I should have. But I didn't. I was far too willing. And you wanted it, too," she said, turning to look down at him.

"I did. I do," he answered, his smile a curl of pleasure as he bent his arm to rest behind his head.

No, he wanted the wager, the release, the excitement, the daring. It didn't matter the woman. And he was looking at her like a cat who'd cornered a mouse, anticipating the final battle. And she realized her breasts were still bare, and his hunger was for that sight. She wasn't a fool, knew he'd not had the same pleasure she had. But he wasn't demanding more.

And then he sat up, and she wished he would continue, make her his wife in truth, and maybe that would somehow stop her from being afraid. But he turned her about by the waist and put his hands on the hooks of her gown.

"Don't worry; you told me to stop, and I shall. But you can't come to bed like this."

Dazed, still aching with desire and disappointment, she spoke without thinking. "This gown is very difficult to remove. Did you plan it?"

"Mrs. Wade, men wish gowns were *easier* to remove."

His hands worked quickly, expertly, on the hooks. When the gown dropped away from the front of her body, she allowed it to pool at her feet, then leaned over to pick it up as she rose.

And he lay there and watched her, no pretty words of seduction, no insistence that he had to have her. She placed her gown across the back of a chair and began to unlace her corset. She met his gaze, lifted her chin, and pushed the corset down her body, along with several untied petticoats.

Leo crossed his arms and arched a brow, as if waiting to see how much she dared.

And she suddenly felt daring, a resurgence of confidence and trust in herself. She knew what she was doing even though he'd surprised her. Turned away from him at the wardrobe, she took off her chemise and let him see her naked back above her drawers. She gave him a look over her shoulder before pulling on her nightgown. His smile had disappeared, she noticed with approval, and he'd risen up to brace himself on his hands.

She leaned back against the wardrobe and studied him. "Did you notice how the Wyndhams didn't even talk to each other?"

"Only you would think deep conversations necessary, Susanna," he said shortly, "especially at a time like this."

Before this moment, she and Leo had been doing nothing but talk, and he'd hardly resisted. But not about things held dearly to themselves, and she was resisting as much as he was. She'd learned something about his childhood today, and he seemed bothered by it.

Perhaps she didn't want him to see deeper than her cleavage. After all, their competitiveness would have to fade eventually, along with this lust that could take over her very will if she let it. But the longer she was with him, the more he was a mystery to her.

In the middle of the night, Leo came awake, gasping, unmanned at how he trembled over a dream. He looked toward Susanna's pillow, and by dim moonlight he could see she slept undisturbed.

There'd been a corpse in his dream again, and this time he'd seen blood, so much blood. Was he going insane? Or was the dream so vivid because it was really a memory? If that was true, why couldn't he remember it?

To distract himself from the violent emotions that ebbed within him, he looked once more upon his wife. He experienced a moment of gradual peace so profound that it shook him. He was being a fool about his dreams.

What was it about her that drew him more than any other woman had? Why was she so able to reach beneath his surface, to pluck at thoughts he'd never needed to share? He wanted to know more about her, to understand why she'd let herself get to this age unmarried. Her crazy hobbies couldn't be the reason—some man would have put up with them. He was.

But wanting to know about her made him understand she'd want more of the same in reverse. And that unsettled him. Men didn't need to discuss emotions best left in childhood. Why did she insist on probing into things that would only hurt her in the end?

He didn't want to hurt her; but, of course, he hadn't wanted to hurt any woman. And it just seemed to happen. He *had* harmed her, changed her life profoundly. His life didn't need to change at all once they returned to London. But he felt different with Susanna, and he wasn't sure he liked it. Why couldn't he simply concentrate on their competition over the wager? There was no need to dwell on anything else. They were married, and it would be a typical marriage. He would make her see they could be content with each other.

* * *

Susanna felt the rumble of the carriage beneath her as they rode toward Newark Upon Trent, and then caught the flash of Leo's amused gaze. They sat on opposite benches, and she had two children beside her, and he had one. It had been Susanna's idea to take the Wyndham children into town, ostensibly to give the tense couple time alone.

But it also enabled her to see Leo surrounded by children, and she couldn't decide if she was surprised or not by how easily he related to them. Eight-year-old Marcus sat beside Leo, a toy soldier in each hand, as he discussed warfare in an adorably serious manner. Leo answered without one hint of boredom.

The two little girls on either side of Susanna were six-year-old twins but dressed differently so that she could tell them apart. They took turns discussing the dolls they'd brought, talking louder and louder as if to drown out the nasty boy talk of battles.

Susanna felt a flush of maternal happiness she hadn't imagined ever feeling, couldn't even meet Leo's eyes in case he guessed her foolish weakness. Wasn't *she* the one who'd vowed to remain a spinster, to be the best aunt possible? Now she was married, and would soon sleep with her husband, she thought with a delicious thrill. Then there might be babies.

Babies who looked like him, she hoped. Babies to love, when at last she had to settle for the understanding that her husband would never love her.

But perhaps they'd have respect, and that would

be something important upon which to base parent-hood.

She had to wonder—did he respect himself? His favorite pastimes were seducing women and gambling. If he found more meaningful hobbies, he would take himself a bit more seriously. He could start by reading more. Young Patience Wyndham had brought several readers with her to pass the hour. Now Susanna tossed one into Leo's lap.

He looked up at her in surprise, and when he smiled his curiosity, she felt again that strange, melting feeling of soft helplessness. Oh heavens, she was falling for him, regardless of his faults and sins and knowing her uncertain future with him.

He could hurt her more than the scandal of a forced marriage ever would.

Swallowing, she managed a smile. "I think you need a new hobby. Perhaps reading? It would broaden your mind."

"I think far too much already," he answered, his eyes merry. He returned to a discussion on knights and sword fighting.

There had to be a more mature way for him to spend his time, so she would keep trying. But today she was going to drag him to another museum. Maybe that would eventually take.

The museum in Newark was small by London or even York standards, just two rooms, but there were collections of paintings by British artists, and artifacts unearthed in the area. To her surprise, Marcus found the paintings fascinating, and she ended up discussing technique, even as she knew most fathers wouldn't allow their sons art lessons.

Leo seemed as bored as the little twins, and the three of them wandered away. She approached them later, and to her surprise, he'd found several Roman pottery shards and was studying them while the girls played with their dolls on the floor beside him. She thought of the curious boy he'd been, and now the man who didn't even read the signs describing the pottery, or the newspaper, or books or—

And then a new realization made the blood drain from her head so fast she put a hand on Marcus's shoulder to steady herself.

Could Leo read?

No, no, how could such a foolish thought occur to her? She'd seen him sign his name and place of residence on their marriage certificate.

But he had to know how to do that, simply to get by. His man of business would only have to point, and Leo could sign. But she'd never seen him read anything else. And he'd openly admitted his brother helped him with his homework, that the teachers thought him incorrigible.

And she'd just flung a child's reader in his lap! Embarrassment brought a new wave of heat into her face, and she sat down heavily on a bench, giving Marcus permission with a wave to join his sisters.

This possibility changed so many things she thought she'd known about Leo, who'd once been curious and intelligent, but now went out of his way to show the exact opposite. A man who felt inferior about something would want to be the focus of the party, to make everyone like him, so no one would question the secrets he was hiding.

How could she bring it up to him? Would she anger and embarrass him so much that their relationship might never recover? She could help him, perhaps tutor him, if he'd allow it. But he didn't trust her, didn't love her; he'd never permit such a thing.

Was this why he expected so little of himself?

Chapter 17

"L eo, why don't you read the newspaper?" Susanna asked.

Leo glanced to where she was sitting at the dressing table, tucking in falling strands of her hair. They were changing for dinner, after a day spent with rambunctious children who actually seemed to enjoy the museum, to his surprise.

He tore his gaze away from her hair and deliberately frowned as he buttoned his waistcoat. "I like hearing news directly from the source. I talk to people. You should try it," he teased, "instead of staying so solitary with all your *hobbies.*"

He didn't understand her mood today. He'd enjoyed watching her with the Wyndham children. Considering she'd at one time meant to remain a spinster, he'd been worried she'd be the sort of mother who'd allow the governess and nurse full control over the children. She'd seemed to find shaping their young minds fascinating. He had seen the tender way she'd looked at the boy Marcus when he asked her questions about art.

But on the way home, when the children slumbered in their respective corners, and Leo could have used the nap, he'd had to tolerate her probing stare. Surely he hadn't given her any reason to doubt him as a father. He *liked* children, probably more than most of his contemporaries.

With exasperation, he wondered why she simply couldn't be the sort of woman who was glad for his name and position and the opportunity to shop. But then she wouldn't be so uniquely . . . Susanna.

The thought of an evening with the Wyndhams, and their loaded silences and Susanna's questions, all seemed like more than he wanted to bear that night.

"Let's have dinner in private," he said suddenly.

At the dressing table, she turned to face him, nose wrinkled quizzically. "But the Wyndhams—"

"They understand we're newly married. They won't mind not having to entertain us."

"But—"

"Afraid to be alone with me?" He unbuttoned the waistcoat he'd just donned.

"Of course not."

"We'll spend another day with them tomorrow."

"We aren't leaving?"

"I know you're anxious to be home and face your parents, but another day won't matter. Didn't you mention another artist lived nearby?"

He'd overplayed his hand, for now her eyes widened briefly before narrowing.

"Yes," she said slowly.

He gave her his most devilish smile. "Then tonight I think you should sketch me."

"It is training for me, of course, but how does that help your cause?"

"I'm going to be nude."

After he pulled his shirt over his head, he saw the way her eyes studied his chest with contemplation—and eagerness, he realized with relief. With her feet yet bare, he noticed her toes curl and thought it far too erotic a sight.

"Surely you've never sketched a naked man before," he said.

She smiled and tilted her head, leaning back in her chair with a languidness that surprised him.

"You'd be wrong," she said. "Perhaps we should call for a servant to relay our news?" She stood up and reached for the bellpull.

He stopped with his hands on the front flap of his trousers. "You've sketched a naked man?"

Spreading her hands wide, she said, "Wouldn't you like to know the details? You should hide behind the changing screen before you shock the maid."

By the time Susanna sent the maid off with a message, Leo emerged with a towel around his waist. She was already sharpening her pencils and watching him with her artist's eye, as if he were simply her subject and not her husband.

"Did you reciprocate and draw Eastfield naked?" Leo demanded.

She met his gaze with wide eyes, then she started to laugh. He enjoyed the sight, the twinkle in her deep brown eyes, the glitter of golden pinpricks teasing him from just beneath the surface.

"Roger? No, I did not draw him. It was no one you would know. Now have you changed your mind?"

She was looking down his body with an appreciation that he wished were about him rather than her art.

"I won't find this drawing hanging in a lady's tea room, will I?"

She smiled. "No, our marital secrets are our own. And I'm very good at keeping secrets," she added slyly.

"So I've noticed."

"Frustrated, are you?" she asked, coming to her feet and walking toward him.

Then she put both hands on his chest and guided him toward the bed. For a moment, he harbored the insane hope that she meant to do more with him than use his body as her subject.

She briskly pointed to the pillows. "Lie on your side, prop your head on your bent arm, and look at me."

Susanna almost laughed aloud at the disappointment that flashed across Leo's face. Yes, she found him desirable—too desirable. More and more the dark world of passion he inspired was luring her in.

But there was so much more to him, or there could be, if he would admit he wanted something out of life. But how to make him see that?

"Pose me, sweetheart," he murmured, smiling up at her.

Sweetheart. An endearment that went beyond *Mrs. Wade*, and he'd used it twice now. Though she knew he could have used it with many women, there was something about the way he formed the word, the softness of his speech, that made her feel a little tremor of longing.

But she was still so very competitive, so she removed his towel, pretended she didn't see how very aroused he was by their game, touched his flank to bring him up onto his side, bent his arm so his head was propped on his hand, then stepped back and admired the figure he made.

"Impressive, yes?" he said.

She grinned. "If only you knew."

And then she stepped away from him, took up her sketchbook, pulled up a comfortable chair, and began to draw.

He didn't say anything at first, and she worked with sure purpose, her thoughts not quite focused. She was thinking about the man himself, his reading problem, and her desperate need to help him. But trust was involved, and she knew neither of them trusted the other—yet.

But they were closer. Could they have that kind of marriage, the trust she saw between her brother and his wife, even between her parents, who spent so many years separated from each other in every way that counted? If her own parents couldn't trust for so long, why would she think Leo could? And he'd certainly never given a hint that she could trust him, not with his past, his reputation.

But reputation wasn't always the truth. She'd been discovering more and more the truths that Leo kept hidden.

She wanted a real marriage, one built on trust—and respect.

And then she realized she was drawing his face, that dimpled smile, the eyes that promised secrets and delights and wickedness. Could she trust that face? Could she believe that he could desire *her*, when she was nothing like the beauties who normally graced his arm?

She heard her thoughts as if for the first time, her doubt in her own desirability, when he'd seemed attracted to her from the beginning. Her own convictions were part of the problem, ruining her confidence about herself and about the marriage they could have. She must somehow unlearn her self-doubts and find a way to trust in him and the future.

Perhaps that foolish wager was part of the problem. It put them on opposite sides, and if it were simply about her, she would abandon it and tell him everything. But it was about her sister Rebecca and cousin Elizabeth, too, two women younger than she, whom she'd guided as they grew up, nurtured, and looked out for. How could she stop now until she knew they were safe and their secrets protected?

"So how do I look?"

Susanna lifted her head, startled. And he was watching her closely, not quite smiling, as if he were serious, as if he cared what she thought.

It made her feel so warm inside.

She turned the sketchbook toward him.

"You didn't even get to my lower body," he grumbled. And then he paused. "But my face . . ."

"You do have one."

His smile grew slowly, those dimples flashing, setting her heart racing so badly she could have flung herself at him. But no, not yet . . .

"I'm a handsome rascal."

She laughed again.

While they ate dinner, alone with each other as they'd been so many other meals, tonight felt . . . different. Leo wore only trousers, to keep Susanna at ease, but they also hid his constant erection. And she still wore only her undergarments beneath that dressing gown, and the neckline kept sagging whenever she forgot it, revealing the faint valley of her cleavage. Desire simmered within him, and every brush of her hand, every soft smile, set him aflame. Nothing else seemed to matter except being with her, winning her over, and that was about more than her body.

Although that body was magnificent even if she didn't think so.

His thoughts also dwelled on the sketch she'd done of him. He'd suggested it as another way to make her think about sleeping with him, but it had turned into something else. She'd drawn his face— he felt almost ridiculous dwelling on that, but it seemed somehow important, another step toward a comfortable marriage.

As if sensing his thoughts, she set her fork aside and smiled at him. "We have played quite a game together these past few weeks."

"That makes it sound so temporary, when you're with me for life."

"But you love the game—you're a gambler after all."

His smile faded, and something in him seemed to go still as he looked at her face, so alive with possibilities and the challenge of their marriage. Words he hadn't meant to say tumbled from his lips. "You're a gambler, too, sweetheart. Gamble on me."

Her face took on a peculiar stillness as she studied him. He couldn't decipher her expression, whether she was pleased or wary. And when she stood up, he thought he'd miscalculated.

She walked around the small table toward him. He pushed back his chair, uncertain what she wanted—and then she sat in his lap and draped her arms about his shoulders.

"Make love to me, Leo," she whispered against his mouth, then kissed him.

The desire for her that never went away now flared to impossible heights. He dropped her back in his arms so that she was sprawled across his thighs, and kissed her with greedy possession. The time for sweet seduction, slow tenderness, was past, and all he wanted to do was devour her.

He broke the kiss, breathing heavily. "I don't want to rush, I want to savor this, give you all the pleasure—"

She cupped his face in both hands. "But I've waited so long, Leo."

With a shared groan, they kissed wildly again. Before he knew it, she was straddling his thighs, her arms wrapped about his shoulders. Their tongues mated and danced, and when she flung back her head, he buried his face in her neck, inhaling the lemon scent of her hair. He suckled her earlobe and the soft skin where her neck met her shoulder. When he parted the dressing gown further, she shrugged it to the floor. But as he touched her corset lacings at her stomach, her hands covered his.

"No," she whispered.

He froze, staring at her. She would stop him *now?* She got to her feet and his arms dropped away.

"But—"

With a wicked smile, she bent to give him a swift, eager kiss. "Leave it on. I like our games."

With a groan of relief, he tried to embrace her again, but she held him off and watched him closely as she said, "But I don't think I'll need my drawers."

When she would have turned away, he caught her hands, spread them wide. "Allow me."

Closing her eyes, she bit her lip endearingly as she nodded. He slowly reached down, and when his fingers brushed the tops of her bare feet, she noticeably quivered. He would make her shake uncontrollably before the night was through.

He explored her calves with delicate touches, slid beneath the hemline at her knee until she caught his shoulders as if she could no longer stand. Her chemise and dressing gown pooled in his arms the higher his hands moved beneath. The scent of her enveloped him, and he almost wanted to bury his face in the fabric that was so intimately close to her.

At her waist, he loosened the laces, then slid his fingers inside, embracing her hips with his palms and sliding downward. The drawers fell in his wake. He watched her face as he cupped her ass, kneading her, pulling her closer, spreading her thighs until she stood, straddling him. Eyes closed, lips parted and trembling, she gave every indication of a woman enthralled by his touch, by the possibilities of lovemaking.

The fact that she'd once thought to remain a spinster briefly crossed his mind, then he put it away for good. Her body was made to be worshipped, and he would show her that.

He let his hands come forward, sliding them down her stomach until his thumbs could part her curls and explore the moist depths. She gasped and shuddered as he rolled her clitoris between the pads of his thumbs.

"Oh, Leo," she breathed unsteadily. She opened her eyes and leaned into him. "I want to be with you, to experience everything . . . with you."

"You mean you want me inside you." He practically growled the words.

"Yes, oh yes." She shuddered and sank onto him, her hot depths cradling his erection through his trousers.

She arched against him, falling back in his arms,

their hips pressed hard against each other. With a tug, he had her breasts free, and he took their sweetness into his mouth as if he were starved for the fruit of her. She kept thrusting and moving and squirming, sending them both higher and higher.

"Wait, wait," he said hoarsely, fumbling between their bodies for his trouser buttons. He didn't think, couldn't think, about anything but being inside her.

With his erection free, he lifted her, then thrust inside so quickly that he took her virginity without any warning, any easing. She cried out, and he went completely still, in shock.

Chapter 18

The pain was sudden and unexpected, and Susanna gasped. She thought she might have cried out, and by the stunned surprise on Leo's face, perhaps she had. He was so deep inside her, stretching her, filling her, but the pain at least had begun to fade.

She hadn't even known two people could make love like this.

"I've hurt you," he said softly, tightly. "I forgot you hadn't—"

"Or you believed I had slept with Roger Eastfield." She gave a crooked smile.

He kissed her with tender worry, still searching her eyes. "No, I didn't believe that for more than a moment."

She laughed, embarrassed and uncertain now that her mindless passion had faded. "True, it would seem hard to believe that a free-spirited artist would take up with a spinster."

He suddenly cupped her face in his hands, forcing her to meet his eyes. "Don't put words in my mouth.

You are a woman who values herself highly, who doesn't lose her control without deep provocation. Hell, you made your *husband* wait—of course you'd think through the consequences of an affair."

The sting of grateful tears took her by surprise, but she couldn't let him see that. Now that the shock had passed, she could feel him pulse within her, and the faintest tremble in his hands where they rested on her cheeks.

It was her turn to cup his face. "Don't stop, I want to feel it all . . ."

He shuddered as if it were difficult to hold himself back. "I'll try to be careful."

"Leo, I'm not a fragile teacup. My virginity is gone—and shouldn't that be the worst part?"

He kissed her hard, then lifted her body, almost completely separating them. Just as she was about to protest, he surged back inside.

There was no pain, only an arrow of pleasure that made her say, "Oh!"

He gave her a triumphant grin, then bent her over his arm to tease her breasts, and there went the last of her reasoning. She felt his hot mouth suckling her nipples, his teeth even scraping against them, inducing a violent spasm of gratification. His body surged over and over into hers. She caught the motion and met him eagerly, using her thighs to lift herself, then come down to meet each ascent. Passion wound her higher, and she recognized it now, welcomed it eagerly, pushing herself against him in ways that only made her need worse.

"Now, Susanna, now!" he said on a groan.

He urged her higher, faster, wilder, until her release shattered her. And it was only made better when he arched and gripped her hips hard, shuddering as he gave everything to her.

She collapsed into his embrace, head on his shoulder, arms linked loosely about his broad, damp back. The air heaved in and out of their lungs, the hair on his chest rubbing sensitively against her breasts. He was still deep inside her, and she wished she could somehow keep him there forever, that this perfect moment could be the sum of their marriage.

But she knew this was something he had done often—how many times she couldn't even begin to imagine. It could not be as special for him as it was for her. He was the only man she'd ever wanted to risk her very soul with, and now she was married to him. She reminded herself that he'd wanted her badly, and it helped take some of the sting of melancholy away.

She simply had to keep the game going between them, to make him still excited and interested in her for as long as she possibly could.

At last she sat up slowly, and felt him go even deeper. His laughter was part groan.

"Does this mean we're . . . making love again?" she asked.

"Oh, we will, believe me, sweetheart, but right now you need to recover. Hell, *I* need to recover."

She found herself giggling, then gasped as he stood right up as if she weighed nothing. And still he held her hips to his, and they remained blissfully as one, with her chemise draped over his arms.

She stared at him wide-eyed. "This brings to mind so many possibilities."

"That's what I like to hear."

He walked to the bed and dropped her into the softness, shucking his trousers and climbing in beside her. She was ready to snuggle against him all night long, perhaps the first, deep restful night of sleep she'd had since Lord Bramfield had found them together.

"Aren't you forgetting something?" he asked. "Or do you plan to sleep in your corset? Much as that pale blue of your first corset excited me to no end—"

"Really?" she asked, delighted.

"I expected plain spinster white, and when I saw it, I almost forgot myself. I chose this one specifically, because I knew it had some give."

He knew it had "some give" because other women had worn the same kind for him. She could deal with that, she told herself, releasing the laces at her stomach. She'd known all along that he was a rake, that women lined up to spend a night in his bed. Now she knew why.

She had to find a way to make sure he never wanted another woman's bed again.

When her corset and dressing gown were heaped on the floor, and only her lightweight chemise hid her from him, she turned toward him, feeling suddenly shy. Shy? Surely she'd conquered such childishness long ago.

He opened his arms to her. "Blow out the candle, sweetheart."

As Madingley Court came into view two days later, Susanna watched Leo's face.

When he saw the towering ducal palace of turrets and battlements and hundreds of windows reflecting the sun, he only grinned at her, and said, "If this is where you were raised, no wonder you prefer the country. It's magnificent."

She tried to smile as she settled back beside him.

He took her hand. "Your skin is chilled and damp." He rubbed her hands between his. "Cold?"

"You know I'm not cold."

"It's your parents."

"I love them deeply. But this situation . . . I am beginning to regret not writing them a letter. Perhaps they are still in the city. This could be a wasted trip."

"It can't be a waste to see where you spent most of your life. Your mother is the daughter of the late duke?"

"Yes. My uncle was the duke afterward, and now it's my cousin, of course. Do you know him?"

"I haven't had the pleasure."

"He's always been very focused on his duty," Susanna mused, staring out the window again, her stomach doing a little dance of nerves. "He never used to enjoy himself much at all."

"Unlike me," Leo said dryly.

She gave him a swift glance. "You know that's not what I meant." If he could read, she guessed he would be a different sort of person, one who didn't have to entrust his money to a hired man. Was this the moment to mention it, to ask?

"We're almost there," he said.

When he betrayed no emotion, she found herself studying him. "Am I the only nervous one?"

"You have nothing to be nervous about, for you were only reacting to a situation beyond your control. As for me, I will understand whatever your father feels he needs to say to me."

Susanna briefly pressed his hand, then turned her head to see that the carriage had swept into the courtyard and beneath the columned roof of the portico. Servants swarmed to take down their trunks, a bewigged footman opened their door, and she breathed, "This is it."

At the top of the stairs, Susanna broke form and gave the plump housekeeper a hug.

"It's so good to see you, Miss Susanna," Mrs. Townsend said, then her eyes widened on seeing Leo.

Susanna's nerves bubbled higher. "Mrs. Townsend, this is Mr. Wade." It wasn't fair to name him her husband before revealing it to her parents.

Leo nodded to the servant and winked at Susanna as if he could read her mind.

"Are my parents here, Mrs. Townsend?"

"They only just arrived yesterday, miss. Much excitement in London delayed them."

"What excitement?" Susanna asked tightly.

"I'll let them give you the news," the housekeeper

said. "They're in the drawing room awaiting an early dinner."

Leo caught up with Susanna as Mrs. Townsend led them through the marble entrance hall lined with statues in recessed alcoves. "Calm down, Mrs. Wade," he murmured in her ear.

"If one of your friends has done something—"

"She said 'excitement.' That doesn't sound dreadful."

Susanna realized she was panicking for nothing but couldn't help her feelings. It wasn't every day a woman faced her parents after an elopement. Surely they'd heard the embarrassing state she and Leo had been found in. Queasiness settled in on top of her nerves.

Mrs. Townsend opened the double doors to the drawing room, where crystal chandeliers hung beneath the painted frescoes on the ceiling. The naughty angels carved into the walk-in hearth seemed to be laughing at her.

But then she saw her parents, and their smiles and open arms made her feel so much better. She rushed to them, to be enveloped by both at the same time. Professor Leland's hair had been the same auburn as Susanna's before being touched by gray, and was as mussed as always. She smiled up at him as he kissed her cheek, and she felt as close as ever, as if nothing could come between them.

Except perhaps an embarrassing son-in-law.

Her mother, Lady Rosa, had regained the weight

she'd lost when she'd thought her son dead, and looked the picture of health. Ever conscious of her girls' need for a good marriage, she used to fuss over Susanna's disinterest, until at last she'd focused all her attention on Rebecca's coming out. With Matthew's return, Susanna had smoothed out her relationship with her mother and even shown more interest in Society.

Susanna felt her mother stiffen, and knew her father looked over her head toward the door. Now they would tell her what they thought, that she'd embarrassed them, that Leo was hardly a suitable husband, and she'd have to explain that . . . she might eventually be happy.

"Good day, Mr. Wade," her mother said slowly, pleasantly, but with obvious confusion.

They didn't know! Susanna suddenly realized, and glanced wide-eyed at Leo. If they didn't know, perhaps no one in London knew, but . . . how could that be possible?

Leo stepped forward and bowed, and behind him, Mrs. Townsend retreated and shut both doors.

Her father stepped toward Leo, his spectacles glittering in a sudden shaft of the setting sun. "I don't believe we've met, sir." He spoke in a reserved voice that told Susanna he'd definitely heard a story or two about Leo's escapades.

Susanna knew there could be so many ways to reveal the truth, and most of them involved delaying. But she couldn't. "Papa, allow me to introduce Mr. Leo Wade, my husband."

That caught her father in the act of politely bowing, and he froze, then turned to stare at her. Lady Rosa gasped and clutched her husband's arm.

Wearing a smile, Leo bowed. "I am honored to meet you, Professor."

Oh, if only his dimples didn't make him look so very amused in an inappropriate way. He seemed somehow larger to her, even in the immense drawing room, a man who drew everyone's eye with his bold handsomeness and easy confidence. What was *she* doing with such a man?

"Your . . . husband?" her mother breathed. "Oh, Susanna, what did you do?"

Susanna hesitated, knowing she had not planned for this surprised reaction at all. Hadn't someone seen them kissing at Lord Bramfield's? Why hadn't that person gleefully spread the news all over London?

And then Leo rescued her, linking arms and smiling down at her so sweetly that her heart simply tumbled in her chest. No, no, she could *not* fall in love with him, she told herself sternly, desperately.

"Professor Leland, Lady Rosa, it's all my fault," Leo said, his voice deep with sincerity.

What was he going to say? The complete truth would make everything worse.

"Your daughter and I spent much time together at Lord Bramfield's country house party. I became so smitten with Susanna that I could not wait to make her my bride. I am profoundly grateful she agreed to have me. We have just returned from Scotland."

She had to be strong, to make her parents see that

everything would be fine. It was too late to change what had happened.

Thank God, they didn't know what had *really* happened.

But her father's lips were pressed together in a grim line. "You've mastered just the right tone for a man who's stolen an innocent girl to wife without speaking to her parents."

Leo opened his mouth, but Susanna quickly intervened. "Innocent girl? Papa, I am seven-and-twenty! You should be relieved at my good fortune."

Lady Rosa sent several uncertain glances toward Leo, but she looked back at Susanna, wearing a trembling smile. "Are you happy, my dear girl? That is what matters most to me."

"Yes, Mama, I am happy." Susanna felt tears threaten, but it was only in relief that this homecoming had not gone too terribly wrong so far. And she truly was resolved to find a way to become happier.

Her mother looked between them, a tear spilling down her wrinkled cheek. She'd always wanted Susanna to marry. At least she did not show the rigid disapproval the professor did.

Susanna wouldn't have thought her distracted, scholarly father capable of such emotion. He didn't glance at her, but focused his attention on Leo, whose expression remained pleasant.

"Oh, Susanna," Lady Rosa said, "I had almost given up hope at seeing this day come."

Susanna felt her own stirring of hope. "I had once thought the same, Mama, but Mr. Wade convinced me otherwise." He could convince angels to descend to earth if he wanted to.

Her father's frown only deepened. Leo had certainly seen such disapproval before. But for once, she'd wanted him to be faced with something better, to know he could be accepted for who he was, for the man he could become with her help.

"Wade—" the professor began in a low voice.

"Randolph, please," Lady Rosa interrupted. "We can ask questions at dinner. But for now, let the children go recover from their travels. I'm certain they have so much to tell us," she added brightly, pointedly. "Especially about the wedding. I wish . . . ah well, one always imagines watching one's daughter marry."

Susanna winced. It might be a long time before her mother could forget that.

"And we have so much to tell them," Lady Rosa added.

Susanna's attempt at a relieved smile faded. "Mrs. Townsend mentioned some excitement in London?"

At last her father looked at her, then cleared his throat, speaking gruffly, but still with love. "Go change, my dear. We have all night to talk." Another pointed glance at Leo. "I'll have Mrs. Townsend prepare a suite of rooms."

"No, that won't be necessary," Susanna said. "We'll simply take my usual room. It's large enough, with its own dressing room, so the servants won't have to move my belongings."

When Leo arched a brow, she belatedly realized

she hadn't even allowed them the fiction of separate beds.

Well, her parents were married, too, and recently reunited in quite a romantic way. They would simply have to get used to it.

Leo had been prepared for a girlish room of ribbons and lace, but then, that wasn't his Susanna. Instead, almost every inch of wall was covered in paintings, watercolors, oils, even the occasional framed sketch. He peered at the signatures, but to his surprise, they weren't hers. They must have provided inspiration. But did not her own work inspire her?

Behind him, he heard Susanna let out a great sigh and turned to find her slumping back on her bed, arms spread wide, eyes closed.

"If you insist," Leo began, leaning over to pin her arms and planning to kiss her senseless.

But she turned her head away. "Leo!" She practically hissed his name.

"You did make certain we shared a bedroom. That was brave of you."

She struggled until he released her, then surged to her feet to face him, hands on her hips. "I wasn't even thinking. And my father's expression!" With a groan, she slapped both hands over her face.

He pried several fingers away so she could see him. "We're married. Every father of a daughter must accept such a thing at some point in life. You simply waited longer than most."

"Ooh!"

She gave him such a push that he staggered back and caught the bedpost with one arm.

"My, such strength. I have ideas what to do with it."

"Please, can you be serious for once?"

He bowed dramatically. "I imagine you wish to discuss your parents' ignorance of our marriage?"

"Yes! If they don't know, no one in London does, for the news would surely fly. Lord Bramfield said he saw someone watching us. I cannot believe such a person would remain quiet."

"Or he lied to protect you by forcing my hand," Leo mused. "I wonder what he told the other guests about our mutual disappearance."

"Lied?" she echoed, distraught. "You mean we wouldn't have had to . . ."

"No, he felt I'd taken advantage of you, that it was only a matter of time before others knew. And he was right. You cannot blame him."

"I don't," she said, walking to the window seat and sitting down.

She kept her head turned, eyes on the horizon, and Leo could see why. All of the rolling hills of the countryside spread out before them, with the sun hovering low in the sky.

"How can I blame him," she continued, "for what the two of us were doing?"

"You can blame me. It would be the truth. I told you I meant to seduce your secrets away from you. Hell, I haven't even done that yet."

She sent him a wry smile. "I was not naïve about your motives, or my response. And I thought myself so capable of resisting. No," she said, hands slapping her thighs as she rose, "this is as much my fault as yours. So I suggest we accept the consequences."

"Spoken like a rebel." When she walked past him, he caught her by the shoulders and kissed her. "It will be fine. Your mother likes me." He flashed his dimples.

With a roll of her eyes, she said, "Women do, it seems."

But at dinner, Leo experienced the unease he was trying not to show for Susanna's sake. He'd hoped there would be more people in attendance, but all were in London for the Season except the four of them. The impressive dining room could have seated fifty, so they headed toward one end of the massive table while the servants began to arrive with the first course.

"This is the only dining room?" Leo whispered to Susanna before they were separated.

"Of course not. But I think intimidation is coming into play."

Her father gestured for Leo to sit alone on one side of the table, while Susanna and her mother sat on the other side.

"Mr. Wade," the professor said as he took his seat at the head of the table and nodded to the waiting footman, "my wife tells me that your brother is Viscount Wade."

"Yes, sir."

"An impressive and upstanding man."

"For our entire lives, to my dismay." He grinned.

The professor did not respond in kind.

"I have a sister, Georgiana, who is engaged," Leo continued, straightening so that the footman could ladle soup into his bowl. "My grandmother and mother occasionally reside with my brother. That is the sum of my family."

"As a younger son, what plans had you made for yourself?"

"I invest my money, sir, but I fear I was never meant for service under God's eyes or the Queen's."

Leo knew he wasn't the sort of man the Lelands had wanted for their daughter. He had thought he wouldn't care if they assumed he was after her for her money or ducal connections, but he found it bothered him in a way he hadn't imagined, and he wasn't certain why. At least Lady Rosa smiled at him.

"And what money do you invest?" Professor Leland pointedly asked.

"My gambling winnings, sir." He took another spoonful of his oxtail soup.

"Gambling winnings tend to disappear as fast as they arrive. Will you then make use of my daughter's dowry?"

"I have already sent word to my solicitor that Susanna's dowry is to be put in trust for her and our children."

The professor blinked at him, then said, "A sound decision."

It was as if a sigh emerged from all their lips. Leo

saw that even Susanna stared at him, not masking her surprise. Well, he'd always told her he didn't care about her money.

And then she smiled at him, not bothering to hide a show of happy tenderness. Her eyes were soft and lovely, and he realized he could look at her all day. Or a lifetime. Then she winked and turned to her father, leaving him feeling . . . bemused.

"Papa, I can hardly contain my curiosity. What news was Mrs. Townsend referring to?"

Lady Rosa clapped her hands together. "You are not my only daughter to find happiness. Rebecca and Lord Parkhurst are engaged!"

Leo watched Susanna's jaw drop, even as she sent him a wide-eyed stare. He shrugged, rather surprised himself that straightlaced Julian had so quickly fallen under Rebecca's spell. Unless something like their own situation had occurred. . .

"And Rebecca is . . . happy?" Susanna asked with obvious hesitation.

"I have never seen her eyes sparkle like this," Professor Leland admitted, a smile relaxing his face.

"And Lord Parkhurst looks upon my dear daughter as if she were his sun," Lady Rosa said dreamily.

Susanna squeezed her mother's hand. "That is wonderful news. I cannot wait to hear all about it." Another surreptitious glance at Leo.

"But that's not the only news," Lady Rosa said with an excited laugh. "Your cousin Elizabeth is also engaged, and you'll never guess to whom! Peter Derby!"

Good God, Leo thought, how had one drunken wager—proposed by him—led all three of the men into the marriage trap? Should he apologize to his friends? he wondered dryly. Or should he be congratulated? he thought, as he looked upon Susanna with a surprising feeling of tenderness.

When Susanna said nothing, Leo studied her, curious about her uneasiness.

Lady Rosa cried, "Can you imagine? And to think, I once thought you and Peter—" She broke off, blushing as she glanced at Leo. "But that is long in the past, of course."

Ah, there it was. Susanna and Peter? Leo looked at his wife with open consideration, and she made a little frown of annoyance that he found fetching.

"I'll have to hear that story," Leo said. *When he was alone with her.* He turned to the professor. "Sir, I know you teach at Cambridge, but I would be interested in learning more. It's not every man who can say one's father-in-law is a famous scholar."

Susanna froze in obvious worry, as if he'd gone too far, but Professor Leland cleared his throat and studied Leo thoughtfully.

"I'm an anatomist, Mr. Wade. I'm surprised Susanna has not explained my work to you." Then he glanced over his spectacles. "Or perhaps there wasn't time."

To Susanna's surprise, her mother led her into the drawing room after dinner, leaving the men to their brandy. Susanna had long since stopped worrying about Leo—he had her mother openly laughing through dinner, and even her father had smiled. Leo understood people well. They were different in that way—Susanna often struggled to hide her incomprehension at the behavior of others, and it was so much harder for her to make easy conversation. And humor? That was Leo's forte.

She and her mother sat side by side on a sofa.

"You look happy," Lady Rosa said softly, touching her daughter's arm. "I feel immensely relieved."

"And you see the same thing in Rebecca's face?"

"Of course!"

"I thought Lord Parkhurst far too sober and judgmental for someone as adventurous as my sister. And Rebecca had been determined to remain unmarried as long as possible."

"You and I did see them together before she left for Aunt Rianette's. I don't know when they had time to become better acquainted. And she was only home for several days before I heard the news. I was quite shocked."

Susanna knew that Julian had followed Rebecca out of London, and she found herself terribly curious to know what had happened. Susanna had vowed to protect her sister and cousin—had she succeeded? Were they truly happy, or trapped because of the consequences of that dreadful painting? The only way to know for certain was to talk to Rebecca and Elizabeth herself.

"But that was nothing compared to my shock this afternoon," her mother said, shaking her head and giving Susanna a hesitant gaze. "When I saw you with Mr. Wade . . ."

Susanna smiled. "I understand, Mama. He is surely the last man I ever thought I'd be drawn to. But there is something about him . . ."

"Of course, of course. I did not doubt you knew your own mind. You always think everything through."

Susanna could have choked.

"But Mr. Wade has such an . . . interesting reputation."

"Some men have wild youths, and his might have lasted a bit longer than most, but it is in the past now." She hoped. "Do you think Papa will eventually understand?"

Her mother's smile was rueful. "Give him time. He has not been impressed with Mr. Wade's reputation. I told him you would make a wise decision, but he seemed to think you could be led astray by the right man."

"I cannot imagine why he thought that." Perhaps because he knew her better than anyone.

"I know! I am your mother, after all. But now I can rest easy, knowing that my daughters and my son are happy and taken care of."

Susanna allowed her mother's hug and wondered how Leo was doing alone with her father.

Chapter 19

Susanna sat in the middle of her bed later that night, drawing the counterpane up around her waist, staring at the dressing-room door as it opened and Leo came striding in. He wore a robe, and his legs were bare. Susanna stared at him, feeling strange with a husband—a very attractive, dominating man—in her childhood bedroom.

"Your father sent up a valet," Leo said as he walked toward the bed. "I didn't know how to tell him I haven't used one on our whole wild journey. He might think you've been providing everything I need."

She shuddered. "What did you possibly say to my father since we've never even discussed if you went to university?"

He eyed her with amusement. "I'm a Cambridge man. I had no choice but to follow my brother."

Follow his brother . . . of course! He'd said Lord Wade helped him with all his work. Should she tell Leo that she knew the truth, that she understood?

And what if he took it poorly, here, with her parents

within earshot? No, his secret would have to wait.

"But you didn't know my father?"

"Anatomy? No." He laughed. "I studied the classics, just like my brother. He was convinced I couldn't get into any trouble that way."

"But he was wrong."

"Very wrong."

Leo put a knee on the bed and began to crawl toward her. She shrank back against the pillows—what could he be thinking? *Here? Now?*

"So, sweetheart," he said softly, when his head was above hers, "what is this about Peter Derby, friend of mine, participant in a wager that has seen him shackled to your cousin? But first he was interested in you?"

She let out her breath shakily and couldn't quite meet his eyes. "Oh, that. Nothing, truly. Many years ago, when I first came out, he expressed some interest in courting me. We didn't suit. Believe me, he courted many women, even my brother's supposed widow."

She expected Leo to laugh, his usual response. Trying to distract him, she reached up to touch his face—

He caught her wrist even as he studied her. "I need the story."

He retreated to sit cross-legged on the bed, and she could see his bare thighs. Without thinking, she ducked her head to see more beneath his robe.

"None of that," he said.

"None of that?" she echoed. "From *you*?"

"Believe me, it's taking every bit of control I have not to toss you onto your back and have my way with you." His eyes smoldered as they meandered down her body.

She felt flushed and pleased and suddenly breathless.

"But you're my wife; you have to tell me your secrets."

"That goes for you, too."

"It does."

"Then I'll take you up on that, soon," she promised solemnly. "Be prepared."

He frowned, studying her. "My question first. Tell me about Peter."

"That's not a question."

"Susanna."

She gave a heavy sigh and looked away. It should be easy to explain her silly, self-conscious youth. "I don't usually dwell on it. I've changed much since then, become confident in my own worth."

"I'm glad to hear it. But about Peter . . ."

"I wasn't so confident then, merely awkward and uncomfortable and inept. I didn't seem to care about the same things other young people did. Men . . . did not pay much attention to me, and if they did, I could easily tell it was because of my dowry or my family connections. I was not exactly a proper debutante."

"Ah, no wonder I was suspect."

"You can hardly blame me for assuming you

needed my money. But you're putting it all in trust," she said, staring at him in wonder.

He only shrugged. "I've told you from the beginning that I didn't need it. I was pleased you seemed to believe me even before I revealed my plans."

"You were?" she said softly, taking his hand again.

"But it took you long enough. Now go on about your suitors."

She sighed. "I couldn't even blame their lack of true attention on the lure of Rebecca or Elizabeth because neither of them were out of the schoolroom yet. And then there was Peter. We'd practically grown up together, neighbors. We were comfortable, and I began to think that such a feeling would make a good marriage—"

"'Comfortable'?" Leo interrupted in obvious disbelief. "You've used that before, and it is the most unromantic word I've ever heard."

"Allow me to finish. I'd begun to hear that Peter was spending time with another young lady as well, and I understood, for there was no commitment between us. At a party with the young, fashionable crowd, I overheard this lady making a joke at my expense. Peter was with them, and I kept waiting for him to defend me, but he didn't. He only laughed, too." She briefly closed her eyes, not wanting to see a pitying look. "We were both young and foolish, and I've forgiven him since, but that was the end of my brief flirtation with Peter." Her forgiveness took a bit longer than she was making it sound, for his behavior had been the final straw in her terrible battle with trying to find a place in Society.

"So you retreated to your books and your art and gave up on marriage."

She said nothing.

"You gave up on marriage for many years."

She shrugged. "It was Matthew's return that woke me up. His wife Emily thought I was being far too safe, taking no risks, that someday I might regret it."

"Life is about risks," he said, nodding. "You took one with me, and look what happened."

"Not a good thing, or so I believed at first."

"Then you regret taking Emily's advice."

Those eyes that could be so light with amusement, as green as new summer grass, now seemed opaque, impassive, showing no emotion.

"Only briefly," she admitted. "But now . . . I don't know."

Though his voice had seemed emotionless, Susanna thought she detected something else beneath. Could she have the power to hurt him? It didn't seem possible. He was so full of vitality and belief in his own worth, even with the secret he kept hidden.

Or did he have doubts about himself, too?

There was only a single candle lit on her bed table, and Susanna leaned to blow it out.

"No," Leo said. "Leave it. I want to see you. And I don't mean while you fall asleep."

She gave him a slow smile, conscious of her need to keep him curious about her. "What if I want the mystery of the dark?"

He met her eyes, and his twinkled devilishly in the flickering candlelight. She caught her breath at the promise there.

"Then let me show you why girls should be afraid of the dark."

She blew out the candle, and while the acrid smell lingered briefly in the air, she felt the disturbance of the bed as he moved.

She tensed with excited expectation. "What are you—"

"Lie back." His command was a soft growl in the darkness.

And then the counterpane started to slide down her body. She wore her nightgown, but the moment the air hit her bare feet in a swirl, she shivered.

"Afraid?" he whispered from somewhere away from the bed.

"Come to me, and I won't be."

"Not yet. Be quiet. Spread your legs, and then don't move."

In the darkness, she could see nothing, and his command made her tense with a new thrill. But still he didn't touch her. She lay blinking, feeling fluttery and nervous and—

And then she felt a whisper of moistness on the arch of her foot, and realized he'd kissed her there. She shuddered, her every awareness centered on her skin, as she wondered where he would touch her next.

It took too long, and her anticipation grew to the point that she was about to beg him. Then she felt the slow slide of his tongue up the inside of her calf, pushing her nightgown up at the same time. She let out a fluttery moan and did her best to remain still, when her skin seemed to be shrinking on her bones, and she had to move or she would be smothered.

He nipped the inside of her knee, and this time she did jerk. His silent laughter was only a puff of breath against her moist flesh. And still he moved higher, and the linen nightdress sliding upward was an unbearable announcement of his intentions.

Now there were kisses, slow and steady, advancing up her inner thigh, higher and higher, until she realized she was arching her hips off the bed, her body taut with pleasure. It coiled deep inside her, stirring, and she wanted to give it free rein to sweep through her again, to take her to heights only Leo had ever provided.

When his mouth left her, she collapsed back onto the bed with a groan.

And then he started up the other inner thigh, this time spreading her legs wider, until she was so open to him, vulnerable. Wasn't it time he should be inside her? Shouldn't he—

And then he nuzzled her entrance, and it wasn't with his fingers.

"Leo!"

His mouth against her, he chuckled, and that made her spasm under him even more.

"No talking," he murmured.

"But—but—surely—"

And then he licked her, his tongue delving so slowly that her moan became strangled in her throat.

She was hot with embarrassment, greedy for passion, her every sense concentrated on what he was doing to her. His tongue darted lightly, then made long slow strokes, tasting her, tormenting her. She was restless with need, her head rolling back and forth, her limbs quivering, feeling the climb toward unbearable pleasure.

And then she felt his hands cupping her breasts at the same time, and she cried out. His fingers tweaked and rolled her nipples, then he suckled her down below, until the explosion came over her in a shuddering eruption of heat and power and release.

"Oh God," she gasped, still trembling, even as he slowly climbed up her body. "Leo, Leo, please—"

She bent her knees to capture his hips; and then he was inside her, deeply penetrating, powerfully stroking. His entire body pressed her into the bed, and it felt wonderful and dominating and intense. She came again almost immediately, letting him ride her through it, rocking against him, feeling the perspiration on their bodies mingle.

Everything mingled—as if they were one body now, one being. He shuddered and groaned above her, and she felt the satisfaction of knowing she'd done this to him—that they'd pleasured each other.

He collapsed onto the bed at her side with a final groan. "Next time I promise to take my time. Maybe. I feel like a randy boy."

"And is that so bad?" she asked, rolling onto her side to cuddle against him. She inhaled, surprised to find how much she enjoyed the scent of him. "I thought it wonderful. I still can't believe what you did to me. Do you like the same thing in return?"

Another groan in the darkness, this time mingled with a chuckle that shook the bed. "There's so much I'll show you, Susanna."

She took that as a promise. But as she lay there listening to him fall asleep, enjoying the intimacy of the way his body relaxed and his breathing evened, her insecurities began to nibble again on her satisfied mood.

She'd told him about her foolish problems with men, and he hadn't laughed at her. He was tolerating her eccentricities as he spent every moment of the day with her, but once they were back in London, there might be days when they only saw each other in passing. Would he tolerate her differences then, when it was obvious Society thought her an outcast?

He had to understand how very different she was, and if it was a test he would fail, she had to know the truth.

Suddenly, she felt him flinch and twitch, and she spread her hands down his arm and across his chest. His breathing became erratic and harsh. She wanted to hold him to her, to soothe him. It was another dream, but why the same thing over and over again?

Leo awoke to a silent bedroom, and realized that although it was just past dawn, he was alone. He relaxed and let weariness overtake him again. He hadn't slept well, even with Susanna a soothing presence at his side. He could only hope he hadn't kept her awake. He didn't think he'd called out in the night, but he could never be certain.

He was beginning to feel helpless, as if his dreams were trying to tell him something, but he couldn't understand the message. And did he really want to know, if it involved a corpse and suffocating darkness? The darkness kept him from knowing where the corpse was, so he had no way to follow the trail in real life and discover the truth.

He was . . . helpless.

He felt the need to be outside before he faced Susanna and her family, so he went for a long ride on horseback. After far too many days in a carriage, it refreshed and cleared his mind to be out of doors, even though the overcast sky threatened rain. He ate a solitary breakfast, then began to explore the palace but couldn't find Susanna in any of the public rooms. There must be rooms reserved for the family alone, and though he was family now, he wasn't certain he'd been given permission to act as one of them.

At last he found Lady Rosa in the morning room, going over the evening's menu with Mrs. Townsend. Lady Rosa dismissed the servant, then smiled at him.

"Mr. Wade, I do hope you enjoyed your ride."

"I did, my lady, thank you. But now I seem to have misplaced my wife. Have you seen her?"

She briefly looked away, her hesitation obvious. "Let me see . . . did you try the music room?"

By her manner, she knew very well Susanna wasn't there. He played along. "It was empty, my lady. But if you have an idea, I would be glad to hear it. In fact, I haven't seen the professor either. Could they be together? I'll ask one of the servants."

He turned to go, then smiled with satisfaction when she called his name.

"Mr. Wade, I do believe I might know where they are. My husband has a laboratory here in the house, in the servants' wing on the ground floor. Susanna might be . . . with him." And then she gave him a nervous smile. "I hope you understand that before your marriage, Susanna needed to fill her day with her hobbies, and I'm certain that now she'll be so busy with her own household, that she will devote more time . . ." And then her voice faded on a sigh.

They both knew how stubborn Susanna could be.

"Lady Rosa, you do not need to explain her passion for her art to me. I think she's quite talented."

"Have you seen the work she's done for her father?" she asked flatly.

He cocked his head with interest. "No."

"Then see it, and I'll pray you won't think differently." She shooed him away.

Filled with growing curiosity and intrigue, Leo found the servants' wing with help, then was led to a closed door by a very nervous maid, who bobbed a curtsy and fled.

He knocked, and after a moment, it swung open. The smell of rotting flesh mixed with a layer of an unrecognizable masking scent almost made him take a step back. But he'd known what the professor did, of course. Susanna stood in the doorway, wearing a plain navy gown covered with a heavy apron that

was spotted with a dark brown substance—blood.
Beyond her, he could see a room with many windows, oil lamps blazing, and a large slab of a table
in the center of the room. The professor, gowned and
spattered as well, stood over what could only be a
man's naked corpse.

Professor Leland glanced over his spectacles and
saw Leo.

"Your husband needs you, Susanna," he said. "I
can do without you."

"Thank you, Papa." And then Susanna closed the
door.

"These are the naked men you've seen," Leo said
slowly, as everything began to make sense.

She gave him a nervous smile. "Does it bother
you? I have never told you what I do because even
my family believes it to be quite . . . ghoulish."

"What exactly do you do?"

She took off her apron and hung it from the door-
knob, tossed her gloves nearby, and slid her hand
through his arm as they walked down the hall. "I
sketch father's dissections in detail, the muscles and
organs, so he has a record of what he's done. He's
often put my work on display when he lectures," she
added proudly.

How Susanna must enjoy contributing to scientific achievement. When he smiled, the worry in her
eyes faded away into happiness. He clasped her hand
where it rested on his arm.

"Why did you feel you had to hide it?" he asked.

"I've been warned for many years not to bring it

up, and I think the habit became ingrained in me. There are many superstitions regarding using the dead for such research. Years ago, my father was interrogated because of a crime committed by men he'd hired. It was a terrible scandal that tore my parents' marriage asunder."

She opened a door leading outside to the park, then led him to a bench surrounded by rosebushes.

Sitting down with a sigh, she continued, "My father's studies consumed him, and much as my mother fell in love with his very differences, she did not realize what being the wife of a scientist would be like. They met when my grandfather—who enjoyed his own scandals—leased a cottage on the property to my father so he could work in peace. Papa paid his employees to purchase the corpses of criminals condemned to death, but it was much more difficult to find female bodies. Little did he know, but his employees had become resurrectionists."

"They stole bodies from graves," Leo said, nodding. "I heard about the scandal."

The wind had picked up beneath gray skies and caught several auburn curls and swirled them across her forehead. He lightly tucked them behind her ear, and to his surprise, she shyly blushed.

"Go on," he urged.

"When the scandal broke, he had committed no crime, but the notoriety was terrible. My mother was furious and appalled, from what I heard. I was a very young child, you see, so I knew nothing then. My parents only truly reconciled, putting aside their pride and long-held anger, just last year, after Matthew's return."

"So secrets kept them apart," Leo murmured.

To his surprise, Susanna was searching his eyes as if looking for some truth. Did she suspect he kept things from her?

"Truly, your work for your father does not bother me," he said.

Her shoulders seemed to slump a bit, but she didn't look exactly . . . relieved. Curious.

"Good. Then I hope you will understand what I have to say next."

She took a deep breath, as if fortifying herself, and Leo frowned.

"He's approached a publisher with his work, and they would like to use my sketches. They need my permission, of course. And I would have to contribute a few new sketches as well." She hesitated, watchful eyes on him. "I would hate to refuse him."

"Are you asking for my permission?" A dozen different thoughts rotated in his brain, and he had trouble deciding which one should be the most important.

She sighed. "No. But I want you to be supportive of this book and my work because I've given much of my life to it, and it has such meaning for me."

Unsaid was the fact that he'd given much of his life to . . . enjoying himself. That restlessness he'd been feeling had gone away since this seduction and his marriage to Susanna, but was marriage to a scandalous artist enough to replace it?

And if he didn't like it, what was he supposed to

do about it? Deny her? See the light in her eyes that he'd only just begun to inspire, disappear? He enjoyed her passions—all of them—and admired her dedication.

"Leo?" She said his name tentatively.

"How could I deny you my support?" he asked lightly, then gave an obvious shudder. "Fathers of brides frighten grooms."

She closed her eyes and leaned her head against his shoulder. "Thank you."

They spent several quiet minutes, watching the distant storm that slowly pushed graying clouds toward them. Leo hoped his reaction had given Susanna some peace, that her trust would truly flourish.

And then what? he thought, feeling uneasy. He'd never been in such a relationship before, of course. He wasn't certain how one honored a woman's trust. He never saw his own parents reconcile and come to love each other, as she had. But some part of him had always thought London had the answer. He'd been trusting in his return to what he knew best, the Society, the parties, all the things the *ton* did. He'd thought he would feel like himself and be able to find a way to live peaceably with his wife.

But once Susanna's work came under public scrutiny, everything might very well change. He was used to being condemned for his own reckless choices—but watching Society treat Susanna harshly was not something he could tolerate. And he would no longer be the devil-may-care Leo Wade. But what would that make him?

Chapter 20

Dinner that evening was a more cordial affair, held in the intimate family dining room. Susanna felt noticeably lighter, glad that Leo knew her oldest secret, and was not appalled, that he supported her work with her father. Surely he now saw that he could trust her with his own secrets, and she was determined to bring up the subject, once they were away from her parents.

In London, she reminded herself, trying not to allow her happiness to deflate. London, where he had his wild crowd, and she had more sedate, intellectual friends. Her friends would come to understand her decisions, but *his* friends could very well make his life hell over what she was doing. He was supportive now, but would that change him over time? And why would he feel free to tell her about his reading problem, when he knew just how to cope, just how to pretend everything was all right? He'd been succeeding at that his whole life.

Lady Rosa seemed to sense Susanna's troubled thoughts. "How long will you be staying with us, Mr. Wade?"

Because it was no longer her own decision, Susanna thought with resignation.

But before Leo could speak, Lady Rosa continued on. "Or will you be visiting your own estate before traveling on to London?"

Susanna almost fumbled her fork and just kept it from clattering to her plate. Leo had an estate? She turned to look at him, blinking, her face set in a pleasant mask to hide her turmoil from her parents. But he was watching her—a sure sign of guilt.

"My wife told me about your land, Mr. Wade," the professor added. "I'm pleased to know that my daughter will have a home in the country to retreat to when London empties after the Season. Where is it?"

Leo cleared his throat. "Woodhill Manor is near St. Albans, Professor."

Near Lord Bramfield's estate—where they'd so recently been? Susanna thought, flustered. But . . . he'd said they'd live in London—with his brother—while they made a decision. Had he kept it a secret because he liked London better?

No, she knew him too well by now to suspect such petty motivation. She should be angry—but she wasn't, only shocked and growing more and more curious about his motive for secrecy. Surely he knew she would have found out eventually. Or did he only want to live in London, leaving his estate under the management of a steward? Perhaps keeping his hands on the reins would involve too much reading, so he distanced himself from it.

She continued to eat dinner, watching the happy

glances Lady Rosa sent her way. Her father and her husband discussed the agricultural pursuits of Woodhill Manor, and it was obvious Leo knew his estate well.

But he hadn't planned to take her there anytime soon. She was certain of it.

When at last the meal was over, and she and her mother were leaving the men to their brandy and their intense discussion, Susanna smiled brightly at her parents, and said, "I'm so sorry we won't be able to spend another evening like this. But I'm simply dying to see my new home, and Mr. Wade has promised to take me there next."

Leo lounged back in his chair and eyed her speculatively. "I thought you wished to see your sister and Lady Elizabeth. You three have much to discuss."

She waved a hand. "They're deliriously happy and planning their weddings, according to Mama. They'd want me to see Woodhill Manor."

Leo saluted her with his brandy glass. And if he looked a bit distant as he stared down into the swirling liquid, it only made her all the more eager. Lord Bramfield would have to make do without one of his carriages for a while longer. Susanna beamed at Leo, knowing that she was only a day or so away from finding out everything he'd been hiding from her.

As the carriage rumbled beneath them, Leo looked down at his wife, who slumped against his side in abandoned sleep.

He had kept her awake long into the night, he

thought with satisfaction. Again, she'd insisted on the dark to cloak them. She was teasing him about the wager, using it against him—claiming that until she spoke with her sister and cousin, it wasn't concluded yet.

But Leo had begun to think there were other reasons for her shyness in their bedroom. The wager might simply be an excuse. Did she think the worst of him, that he would find fault with her nudity? If that were true, he was certainly not gaining her trust. When would she be able to escape the insecurities of her past?

Or perhaps he was doing something wrong and needed to prove himself.

He was certainly proving something by agreeing to visit Woodhill Manor though he wasn't certain what. He hadn't been to the estate since childhood, when it had been held by a member of his father's family but not entailed with the viscountcy.

And with his father's death, it had become his own, but that still hadn't made him want to return. His grandmother lived nearby, and it was easier to stay there, to amuse his relatives rather than be alone with only a few servants. He heard regular reports about the estate, of course, and would certainly never allow its mismanagement. But visit? The very thought never occurred to him.

For the first time, he allowed himself to wonder why and couldn't come up with a reason.

It was late in the evening when they arrived, and the sun had already set, but that could not account for Leo's strange feeling of unease when he saw the two-story manor of simple stone, with several dozen windows, instead of the hundreds that Madingley Court had. Woodhill Manor wasn't a ducal palace; it had been the home of his bachelor uncle, who'd died many years before. Leo had told the history to Susanna on the journey, and she'd been far more fascinated than the story warranted, but he understood why—because he himself hadn't spoken of the estate before now. His secrecy was suspect in her eyes, and even suspect in his.

Inside the house, Susanna walked through the rooms with the housekeeper, delighting in the snug drawing room, the many windows in the dining room, but especially the library. Leo trailed behind, pretending an ease he was far from feeling.

Up in the master bedroom, she continued chattering about her views of the house, and he was still amazed that she wasn't angry with him. She fell into bed talking, would have continued if he hadn't stopped her with a kiss.

He had trouble falling asleep, and although the nightmare didn't return, his sleep seemed only oppressive and deep, as if in waiting.

Susanna could have skipped with delight midmorning as she went to find Leo. The house was cozy and quaint, well cared for and lovely. Several tenants had stopped by with breads and jams and baked goods, all to welcome them to Woodhill Manor.

And it was very obvious they were curious about

Leo. A farmer's wife had actually whispered that she'd lived nearby for many years and never met him. It wasn't all that unusual for wealthy men to own many different estates, some simply for revenue rather than as a residence. But this was Leo's only property.

To her surprise, she found him in his study, account books spread out over the desk, and the steward, a lean blond man who was dressed as simply as a farmer, doing the talking, while Leo frowned out the window. The steward bowed and left them alone, and Susanna seated herself behind the desk.

"I am very good with mathematics, Leo."

"Why doesn't that surprise me?" he asked, wearing a wry smile.

"I'd like to help."

"Of course."

If she'd expected him to bristle, as other men might, she would have been mistaken. When would she ever understand him? she thought, her gaze roaming his desk.

And then she saw a book on Roman antiquities, opened to several sketches of an ancient bath, and it made her pause. He hadn't wanted to see the remains at Bramfield Hall, but since then, in more than one museum, she'd seen his fascination. Perhaps this was a way to reach him.

"You want my help, Leo, and it makes me glad," she said softly. She slid the book toward her, took a deep breath, and spoke. "Since you'll accept my help with the estate, perhaps you'll let me help you learn to read."

He blinked at her for a long moment, and she

found herself holding her breath. He could deny it—perhaps she'd see him in the first rage of their marriage. Or would he simply walk away, ruining their growing trust?

He gave her a tender smile, then leaned over and began to read the book, flawlessly translating into Latin, then German.

She gaped at him as her face heated with embarrassment.

He cupped her cheek. "Where did you come by the idea that I couldn't read?"

She pushed his hand away and rose to face him. "You gave it to me! You don't read papers or books. In museums, you don't read the signs. I thought—I thought—" Words briefly failed her, and she realized she wasn't even angry; she was terribly relieved. "But if you can read, and you were so brilliant as a child that you could take machines apart and put them back together, why did you reject more intellectual pursuits?"

"Other things have always interested me more than reading," he said with a shrug. "Fencing, boxing, riding. And I like to be with people."

"Cambridge," she said softly, shaking her head. Of course he could not possibly have attended if his brother had done *all* his work.

He continued to smile at her, confusing her with his very handsomeness.

Oh, there was still more, she just knew it. She pointed to the book. "Then tell me about your fascination with Roman antiquities."

"Fascination?" he said blankly.

"You reacted very strangely to the remains on Lord Bramfield's estate. I've seen you looking several times at Roman artifacts or paintings when you accompany me to museums. And now this book, sitting right here open on your desk. It seems like a fascination to me."

He shrugged nonchalantly. "It's a recent fascination, I imagine. It was something to look at."

"You deliberately picked this book off a shelf, out of the very impressive library here at Woodhill Manor."

With his casual behavior, she was beginning to wonder if even *he* understood what was going on.

He spread his hands wide. "What can I say? I was avoiding work. Surely, you cannot be surprised."

She stared at him speculatively. Other men might be appalled at her deductions of illiteracy, or believe she'd thought him weak-minded. Not Leo.

And he hadn't even been at Woodhill Manor a full day, and already he was looking for distractions rather than attending to the estate's business. Was it the estate itself? she wondered.

Following her intuition, she said, "Well, if you'd like to avoid work, then let us go for a ride, and you can show me the grounds of your home."

Leo leaned his hip on the desk in front of his wife, watching her, but trying to understand his own emotions. He wasn't used to even thinking about them, so it all felt very strange. He found himself saying, "Woodhill Manor was never my home. In my mind, it's still my uncle's."

The uncle he barely remembered, he thought in confusion. Why did he feel so resistant, so uneasy? He didn't like being here. And even he couldn't tell himself it was because he preferred London. There was more to it—but he didn't know what.

"Are you saying you don't wish to ride?" she inquired almost too politely.

"The steward is waiting to continue our meeting."

She didn't become angry, only said brightly, "Another time, then. I'll go for a walk."

"Perhaps you should wait for me." As if Susanna would believe herself in need of a male escort. He tried to make it sound like a joke, as he said, "You know I wanted a wife who would obey her husband."

She didn't laugh. "And I wanted a husband who was curious about the world. It seems neither of us got what we wanted in this marriage."

Two hours later, the steward had left at last, and Leo sat back, contemplating his satisfaction at how Woodhill Manor had flourished with his benign neglect. It was so quiet. Listening intently, he couldn't even hear servants working nearby. He was used to the sound of London traffic, the smell of coal dust, the glitter of palaces near Hyde Park.

Here in Hertfordshire, he would become a country squire if he stayed for long, shooting his dinner with the locals and attending assemblies with girls who would pester him about his long-ago life in London. He'd always laughed about such men, had sworn never to become one.

And now he was married to a bluestocking who hated London. He sighed and looked out the window, not seeing the view. He was disappointing her, he knew, and that made an uncomfortable tightness grip his stomach. She wanted a husband "curious about the world," and the notion made him smile sadly. With her curiosity, it was a wonder she hadn't tried to become a scientist like her father. She believed she could do anything, and if it could happen with will alone, she would succeed. Whereas he knew—he could not.

"Leo!" Susanna rushed into the room and practically skidded to a stop in front of his desk.

He straightened. "What's wrong?"

"I found a cave!"

He blinked at her, and some distant part of his brain seemed to toll like a warning bell, warding off ships from a rocky coast.

She clapped her hands together. "There were signs about treacherous rock, so I stayed well back, of course. But I could tell that someone has begun excavation there. It could be Roman antiquities, since we're near St. Albans, don't you think? Surely you have heard about this, hence your fascination."

"I don't remember." And he didn't. There seemed to be a suspicious blank space in his mind. "Show me."

The walk took less than an hour, well off the manicured lawns of the park itself. Susanna turned and followed the banks of a small stream, where rocks had tumbled over each other. All of this was familiar, but like an old recollection, a dream long forgotten.

At last she veered away from the water, and for some reason, his stomach seemed to clench. Nothing was making sense, but he needed to know the truth.

The trees thinned, the rocky ground leveled out, and he saw the warning signs now. Rope had been strung all around the clearing, but that would never stop a curious boy, even now. This was no cave one walked directly into, he remembered, coming close and looking down into a dark, gaping maw at his feet.

"What do you think?" Susanna demanded. "I saw something etched on one wall, where the sunlight touched it. Do you see it?"

He grabbed her arm and tugged her back to his side. "Be careful," he said harshly.

She looked up at him in surprise, but whatever she saw in his face stopped her response, except for a faint, "Leo?"

"I've been here," he said softly, forcing himself to look away from the cave though it drew him with a sick fascination. "I think I fell in when I was a little boy and was trapped."

"You think . . . ?"

He strained to look over the edge, and his mind flashed to the dark franticness of his recent nightmares. "This is the place in my dreams. But I don't understand why I haven't remembered before now."

She linked her arm with his. "It depends how young you were. You could have been quite frightened. That sometimes makes people forget. Perhaps it was the corpse you mentioned, Leo?"

"I just remember sheer terror and nothing else. If there was a corpse, surely my family would have discussed it over the years."

"Or would they have banned any mention of it," she said slowly, "because of your fears? We could ask."

"Not yet. Let me think."

She leaned forward again. "Such a shame we don't have a rope."

Once again, he grabbed her arm, this time bringing her right up against his body, using his height to look down on her, to intimidate, something that did not come naturally to him with women. "I know you have your own mind, Susanna, but don't put yourself in danger."

She stared up at him in surprise, and he realized he was holding her arm too tightly. He let her go and thanked God she didn't stumble away from him with anger or mistrust. But her assessing look was almost as bad.

"I can't ignore this," he said grimly. "Let's return for rope."

An hour later, he tied the rope around a tree and lowered the other end into the cave. Susanna handed him a small sack she'd quickly prepared, and he dropped it over the edge, before climbing down and landing silently on the earthen floor. He found himself breathing heavily, although it wasn't with exertion. He could see the rats fleeing into the corners. He remembered the rats.

"Leo?"

"Don't come near the edge. I'm fine."

He removed a candle and lit it with a match, then held it up, inhaling swiftly at the sight. Broken columns littered the floor, evidence of past civilization. More modern tools were stacked in a corner, as if abandoned. Then he held the candle higher and inhaled with surprise. One wall was covered by a fresco, now scarred with time, its colors muted, lines like spiderwebs etched all through it. It was a landscape, with a woman on the edge, as if part of the scene, but not its focus.

Had the nude painting in London somehow connected his mind with *this* painting, one he'd seen as a child during a traumatic time?

"Tell me what you see!" Susanna called.

"Roman columns, but any pottery seems long gone. Some excavation work was begun, then abandoned."

"Lord Bramfield did say the archaeologists were concentrating on St. Albans. Anything else?"

"An old, cracked fresco dominates one wall."

"From Roman times? How incredible!"

"I remember it. Give me a moment."

He closed his eyes and tried to pretend he was a little boy again, concentrating so hard that his head began to pound. But his reward was a murky scene that seemed to emerge from the mists.

"I was walking with someone," he called to his wife, "and together we fell in. I was unharmed, but he was not so lucky."

"The body from your dreams. So it was all true.

Can you remember anything else? Did he die immediately? How did you go for help?"

"I don't think I did. I was young, not yet of age for school. But—I cannot remember anything more. Only a man who died here, and the rats that are scurrying around even now."

"Rats? Oh, Leo, come up from there!"

He blew out the candle and left it below, climbing up the rope with alacrity. He kept Susanna away with a raised hand as he emerged from the unstable opening, then went to her.

"So a man did die here?" she asked softly, her gaze searching his face as if she needed to know he was all right.

She rubbed a smudge of dirt off his cheek, and he took her hand. "I think so. But I don't remember who he was, or how we were discovered. I can't go on being haunted at night. Soon my wife won't sleep with me if I disturb her."

She shrugged shyly, playfully. "I only need you for one thing, then you're free to find your own bed."

"You mean as your model?"

"Oh, I had forgotten all about that!" she answered sweetly.

He found himself laughing, and it felt good and pure, not like the darkness in the cave behind him, not like the senseless, mysterious death that made even the shadows of that cave seem menacing.

Chapter 21

Leo behaved . . . differently after their return from the cave. Susanna did her best to hold a normal conversation at luncheon, but he seemed distracted. She mentioned that perhaps his interest in studying antiquities was a way to put unpleasant memories to rest, then showed him an advertisement in the *Times* for the British Archaeological Association, which met in London. He only thanked her and set it aside.

In their room that night, she watched him undress, enjoying the movement of his body, the very beauty of muscle and bone. But he wasn't just a handsome man, a daring rake, or any of the other names Society had given him. He was gifted with great intelligence, and the thought made her eager as to what more she could unearth about her husband.

"Leo."

He turned from where he'd been hanging up his coat. In white shirtsleeves he looked dashing, a touch of sun darkening his skin after his ride at Madingley Court.

"I went up to the nursery today," she said.

"Surely it is too soon for a happy announcement."

"It is." She answered his smile with a shy one of her own. "I found things that had been marked with your name, books, even a project or two. I thought you hadn't spent your childhood here?"

He frowned, his fingers stopped on the collar buttons of his shirt. "I didn't. I assumed I merely visited on occasion, and that's when I fell into the cave."

"Perhaps there was more going on than a simple walk in the woods. Were you escaping the house? You said you used to amuse your parents to distract them from a bad marriage. Was it better to be a little boy who caused trouble, to draw attention to yourself?"

He smiled and shook his head. "You are looking too deeply into a little boy's motives, Susanna. I liked to be bad, and the attention was better than none at all."

He came to the bed, still wearing his trousers, but the garment didn't exactly hide what else was on his mind. And much as she welcomed him, part of her was still thinking about how she'd misjudged him. She'd been treating him as she'd always been treated, as if what the world saw was all that counted.

He knelt on the bed above her, and his smile faded. "Susanna, this preoccupation with my childhood doesn't change anything. It's as if you're looking for a revelation in me, a misunderstood knight-errant rather than the selfish bastard I've chosen to be much of my life. Marriage cannot totally change me—I'm still what I was, the man who compromised an innocent woman into marriage, who almost ruined his future sister-in-law."

"I beg your pardon?" She came up on her elbow, the counterpane bunching at her waist to reveal her nightgown. She remembered Lord Greenwich's warning back at the house party, but hadn't imagined the whole story.

"She wasn't my sister-in-law then. Louisa was an innocent young woman who enjoyed the parties as much as I did, whom everyone liked, especially the men. I was fascinated with her, and one drunken night at a ball, I followed her down a corridor. She didn't allow my kiss, but my friends assumed she had, and I let them think it."

His voice was clipped and hard, and though he was warning her, Susanna sensed he was also reminding himself of what he'd done.

"Her reputation changed drastically, and all thought her fast. She didn't realize what was going on and thought she was simply even more popular than before. I found out later that men were betting on who could get her to take the next step in her ruination."

"But not you."

"No, not me. But I didn't put an end to it. And when her father died, leaving her penniless, she lost even the friends she'd once had. She took a position as my grandmother's companion."

"And met and fell in love with your brother."

"But in the middle of that, the whole story and my involvement came out. You aren't the first woman it was suggested I needed to marry to restore her reputation."

She relaxed back, saying, "You wouldn't have let her be ostracized for something you began."

His jaw clenched. "You're doing it again, Susanna. You're making me out to have fine motives. I was simply trapped, and my grandmother and mother were there, and Simon—Simon wasn't certain what he should do."

"So your blind brother needed a push from you to realize he loved Louisa. You married me, even when there was no certain proof that I had been openly compromised. Ah, Leo, you are so wicked."

He turned his back and sat on the edge of the bed. She came up behind him, putting her arms around his neck, resting against him, separated by only the sheer linen of her nightgown.

"Leo, I don't believe you even know yourself. There's a childhood accident you can't remember, and an interest in archaeology you're trying to pretend doesn't exist when perhaps you might wish to delve into it further."

She felt his resistance in the stiff lines of his body.

"You've spent your life keeping people at a distance, all while you played the charming scoundrel. You can't keep a wife away, Leo."

"It seems I can't keep my wife properly naked in bed," he said darkly.

She kissed his neck, then beneath his ear. "Surely you don't want every step of our marriage to come easily. We've both been a challenge to each other, and I will see this wager through." She felt some of the tension leave his back, and hugged him closer, saying, "Since you aren't that frightened boy any-more, bad memories can't hold sway over you."

He turned his head, and she could see his severe profile.

"But there's more I can't remember," he said qui-etly. "Part of me doesn't want to."

"That makes sense. It's been hidden inside you all this time. We need to talk to people who can give you answers, and I don't just mean the rumors of servants or neighbors. You said your grandmother's estate isn't that far away—is your brother there?"

Simon nodded. "He spends much of the Season there, close to London when they need to be in town but easier for him to get about."

"Then let's invite them. I'd love to meet them all."

"I won't announce our marriage in the letter," he said.

"No?" she asked with regret.

He grinned. "I want to see his face."

Leo knew that others had to know what happened when he was young. The half dozen servants now working inside the manor were hired too recently, but his steward had records of the woman who'd acted as nurse to visiting children. Leo and Susanna rode their horses several hours to visit her.

Miss Deering was an elderly woman with thin-ning white hair and papery, wrinkled skin that smelled of powder. She lived in a little vine-covered cottage on a village green, where she could sit in the window and watch her neighbors pass by. A maid-servant introduced Leo and Susanna, and when Miss Deering tried to rise, Leo quickly went to take her hand.

She smiled up at him with obvious delight. "Did she introduce you as Mr. Wade? Mr. Leo Wade?"

Leo bowed as Susanna reached his side. "That is my name, Miss Deering. Do you remember me?"

"I do! You often came to stay at Woodhill Manor with your older brother and younger sister."

"And this is my wife, Mrs. Susanna Wade."

Miss Deering beamed as Susanna curtsied. "How lovely to meet you, my dear! I always knew that Leo—I should say Mr. Wade—would find himself the perfect bride. Now please sit down."

As they sat side by side on a delicate sofa across from the nurse's chair, she regarded Leo fondly.

"What a scamp you were, Mr. Wade. Your visits used to turn the household upside down for days."

"He does have a certain reputation for pranks," Susanna said dryly.

"Every young boy has that," Miss Deering agreed with a nod. "But Mr. Wade . . . ah, he was a bundle of liveliness. He wanted to know everything, to do everything. The library was not safe from him, of course."

Leo frowned.

"I imagine you've read every book by now. Insatiable curiosity, Mrs. Wade, but of course you know that."

"I do," Susanna said quietly, but gave Leo an amused glance.

"He demanded to be taught to read, or so his mother once told me. He held up a book at just two years of age and said he wanted to be like his brother." She clasped her trembling hands together. "Such an intelligent mind! And a gift for languages, too. I was not his tutor, but I enjoyed seeing how he could learn. He knew a smattering of three languages by the time he was five years old."

Leo frowned. "Surely that can't be right, Miss Deering."

"How many languages do you know now?"

He glanced at Susanna and gave her an apologetic shrug. "Five."

She stared at him, lips parted.

"Well, I foresaw that," Miss Deering said with satisfaction. "When others tried to tell me about your town ways, I told them they didn't know everything."

"I do have things I'm not as proud of."

"So do we all, my boy, so do we all." She paused while the tea tray was brought in, then insisted on pouring for them though her hand faintly trembled. "I'll continue to rattle on about your childhood if you don't interrupt and tell me why you've come to visit."

Leo accepted his tea black, took a sip, then set it down. "Miss Deering, do you remember an accident I had as a child? Apparently, I fell into a cave, but I have no memory of it."

Her cheerful expression faded, making her look suddenly older. "Yes, I do remember, though I can't be surprised that you do not. Such a sad business. You and your tutor, Mr. Boorde, were having a walk, and you fell in together."

"Mr. Boorde?" he said blankly. The name conjured up nothing, like there was a hole in his head.

"You were inseparable, my boy. You had such a curious mind, and he so enjoyed opening up the world to you."

Susanna was watching him as if judging his reaction. He didn't know what reaction to have.

"I can't even picture his face," Leo said between gritted teeth.

Miss Deering reached across the little table and patted his hand. "You blamed yourself at first, and though I tried to comfort you, you would never discuss it again. Your parents forbade the subject, since you reacted so badly whenever it was brought up. During the twenty-four hours you were trapped in there, you fought to keep the rats from Mr. Boorde."

"Twenty-four hours," Susanna breathed, her eyes brimming with sympathy. "No wonder you can't remember. That must have been truly terrible."

He nodded, but except for knowing he'd been there, the details themselves seemed blurry.

"Let us talk of happier things, Mr. Wade," Miss Deering said brightly. "Tell me of your marriage."

He glanced at Susanna, cocked an eyebrow, and let her answer. He kept trying to remember what Mr. Boorde had looked like, but why that was so important, he didn't know.

* * *

Susanna rode quietly at Leo's side as they crested a hill and saw Woodhill Manor nestled in the valley. Hedgerows separated much of the land into variegated squares of farmland, and the sun seemed to shine down as if blessing the scene.

She glanced at her husband, who studied the view with something less than enthusiasm. And now she knew why he hadn't wanted to come here.

Twenty-four hours alone with a dead man, screaming for help, wondering if you were soon to meet the same fate. Hungry, thirsty, frightened . . . it made her shudder.

"What's wrong?" Leo asked.

She met his speculative gaze. "I'm dwelling too much on what the accident must have been like for you."

"Perhaps it would be better to be like me and barely remember it," he said wryly. "I can't even picture his face, and the man died in front of me."

"We can do something to spur your memory. There are things of yours in the schoolroom. Perhaps seeing where you spent time with Mr. Boorde will help."

"Wait," he said, before she could urge her mount forward. "You don't need to help me with this. You certainly didn't plan for a husband with . . . mental problems when you married me."

"Mental problems?" she echoed, smiling softly.

That smile cut into Leo, and he found himself

wishing he could be a better man for her. He'd drunk and gambled and wasted his life, and now, just when he thought marriage would make him happy, he was less than whole in her eyes. She was patience itself, and never had he imagined, when he'd given thought to the perfect wife, what a blessed virtue that was.

She urged her horse sideways until their knees brushed, then reached to touch his arm. "I never expected perfection, Leo."

He put his hand over hers, and said softly, "Neither did I."

She searched his gaze, then looked away. She was harder on herself than she was on him.

"To the nursery then?" he said, trying to sound determined.

She nodded, tapped her heels into the horse's flank, and called back, "Race you!"

He watched her gallop away and enjoyed the sight immensely. Having a good seat—another attribute for the perfect wife.

But once they reached the nursery, after a quick meal of cold ham and bread in the kitchen, Leo's mood turned dark again. This place he remembered, the little desks, the large windows with their expansive view of the surrounding park.

"Anything?" Susanna asked, spreading out books on a little writing desk. "These had your name inscribed in them."

He ran his fingers over several covers, as if touching *A Guide to the Arrangement of Insects* or *Grimm's Fairy Tales* would help. "I remember these books, of course, but then they're here in front of me. It's like there are faint echoes of ghosts, indistinct, without a face. I remember feeling . . . happy here."

"Happy—learning?" she asked, pretending shock. "Who could believe it?"

He laughed, easing some of the tension, and watched as she opened the door to a cupboard.

"I found these," she said, backing away.

He saw a board with shapes affixed to it, and came closer. "What is it?"

"I believe it's your version of a Roman temple," she said wryly. She pulled forth a piece of Bristol board. "Look, you made a painting of a bird. Not bad for a child. Your tutor must have enjoyed bringing out your talents. Do you remember feeling close to him?"

He studied it, realizing that he could hear the faintest echo of voices in his head, another boy—Simon?—and a man, who laughed good-naturedly. He fastened on the memory, rubbing his forehead as if to wipe away the ache.

Very good work, Leo.

Thank you, Mr. Boorde.

When Simon leaves for school, you and I will become Egyptian explorers.

The missing pieces of his memory seemed to suddenly click into place, and he felt a sick coalition of dread in his stomach. His whole world, everything he thought he was—gone. "Close to Mr. Boorde? Yes, it seems we were."

Susanna clutched his sleeve. "Leo, what is it? You sound—you sound . . ." She didn't go on, only watched him with wide eyes full of growing fear.

He wanted to lie to her, to pretend he'd remembered nothing. It would be so much easier that way, and maybe, eventually, he'd forget it all again.

But Susanna stood there, her concern so very evident in her moist eyes. She cared about him. Somehow he'd been lucky enough to find such a woman. He certainly didn't deserve anything approaching love.

Though Leo cleared his throat, his voice still sounded husky as he said, "He made a confession to me after we fell into the cave."

She blinked at him in confusion. "A confession?"

"He said he was my father," Leo said bitterly. "And then he died."

Chapter 22

Susanna couldn't make a sound—her throat seemed to close up as she stared into Leo's bleak eyes. He was staring down at the childish painting, running his fingers absently across it.

"I'm not a true Wade," he said, sounding dazed.

"How can you be certain?" she whispered.

"Why would he lie as he was dying? I remember him now, and he had green eyes like mine."

"That might mean nothing."

"He took me everywhere, shared his love of learning with me. My own parents were less than interested, glad I was off their hands. They fought all the time, and sometimes I would run to my room and cover my ears for hours, hoping not to hear anything. Do you think they fought because of me? Because of what my mother had done?"

"I don't know, Leo. But perhaps now you can understand why you never had a good relationship with her. Part of you must have remembered what she'd done." She wanted to soothe him, but she understood that his pain couldn't be eased. The father he'd thought of as his own was unrelated, cuckolded by Lady Wade.

Leo set the painting back in the cupboard and closed the door, even as a calmer expression smoothed out his features. "I'm relieved to know the truth, but there's nothing that can be done."

"Leo, you don't have to perform for me."

His eyes were impassive, his thoughts shuttered from her. "I don't know what you mean."

"You may have entertained your family, unconsciously keeping them from thinking of these dark secrets, but you'll never have to do the same with me. I'm stronger than that. Our marriage is what we make of it, and it won't be like your parents'."

He cupped the side of her neck, even as he gave her a faint, tired smile. "It's all right, Susanna. This old scandal isn't important. I'll get over it."

"Over it?" she cried, searching his face. "But Leo—"

"I know the truth, and it can no longer haunt me. I'm looking forward to a good night's sleep." He walked toward the door, then turned and held out his hand. "Coming?"

Silently, she took his hand and followed him, but her worry wasn't going to fade away. Part of her hoped this revelation would help them—at last she knew all of Leo's secrets—but she still had a feeling of impending trouble. Perhaps being with his brother would make him see that having a secret father didn't change the man he was.

* * *

Alone in his study late that afternoon, Leo found himself remembering what it was like as a child, when all the world had been full of exciting adventures. Mr. Boorde had brought him book after book about Roman antiquities, a particular fascination of the man. They'd visited St. Albans together. Leo remembered how patient Mr. Boorde had been with his endless curiosity when his parents had been overwhelmed by him. Leo had led the way on their fatal walk, ignored Mr. Boorde's instructions to remain nearby.

Leo couldn't blame himself for the man's death, but it was his own curiosity that had led to it. And he realized that afterward, along with the memories he'd abolished, he'd given up on everything intellectual. Punishing himself? He didn't know.

He began to page through the book on Roman antiquities, looking for similarities to what had been discovered on his land. Without making a conscious decision, he opened a notebook and began to write.

When he received word that his brother and his wife would arrive the next day, he laid aside the work he'd been doing. Their visit would distract Susanna from following him with her very worried gaze, as if he would shatter like a broken window, and she had to catch the pieces.

He wasn't going to break; the truth was a relief. He'd always felt himself different than his brother and sister, and now he knew why. It didn't make him any less of a sibling to them, he told himself. But after watching his parents' marriage for so many years, he had to face the fact that he didn't know *how* to be a good husband. He could keep her satisfied in bed, but was that enough?

And was it satisfaction, when they took each other in the dark? Perhaps it wasn't just Susanna who was hiding.

As the carriage with the Wade coat of arms pulled to a stop outside their front door the next afternoon, Susanna stood beside her husband and told herself to stop being nervous. How could his family be disappointed that he had a wife to settle him down and give him children?

After the footman opened the carriage door, Viscount Wade descended first, feeling for the folded-down stairs with his foot before placing his weight, then reaching the ground. He turned and lifted up his hand, and his wife, Louisa, leaned out to take it, smiling down at him as if he could see her. She wore a jaunty hat perched on the most flaming red hair Susanna had ever seen, making her own auburn look positively subdued.

Susanna turned to Leo. "You and your brother both married redheads!"

He laughed, and the sound made her feel positively warm with happiness.

Once Louisa was on her feet, she looked up at the mansion with frank interest. It was suddenly apparent that she was with child. Louisa spotted them almost immediately and waved, then her eyes widened on noticing Susanna. She leaned to say something to Lord Wade, whose only response was a shake of his head.

"She's confused," Susanna whispered. "We should go make our announcement."

"Let them enter the house," Leo said. "You're far too eager."

"Nervous, so very nervous."

"More nervous than with your parents?"

"Of course! I trusted my parents enough to know that I could eventually win them over. But your family . . ." She let her voice trail off, then found herself chewing on her lip.

He covered her hand where it rested on his arm and squeezed. "I'm not worried at all. They will love you."

They looked into each other's eyes, and Susanna's breath caught in wonder at the tenderness. It washed over her then, that she had a new life, the companionship she wanted, a family, and could only pray that Leo would stay this close to her once he was back in London.

"Who is this?" came the sound of a strident female voice.

Susanna jumped, knowing she'd been looking so deeply into Leo's eyes she'd almost forgotten about their guests. Leo had stiffened at her side, even as they both turned. Lord Wade was escorting two women, one on each arm, and it was surely the second one who'd spoken. She had light blond hair that was fading to white. Her face was handsome, with the echo of Lord Wade's and Leo's bone structure in cheeks and straight nose.

Leo's mother, she realized, and glanced surreptitiously up at her husband. His face was all that was pleasant, but his green eyes, so open a moment before, now seemed impassive.

As their guests approached, Louisa smiled with excited expectation. "Leo! How wonderful to see you!"

Lord Wade smiled. "And you aren't standing here alone, or so Louisa informs me."

"Simon, Mother, Louisa, allow me to introduce my wife, Susanna."

Louisa gasped, her lovely face full of a happiness that Susanna tried to focus on, because Lady Wade's eyes narrowed. She looked Susanna up and down like the professor might just before a dissection.

"It is a pleasure to meet you all," Susanna said, curtsying. "Lord Wade, I do believe we became acquainted in London some years back."

Though Lord Wade smiled, he didn't get a chance to speak.

"And what was your family name?" Lady Wade asked skeptically.

"I remember," Louisa said, reaching to take Susanna's hand. "You're formerly Miss Leland, cousin of the Duke of Madingley."

Susanna was grateful for Louisa's recognition. She remembered that Louisa was once very popular in Society, just like the Wade brothers had always been.

Susanna had often stood with the chaperones and wallflowers, watching the beautiful people dance. Louisa had captured all the men's fancy, and the Wade brothers, so handsome and charming, always bestowed dances. Lord Wade had insisted on dancing with Susanna, and though it had surely been pity, she'd been appreciative.

Lord Wade bowed his head to her, then flashed nearly the same dimpled grin that Leo used. "I remember you as well, Mrs. Wade. To think my brother has actually given you his name. It will take me some time to become used to the amazement of it all."

"And he told us nothing about his courtship of you," Lady Wade said skeptically. Then she stepped between Leo and Susanna and took her son's arm, leading him inside. "Come tell me what happened, Leo."

Susanna led Lord Wade and his wife into the small entrance hall, and saw that Lady Wade had already pulled Leo into the drawing room.

"Don't worry," Louisa said in a soft voice, smiling at Susanna. "Lady Wade doesn't particularly like me either, but her opinion doesn't matter to the Wade brothers."

"Our mother doesn't believe there's a woman alive good enough for Leo," Lord Wade said.

"Oh, and she wasn't protective of you?" Louisa shot back, laughing up at her husband.

Susanna noticed that Lord Wade's gaze didn't focus on the person speaking, though he turned his head in the proper direction. She could not imagine what it must be like to lose something as important as sight. Her artwork would be impossible, she thought with a shiver.

Louisa turned back to Susanna. "Lady Wade worried that my reputation would harm Simon."

"Yes, Leo told me."

"He spoke to you about what happened?" Lord Wade asked sharply.

"His poor judgment?" Susanna answered. "Yes, he did. And his extreme remorse, then gratitude that everything worked out as well as it did. I hope you don't mind. I would never repeat anything he told me."

"Well," Louisa said, her smile deepening, "you must be something even more wonderful, that he would willingly share his mistakes. How long have you been married?"

As they walked into the drawing room, Susanna answered the questions about their hurried wedding the way Leo had explained it to her parents.

Lady Wade, standing huddled with Leo near the expansive window overlooking the park, turned with a frown as she heard Susanna's final words. "Gretna Green? Leo, how . . . scandalous!"

"I think it's romantic," Louisa said.

Susanna said nothing, well remembering how she'd been feeling at the time. Everything had changed since then, and she couldn't have imagined that she could be so in love.

She choked on a cough and managed an apology. In love? Had she really, finally, admitted the truth

• to herself? The scary truth, the one that put her in Leo's power?

She'd been in his power, under his spell, from the beginning. But was he capable of loving her?

When dinner was served not long after, Susanna sat back and enjoyed the Wade family show. Simon and Leo took turns being charming rascals, and Louisa basked in her role as the foil between them. Susanna felt shy among such powerful personalities, and the dagger glares of Lady Wade did not help.

But Leo was trying to pretend everything was right in his world, even when it wasn't. Susanna wondered if he planned to inform anyone about his discovery. She only hoped that having his brother there would enable him to find some peace with his past.

"So you're an artist," Louisa said, turning to Susanna with interest. "I remember your popularity at my sister's weekly salon for the arts."

"Every young lady paints." Lady Wade sniffed.

"Not every young lady gives lessons," Leo said, "and is well-known for her work. Her paintings could be hanging in any museum."

Susanna blushed and smiled at her husband. She noticed he did not mention her work for her father or the upcoming book. It was new, the work not completed, but she still felt a prick of disappointment. Yet now was probably not the time to inform his mother.

"Louisa is involved in helping shy debutantes come out in Society," Lord Wade said. "It seems we alone cannot keep our wives busy."

"I'll be quite busy soon enough," Louisa said, resting a hand on her stomach.

Susanna found she could not take her eyes off the new life growing inside her sister-in-law. She wanted so badly for the same to happen to her. But she was older than many young brides, and a realist besides. She would accept what God had planned for her.

But she desperately wanted to give Leo a child.

Or did she think being a father would bind him to her, giving him further reason to resist the call of his old life?

Leo watched Susanna rise to lead the way back to the drawing room, and though he came to his feet, he said, "Sweetheart, Simon and I will share a drink before we join you."

She blushed prettily at his endearment, while his mother rolled her eyes and harrumphed.

After the females had departed, Simon said dryly, "I can imagine your expression. I'm sorry Mother just happened to choose yesterday to visit us. Rotten luck."

"You have no idea," Leo murmured.

"It's the baby's imminent arrival, I think. Although it makes me shudder to imagine her a grandmother."

"I don't blame you although I wish you could have brought Grandmama with you. She would have loved to meet Susanna." He poured a brandy and pushed it toward Simon. "The libation is north of you."

Louisa was the one who'd heard about using the points of the compass to help Simon eat and drink in public. Before that, his brother had closeted himself away at every meal, a very social man missing the most social part of the day.

"Grandmama went to London," Simon said, "happy to be wherever her daughter-in-law isn't."

"I'm glad to hear of her continuing good health." Leo stared into the liquid, swirling it absently. He was trying to find a way to broach awkward questions.

"Spit it out, Leo. Tell me about this marriage, and not the sanitized version you gave our mother."

Leo grinned. "Surely you don't want to hear about my newest scandal."

"I suspected as much," Simon said with a grimace. "What did you do, compromise the girl?"

"Well . . ."

"You didn't."

"It's a long story. Suffice it to say, we'd become a part of wager with a group of people in London. I followed her to Bramfield's house party, and we spent a pleasant few days annoying each other. But it went too far, and we were discovered."

"Discovered doing what?" Simon demanded.

"Just kissing. But apparently we'd been a bit obvious during the party, for Bramfield urged our immediate marriage."

"Leo." Simon gulped his brandy and then ran a hand through his hair. "Damn."

Leo leaned across the table. "You probably think I should have learned my lesson after Louisa, but there was something about Susanna that made me a little . . . crazy. I didn't have to be forced to marry her—I wanted to. *She* had to be forced to marry *me*."

"I wonder why," his brother said dryly.

"I kidnapped her, before she could go live in disgrace in the country, and took her off to Gretna Green. It was not an auspicious beginning."

"But she sounds happy now."

"I think she is—I hope she is," Leo added. He reminded himself that he'd felt relief when Simon and Louisa had arrived, seeing that they were still so happy together. It was as if he'd been holding his breath, waiting for the inevitable arguments. But they only seemed even more in love. "The thing is . . . how do you know how to be a good husband? We didn't exactly see a fine example of the ideal marriage."

"No one has an ideal marriage. There are always moments of compromise, and someone is disappointed. Sharing the disappointments is what matters."

"Such words of wisdom from my elder brother."

"I never thought to hear you ask for them," Simon admitted.

Leo grunted a response. It felt foolish to admit how very unsure marriage could make a man, even one as arrogant and confident as himself. "Simon, about Mother and Father . . . did they always argue? From your earliest memories?"

"Yes, but I can't tell you how early that actually was. I was four when you were born, and my memories began in truth then."

"I was memorable," Leo muttered halfheartedly. "But you remember nothing much before that?"

Simon shrugged, his focus intent, even though his eyes remained distant. "You know they kept us with our nurse much of the time when we were that young."

"We weren't interesting enough then."

Simon laughed, then his expression sobered. "Now that you're married, don't look back at every detail of our parents' marriage. You can be happy, regardless of the poor example they set."

"Maybe I avoided marriage because I didn't think I could do any better," he mused.

"You know that's not true. I can't see your wife, but I can hear her voice. You've made her happy, Leo, and that says a lot."

Though further questions crowded his tongue, he couldn't bring himself to mention his tutor and make Simon even more furious with their mother. Leo and the late Lord Wade hadn't been all that close, but to let the truth come out seemed . . . disloyal to his memory. Lord Wade had done the best he could, never once ruined Leo and his mother with the truth in public.

But Simon hadn't been able to assuage Leo's curiosity about the root of his parents' problems.

That night in their bedroom, Leo paced back and forth, and Susanna watched him warily. He'd seemed so happy to see his brother and sister-in-law, but the appearance of his formidable mother had obviously altered his expectations.

"Louisa is wonderful," Susanna said at last.

He lifted the drapery and looked out into the darkness. "She is." He glanced back at her, brow lifted with irony. "Does it feel strange to be near another woman I'd pursued? Trust me, there are no more women I nearly compromised but the two of you."

"Then I hope it isn't a pattern," she said, forcing a light tone to her voice.

He turned to face her, arms folded across his chest. "What does that mean?"

She inhaled and let out a sigh. "I admit I'm frightened to return to London, back to our friends who are so different."

"You mean my friends."

London was beginning to loom large in her mind as a turning point for their marriage. And much as she could not believe he'd betray her, she couldn't know if he'd allow his friends to sway him into his old risky life.

"I've always been a selfish bastard," he said. "It had nothing to do with anyone in London. It was up to me to control my impulses, and I didn't. You could have suffered terrible harm if someone other than Bramfield had found us. What if he hadn't interfered, and instead word spread throughout the *ton*?"

"But that didn't happen, Leo," she said quietly. "You don't need to dwell on this; I've forgiven you, surely you know that."

But had he forgiven himself? she found herself wondering for the first time.

Changing the subject, she asked, "Did you tell your brother about Mr. Boorde's deathbed revelation?"

Leo approached the bed and sat down beside her, taking her hand. "I couldn't do it. The family peace has been shored up so tenuously through the years. How could I tell him that our mother betrayed our—his—father? I'm sharing it with you. That's enough."

"Is it?" she responded, coming up on her knees to kiss his cheek. "I thought Simon would be able to offer you some comfort."

"He does, but . . . he doesn't need to know about this."

"Perhaps your mother—"

"No," he interrupted firmly. "What good would it do?"

She'd planted the idea, and privately thought it would do much good.

Chapter 23

Leo spent breakfast the following morning staring at his mother. Louisa and Susanna made plans for the day, a picnic luncheon, a walk to go painting, and Simon listened tolerantly.

Lady Wade never openly confronted her daughters-in-law, but she criticized every idea, as if she had to have her approval stamped on everything. He would spend the rest of his life looking at her, wondering, the secret inside him like a heavy weight.

When the women left, and Simon's secretary was consulting him about business, Leo excused himself. He discovered from his housekeeper that Mr. Boorde had been buried in the graveyard next to the family chapel, as if he had no relatives to claim him. The only people he had were Leo and his mother. Leo had forgotten him, and Lady Wade—well, he didn't know anything about what his mother had thought or intended.

It was easy enough to find Mr. Boorde's headstone, and Leo looked at it for a long time after clearing away some of the weeds at the base. He'd have flowers planted there, and it would be as well taken care of as the rest of the family plots.

His mother's relationship to the dead man would haunt Leo unless he discovered answers. No secrecy or detective work necessary. He would simply confront her, just as Susanna had suggested. He couldn't let his inclination to cover up problems harm his marriage.

Would his wife always be right? he wondered wryly.

He found his mother writing letters in the library. She looked up when he entered, and her face softened into a satisfied smile.

"Leo, my dear boy."

He closed the library door, and her smile faded.

"Is something wrong?" she asked. "Has Susanna complained to you about me?"

"Susanna never complains about anything, but I have eyes. She is a good wife, and I expect you to treat her well."

She sighed. "You married so quickly that I worry about you."

"I love her, Mother, and that should be enough for you."

The words he hadn't even said to Susanna surprised them both, and his mother's eyes widened.

"I don't want to talk about Susanna," he continued. "I want to talk about Mr. Boorde."

Her frown was delicate and convincing. "Mr. Boorde," she began slowly. "I do not believe I—"

Her eyes widened. "Your old tutor here at Woodhill Manor?"

He pulled up a chair and sat down opposite her at the writing desk. She was staring at him, then dropped her pen before looking away.

"You've never wished to discuss him after what happened," she said in a low voice. "I thought you'd forgotten that terrible tragedy, but I imagine being here made you remember it all."

"I *had* forgotten, and it turns out there was a reason I'd blocked it from my mind. Once I saw the cave again, I finally remembered his last words as he lay dying. He said he was my father."

He expected her to deny it, to be angry and offended. But her shoulders slumped, and her bottom lip trembled before she caught it between her teeth. He'd never thought his mother vulnerable, but she looked so now.

"Your father—Lord Wade—never gave me even a moment of the joy that I found with Mr. Boorde," she said quietly.

Leo sat back slowly, surprised that he was still capable of being stunned. It sounded as if she'd had an unhappy marriage from the beginning. It hadn't started with his birth. He took a deep breath for what seemed like the first time since he'd remembered the tragedy. But if he'd expected to feel better, he was disappointed, for sadness at the whole situation lingered.

At last, Lady Wade met his eyes. "I—I had no idea that you knew."

"Neither did I," he said dryly, "until just a few days ago. I guess being trapped in a rat-infested cave with a man whose dying words changed your life, might make a seven-year-old want to forget absolutely everything. And apparently, you and Father went along with that. Did Father know?"

"I think he suspected I might have . . . found someone, but he never asked, for that would have opened him up to questions about his own conduct," she said with the faintest trace of bitterness. "He did not treat you any differently than he did Simon, so I assumed . . . I hoped . . . that he didn't know. You both resemble me."

"Then Simon isn't—"

"No! Oh my, no! Simon is the viscount in all respects. I only let myself have a . . . private friend after his birth. I had done my duty."

Private friend? That was a novel title.

"And were you still *friends* at the time of Mr. Boorde's death?"

"Yes." The first tear slid down the side of her nose, and she wiped it away with furtive fingers. "I was . . . devastated. I did not take a lover even after Lord Wade's death, as so many of my friends do."

He found himself grudgingly admiring her for having some sort of loyalty.

"What will you do now that you know?" Lady Wade asked, her gaze searching his face.

"Nothing. Simon and Georgie don't know, and I plan to keep it that way. They would only worry about me and be angry with you."

Her lips trembled again, and she pressed them together, nodding. "Thank you. Did you want me to . . . tell you about him?"

"Someday, perhaps. I have my own memories, too."

"He loved you. The joy he felt being your tutor gave him great purpose. I was always very sad that you did not care to continue your studies after his death. Now I know the reason."

He studied her for a moment, deciding to take advantage of this rare, quiet moment. "Why were you and Father so unhappy?"

"Our families insisted on the union, and we did our duty. But we were very unsuited to each other, and sadly, we made no great effort to make things better. It was easier for him to spend time with his cohorts in the evenings, rather than me." She tilted her chin, and her pale skin flushed, as if she remembered the humiliation.

"I'm sorry."

She nodded and gave him a brief smile, turning the pen aimlessly in her hands.

After leaving her, he wandered the house as his thoughts wandered in his brain. He didn't want to be like his parents, letting his marriage go out of indifference or laziness. He would do far better by his wife. In his study, he looked out the window and saw Louisa, arm linked with Simon's, following Susanna through the garden. Susanna turned back to them, wearing an animated smile, and it was as if Leo's very soul softened in response.

He loved her.

How had he not realized it, after the way he was obsessed with her, and how easily he agreed to marriage once he'd harmed her? Her confidence and prickly pride made him admire her, her determination and passion for her work only increased that admiration. She didn't care what people thought of her—hence the acceptance of her father's request for help on his book.

Leo never thought he cared what people thought of him either, but it was far easier to be a man and a scoundrel than it was to be an outcast among all the other young ladies. She was the one with the true courage. He'd merely wiped from his memory anything that made him different.

It was time to confront London, and everything it meant. Susanna sat beside Leo and found herself watching her husband more often than not. When he met her gaze, his smile seemed almost forced. The revelations of these past days were not something easy to put aside.

She smiled back with a confidence she was far from feeling. Oh, the wager would be resolved—and she hoped the women would win the painting outright.

But once the wager was finished, and their heated competition over—what would she and Leo have? Would they become like Leo's parents, who never even tried to find things in common? Or perhaps Leo, who now knew he wasn't a true Wade, would do his best to fit in with his friends the way he always had.

But she couldn't put these foolish doubts into words. She had to trust herself, trust in her love for him, and hope he could come to love her.

After a long day, and several changes of horse, they arrived late in the afternoon at Lord Wade's town house, where they left the Bramfield carriage to be unloaded and returned to its rightful owner. They requested a Wade carriage to visit Susanna's sister and cousin at Madingley House.

As they traveled through the crowded streets of London, Leo asked, "Are you certain you don't want to wait until morning?"

"Frightened of hearing that you lost?" she asked sweetly.

He gave her a distracted smile. "You assume Julian and Peter have not found proof. So that must mean *you're* the model."

At least he still had some humor after everything that had happened. "Your supposition is not actual evidence."

"Perhaps you should spell that for me," he said.

She leaned against him, and whispered, "I would love to."

At his rumbling laughter, she closed her eyes, grateful she could still make him laugh.

Madingley House was a palace by London standards. Warrior angels lined the roof as if to guard from above. Inside, a marble staircase circled the entrance hall, rising all the way up to a stained-glass dome four stories above. But Susanna noticed it only with a passing glance. This was her home during the Season, as familiar to her as her name.

The butler, Grimes, tall and thin and bald, bowed as he took Leo's hat. "Miss Susanna, how good to see you."

"And you, Grimes." She forced a smile, even as she tried to look beyond him up the stairs. "I believe you've met Mr. Wade."

The butler bowed to Leo.

"Can you tell me who is home at the moment?"

"Your parents just arrived after a brief visit to the country. Miss Rebecca and Lady Elizabeth are also in the drawing room with the rest of their guests. Though the duke and his wife are at the opera, your brother, Captain Leland, and his wife are also in attendance."

"We cannot wait to make our announcement in private," Leo said.

They both followed Grimes up the curved staircase to the first floor. Huge paintings covered the walls of the entrance hall, and Susanna touched the edges of her favorites for luck.

"I'd hoped to have our audience be just family," she said.

"Luck is against us." He held out his arm as Grimes opened the large double doors. "Ready?"

She took a deep breath and laid her hand on his firm arm. They entered the drawing room, where several dozen guests milled about the clusters of furniture. Carved archways decorated the walls beneath a frescoed ceiling. Beyond were French doors leading out onto the terrace, and as dozens of eyes focused on her, Susanna thought escape was looking appealing just then. Oh heavens, even Lord and Lady Bramfield were in attendance. His lordship glowered at Leo.

"Susanna!" Rebecca cried, and rushed to her, followed by their cousin Elizabeth.

Both of them threw their arms about Susanna, and a part of her world righted itself as she saw that they looked well. Unlike Susanna, Rebecca had their mother's brown hair and eyes, and with her heart-shaped face, was the true beauty of the Leland family. Elizabeth had the raven hair of her Spanish mother, and in her usual manner, she was laughing at the sisters, even as they broke apart.

"Look at us!" Elizabeth said, as the three of them continued to hold hands. "None the worse for wear."

But Rebecca was studying Susanna thoughtfully. "Something is different about you, Susanna, and you'd better tell me what it is." She looked beyond to Leo, and frowned.

Next, their brother Matthew gave her a hug, tall and auburn-haired like her, with the happy grin he'd been sporting ever since his return from India. "You look wonderful, Susanna. Pay Rebecca no attention at all."

Susanna stared at all the openly curious people, saw her father nod to her with encouragement, noticed her mother producing a handkerchief as if prepared to dab her eyes. As Lady Bramfield worried at her lip and looked hopeful, women with speculative expressions leaned together to talk. Susanna had arrived with Leo Wade, as if they'd been traveling together. And certainly people knew they'd left the Bramfield house party on the same day.

She looked at Rebecca and Elizabeth, squared her shoulders, and said, "I'm married."

Their mouths dropped open, Matthew frowned over her shoulder at Leo, and the noise level in the room doubled as the guests began to buzz at the announcement.

"Married!" Rebecca cried. "To Mr. Wade?"

Leo took Susanna's arm. "You cannot be surprised, Miss Leland. You know how wonderful your sister is, and how she's been hiding herself for far too long. I'm the man lucky enough to deduce the truth first."

Though Lord Bramfield smiled with obvious relief, Susanna felt the tide of curiosity and malicious speculation as it swept the room, saw the looks of pity, as if she settled for a scoundrel desperate for her money instead of being an old maid. She knew Rebecca's and Elizabeth's worry and confusion, saw her brother's doubts. But all she could do was look up at Leo, those warm green eyes full of mischief and tenderness. Even in the midst of his troubles over his parents and his real identity, he focused on her. She smiled and let him take her hands in both of his.

"You knew about this!" Rebecca called to her parents.

"It was not our announcement to make," Lady Rosa said. "But I am very glad I did not have to keep quiet for too long!"

Leo laughed, then Susanna watched as he met the amused gazes of his friends, Peter Derby and Lord Parkhurst.

With a wry glance at Lord Parkhurst, Peter said, "We've been upstaged." He was tall and slim, with sandy brown hair and a habit of using his hands as he talked. "All we did was propose."

Lord Parkhurst, a far more serious man of business, with a boxer's body that belied his noble lineage, seemed at ease as he put his arm around Rebecca. "Are you disappointed in me, darling?"

She playfully pushed at his chest. "I'll have to let you know after I hear Susanna's story."

"We all have much to discuss," Leo said meaningfully.

Susanna looked around at the four other participants in the wager that had changed the very course of their lives. It was almost over, but the outcome could still affect her marriage. "First, I need to speak with Rebecca and Elizabeth alone."

"Should we allow it?" Peter drawled.

Leo sighed. "We have no choice."

"Is this Leo talking," Lord Parkhurst asked with exaggerated astonishment, "bowing to the wishes of a woman?"

"You aren't married yet," Leo responded.

Susanna found herself smiling before a thought made her hesitate. To Leo, she said, "I would understand if instead of waiting for me, you wanted to see some of your other friends tonight."

Would he desert her now that he was back in

London? She told herself that she had her own friends she wished to spend time with. She could not deny him the same.

He shrugged. "If your family will have me, I'll remain until you're ready to leave. We can gather the rest of your things another time."

Susanna tried not to show her relief.

The three women retired to Susanna's bedchamber, where she sat her sister and cousin on the bed and stared at them, hands on her hips.

"This is surely too much of a coincidence," Susanna said in her best governess voice. "All three of us engaged or married to the three men who humiliated us with that foolish painting? How did this happen?"

Elizabeth grinned and shrugged. "I never imagined it *could* happen, but it did."

"We're only engaged," Rebecca grumbled. "But you—married? To *Leo Wade*? Susanna, I would have thought . . . I would never have guessed . . . do you love him?"

"I do." The truth came so easily to her now. She drew up her dressing-table chair to sit and face them. "He's nothing like I imagined."

"But . . . what do you possibly have in common?" Rebecca asked plaintively.

"What do you have in common with Lord Parkhurst? I do believe you called him staid and dull."

"Well . . . that isn't exactly true."

Susanna rounded on Elizabeth. "And haven't I heard you call Peter Derby an old family friend, more a brother than—"

"No! Don't even say it!" Elizabeth said with a shudder. Then she gave a slow smile. "He definitely doesn't treat me as a sister."

Rebecca and Elizabeth shared gazes and grinned.

Susanna frowned. "And how have you been treated? Neither of you is married."

They both looked so innocent that Susanna gasped. "Do not tell me—did you both *have* to become engaged?"

"Why would you think that?" Rebecca asked. "Unless . . . oh, Susanna, did that terrible Leo Wade do something he shouldn't have?"

"The beginning of our marriage was less than . . . favorable." She told them how she'd foolishly allowed herself to be compromised, how angry she'd been with Leo, but how very different he turned out to be.

"I love him," Susanna reiterated, "but I don't know if he can love me. Now that we're back in London, he has his bad reputation to uphold. With so many temptations, perhaps being a husband won't interest him anymore. Perhaps I . . . won't interest him anymore," she ended with a whisper.

"Don't think that," Elizabeth said, reaching to take her hand. "You are a wonderful woman, and he certainly didn't have to marry you if he didn't want to. His reputation couldn't have been any worse, after all—oh, dear, I didn't mean it quite that way."

Susanna gave a thin smile. "No, it's the truth. I have to overcome my silly doubts. So tell me about your adventures!"

Elizabeth talked about almost being forced to marry another man, and Peter stepping in as her pretend fiancé, when all the while he meant to become the real thing. Rebecca's adventure was far more dangerous, concerning the necklace in the painting that turned out to be real, a rare diamond called the Scandalous Lady that had been stolen from Lord Parkhurst's family years before. They'd been pursued by villains, and while Rebecca spoke, Susanna found herself gasping more than once in shock or worry.

"Susanna," Rebecca said after a quiet moment, "you should know that Roger Eastfield was killed because he used the diamond in the portrait."

Susanna gasped. "Killed? Roger is . . . dead?"

"I know he was a friend to you," Elizabeth said with sympathy. "I'm so sorry."

She and Roger had shared a love of art until his betrayal over that painting . . .

As if Roger's name had struck a chord, Elizabeth gave a start, and said, "About the painting. It's gone."

Susanna gaped at her. "Gone? Someone bought it?"

"No one knows," Rebecca said with a shrug. "It simply disappeared from the club."

"So our wager?" Susanna asked.

The three women shared an uncertain glance.

"Have either of you told the truth to your fiancés?" Susanna demanded.

"Of course not!" Rebecca said. "We were waiting for you so we could make a determination together. But we wanted to win the painting, and now the painting is gone. It seems our part of the wager is over."

"We can let the men hash out the money," Elizabeth added.

"Regardless, the deadline is past, so it seems we won," Susanna said. "Do we all agree that we can tell them the truth now? It seems like it's time to go on with our new lives."

Elizabeth's eyes watered. "Oh dear. I never imagined not seeing each of you every single day."

"Come now," Susanna said gruffly. "We were not glued to each other's sides. We spent time apart."

"But we always knew we'd be together," Rebecca said. "Now, we'll just have to make sure we see each other several times a week. And soon there'll be children, and walks in the park, and birthday parties."

"No more waiting for the perfect husband," Elizabeth murmured, smiling through her tears.

"I think you were the only one waiting for that," Rebecca countered. "I had decided not to marry at all, that I wanted adventure. Well, Julian certainly gave me that."

"It puts me at ease to know you're both happy," Susanna said with a peaceful sigh.

"And in love," Rebecca added. "Take heart, Susanna. I saw Mr. Wade's expression when he looked at you. I think he returns your love."

A great weight of responsibility was now gone,

and Susanna knew she no longer had to worry about Rebecca and Elizabeth.

It was time for Susanna to face reality. She had to see if Leo could be honest with her, when he'd spent so much of his life hiding ugly truths.

Chapter 24

They could easily have had a suite of rooms at Simon's town house, but Leo was secretly relieved that Susanna wanted to share just a bedroom and dressing room with him. Part of him had wondered if being with her sister and cousin might somehow affect their marriage, but she'd been calm and smiling in the carriage back to his brother's home. They were able to surprise his sister with the wedding news, and Georgie had actually cried with happiness, to his embarrassment.

But now they were alone in their room, and Susanna had seemed distracted. Leo waited, knowing she'd eventually tell him what was wrong. He began undressing, and was down to his shirtsleeves when at last she stepped in front of him.

"Leo, I have some things I need to say to you."

He wondered what Rebecca and Elizabeth had said to her.

"We're married now, and I want to be totally happy—but I'm not." Her voice softened. "I love you, Leo."

That wasn't what he'd expected to hear after the way she'd begun, but it brought him immense satisfaction and relief. "Susanna, sweetheart—"

"Let me finish. I love you, but that doesn't mean I'll accept any way you decide to treat me. I want all of you, even the truths you've kept hidden, the things you think might hurt me. Can you be faithful to me, Leo? Can you forget I'm not the sort of wife you wanted?"

He took her shoulders. "Of course you're not the wife I wanted."

He felt her stiffen.

"I wanted someone who only cared about my looks or money or standing in Society. You—you see too much, you know me too deeply. I can't hide myself from you."

Her posture softened, loosened, and she gazed at him with sweet longing in her eyes.

"Sweetheart, this is a more intimate relationship than I've ever had. I never thought I could be this happy."

"Oh, Leo!"

She fell into his arms, and then they were kissing passionately, stripping off each other's clothes, the lamplight revealing the creamy curves of her body at last. Every inch of skin he'd touched now shown with just as much beauty in his eyes. When he would have taken her to bed, she held up a finger, then rummaged in her open trunk and pulled out a long scarf.

"I can't believe I never thought to look for the scarf

from the painting!" he exclaimed, disgusted with himself.

"You wouldn't have found it. It was in London all along." She draped it about her and fell back on the bed, arms stretched over her head, back arched. She was the painting come to life even though she'd hid her identity well.

He came up on his knees beside her, let his fingers trace her curves, from the tips of her trembling breasts, to the curling hair at the juncture of her thighs.

"No wonder he wanted to paint you," Leo said in a husky voice.

She laughed softly, catching his hand and holding it briefly to her cheek. "He certainly didn't know how I looked beneath my clothing, Leo, but he made me feel beautiful enough to take the risk. I always thought of the painting as removed from me, the image improved by his talent."

"Susanna, you were so wrong. He was only painting what he saw—a beautiful woman coming into her own, seeing herself as a sensual creature for the first time."

Her smile faded as she stared up at him, and suddenly he thought she might be waiting for something from him. It seemed . . . pivotal, this moment in their marriage, and he felt uncertain. He retreated to the lightness that was so easy for him.

He let his fingers trail over her upper thigh, then stopped when he saw the small mole she'd been hiding from him. He chuckled. "This has been eluding me."

She blinked at him. "I beg your pardon?"

"I noticed this on the painting from the beginning."

She sat up suddenly, letting the scarf cover her. "And you were trying to see it, to seduce it from me."

"I told you my intentions all along." He smiled at her. "We've both been trying to win the challenge, but now you'll have to concede defeat."

A terrible dread settled over Susanna, much as she fought it. Her mistrust was always there, and now it struggled into prominence as if swimming up from the depths of a pond. She'd told him she loved him, and he hadn't answered the same. She'd been a challenge to him all along, but she had no more passion to continue the game.

"Susanna?" He was frowning down at her.

"I let myself believe that you could change . . . just like I let myself believe I could trust Roger. He shared my sensibilities more than any other man had. He sympathized with my regret that I could never be a serious artist."

"But you can now, with your father's book."

She made a sound of dismissal. "You couldn't even tell your family about it."

"Susanna—"

"Never mind. I'm used to betrayal. Roger betrayed me over that painting just for money. What I thought was private between us, he put on display for all of London to see, taking a great chance that

I'd be discovered and ruined." She closed her eyes and brought her knees up to her chest to cover her nudity, her vulnerability. "He's dead now—did you know that?"

He shook his head. "I'm sorry."

"All for money. The same reason I once thought you married me—money from the wager, money from my dowry."

"You know I regret how our marriage began. I never meant to hurt you."

"You never mean to hurt anyone," she said softly. "I don't know if you can change."

He looked as if she'd slapped him, but the truth had to be said. They stared at each other, and in that moment, she wondered if her foolish behavior might very well drive him back into the arms of his London friends, bringing about everything she feared.

"I can't talk right now." She stood up and donned her nightgown. "I'll cry and embarrass myself and prove how little strength I really have. I need time to reconcile myself to the truth of our marriage. Everything will be fine." Her mouth trembled too much for her to continue speaking. She lay down next to him and turned her back, only then allowing her tears to fall.

Angry and indignant, Leo slammed to his feet. He was still dressed. There was no reason he couldn't leave, because he certainly wouldn't sleep now, after all the things they'd said to each other. He could go to his favorite gaming hell, where the bets were steeper, the clientele dangerous, the excitement greater.

And then he realized what he was thinking, and was ashamed of himself. Here she was worried he couldn't change, and when things got difficult, his first instinct had been to return to his old haunts. How could he blame her for doubting him? He was doubting himself.

But he didn't need his old world, where the glitter was tarnished, the clientele reckless, the air stale with desperation. Those people had nothing to live for but the roll of the dice. He had so much more than that.

Quietly, he removed his clothing and lay down next to Susanna. He could tell she was tense, but when he settled down, he heard her faint sigh. He lay still while his mind raced.

Leo awoke without Susanna. Before his marriage, he'd always slept alone, made it a policy never to sleep in a woman's bed.

But now the bed felt empty without Susanna beside him. He closed his eyes, reliving her pain. He hadn't known what to say, how to convince her. He knew he should have told her he loved her, too, but she was so upset, she might believe he only mouthed the words to pacify her. He'd never said them before, never used them in a seduction, but she wouldn't know that.

He sat up, feeling like deadweight. No matter how much he wanted to change, to face down what he'd become, he was still a man who thoughtlessly hurt women. Her pain last night had etched itself on his very heart, as if he could bleed.

Since discovering he wasn't a true Wade, he'd been buffeted by emotions he'd tried to suppress, telling himself that eventually he'd come to peace with it.

But he felt . . . removed from his own brother and sister, as if he wasn't one of them anymore. He'd had the solace of his marriage to Susanna, but now he worried he'd harmed that permanently.

She obviously didn't trust that he could love her; she had insecurities about herself, but he thought they'd gotten past them. He'd been wrong.

He wasn't the same man she'd married—he knew the truth about himself now. He was the son of a good man, born of love, not duty. His parents' misery had nothing to do with him, and he didn't have to let it rule his life.

How could he prove to Susanna that he *had* changed, that he really loved her, enough that she'd believe?

As he dressed, he discovered the note she'd left, saying that she was going to visit her sister for the day. He balled it up, taking out his frustration. She was going to talk to Rebecca instead of her own husband. They couldn't ignore each other and this rift between them. Susanna needed some kind of sign from him, more than words she might not trust.

And then the answer hit him square between the eyes.

He finished dressing and ran down the stairs to

the entrance hall. He started to pen a note for Julian and Peter, canceling their breakfast at the club, but they arrived before he'd finished it.

"I can't go with you," Leo said. "I have to locate the British Archaeological Association."

Peter stared at him. "What are you talking about?"

"Susanna doesn't believe that I've changed, that I can love her. I have to prove it to her."

"At the archaeology association?" Julian said dubiously, folding his arms across his broad chest.

Peter rolled his eyes. "Wouldn't flowers, or something romantic, work better?"

"That won't impress her. It's not what she cares about. I have to go."

Susanna sat alone in her favorite parlor at Madingley House, looking out the window. She'd spent much of the day alone, her thoughts awhirl, her guilt at her own behavior warring with her knowledge that she *deserved* Leo's love.

"An invitation came for you," Rebecca said as she entered the room. "Hand delivered."

Susanna frowned. "I imagine there are people who still don't know I married . . ."

"You're married?" Rebecca shot back. "You spent the day here—how was I to know?"

Susanna glared at her sister even as she snatched the invitation. When she opened it, she read through it quickly, felt a hitch in breathing, and read it again in growing surprise.

"What is it?" Rebecca demanded. "Your expression . . ."

Susanna covered her mouth before a giggle could escape, as the first tears slipped down her cheeks. She held out the invitation.

Rebecca read it, frowning. "I don't understand. This can't be *your* Leo Wade."

Susanna nodded, wiping her cheeks with both hands. "It is—oh, it truly is."

"But . . . he's presenting a paper to the British Archaeological Association? On what, for goodness' sake?"

"Roman antiquities, a study he began as a child and put away for far too many years." Susanna hugged herself with giddiness.

"He's going to lecture . . . ?" Rebecca stared at her with consternation.

"It's not for two months. Plenty of time to sort the remains at Woodhill Manor."

"Oh. So . . . this is a good thing."

"It's a very good thing." Susanna threw her arms wide. "It means he loves me! Oh, Rebecca, this mess was partly my fault. I could never trust that someone like Leo could love someone like me. I thought we had nothing in common. With one doubt, I let all my insecurities back in, the very ones I'd struggled so hard to overcome. I was the quintessential bluestocking, getting my revenge for being compromised, but maybe I was forcing him to reject me because I thought it was bound to happen. Rebecca, he took everything I sent his way without blinking. He—he really loves me."

"Then what are you telling me for?" Rebecca asked, wearing a broad grin. "Go!"

Leo buried himself in Simon's library while he awaited Susanna's verdict. There were books on antiquities from all around the world, Greece, Italy, Egypt. It was as if, now that he'd admitted a fascination, he couldn't read fast enough. He'd almost filled a notebook with thoughts and analyses, and begun to keep a list of things he needed to do, starting with visiting the collection at the British Museum. He was filled with new purpose, a new goal, and it was as if the aimlessness of his life was in the unfocused past, something he had to go through but no longer needed.

Yet nothing distracted him from thoughts of Susanna. Every so often, he'd come upon an interesting fact, and think that he wanted to tell her, but she wasn't here. He consoled himself with believing that when he was finished, she would sit in an assembly room and listen to his conclusions.

He hoped to God she didn't expect him to wait the whole two months before she forgave him.

He worked late into the night, barely noticing when the servants lit lamps or brought food. When the door opened, he didn't look up until he heard Susanna's voice.

"Leo?"

He dropped the pen and came to his feet. She had the invitation in her hand, and she was staring at him in wonder.

"Did you do this . . . for me?" she asked softly.

"Only partly," he admitted, feeling the first easing of gratitude and relief. "The rest was for me."

"That's good. We should always do something for ourselves, and I so hoped you would find a passion." Her voice broke.

Tenderly, he said, "Besides you?"

She closed the door behind her and walked toward him. He didn't move, afraid to startle her, to make her change her mind. He found himself nervous, something he'd seldom felt before. But she was his wife, and that made everything different.

She clutched the invitation in her hand and looked at it rather than him. "I always thought I was independent, Leo. Though I told myself I didn't care what people thought about my bluestocking ways, I *did* care—too much—what men thought of me." She raised her eyes, and their chocolate depths shone with determination. "I don't want to be that insecure anymore. I know you've changed, that you wouldn't lie to me, that our marriage isn't about some foolish wager. I know you love me, even if you can't say the words. Actions are what matter, and you've shown me—"

He pulled her against him. "I love you, Susanna," he said fervently.

Her eyes filled with tears, and her mouth parted as if in wonder.

"I think we both had doubts that we could ever be loved for who we were, mistakes and all," he continued in a quiet voice. "You came into my life, with your accomplishments and goals, and the restlessness I'd been feeling made me realize I had nothing to look forward to. But I have that now."

"Oh, I'm so glad, Leo," she whispered, then stood on tiptoes to kiss every part of his face she could reach.

He returned her kisses, and it was some time before she broke away, her eyes dazed.

She laughed. "Tell me about the archaeology association. I cannot believe you finally went!"

"I spent this afternoon there, and it was quickly apparent to me that simply studying the remains at Woodhill Manor wouldn't be enough. I will present my work, but then I'll need to travel to the Continent. If only I could find an artist willing to accompany me and sketch what I need . . ."

She gasped, and her mouth widened with an excited smile. "Me! Choose me!"

He laughed and hugged her. "After you've finished helping your father. That's been the work of your life so far."

She flung her arms around him, dropping her head back to laugh as if the world held only wonders from then on. Looking into her beloved face, Leo knew it was true.

Epilogue

The weddings were beautiful. Susanna stood beside her husband in the church, watching as Rebecca and Julian, Elizabeth and Peter, were joined in matrimony. Then they all returned to Madingley House for a celebratory breakfast, where Susanna and Leo were feted at the same time since their wedding had been far from traditional. Susanna looked around at the overflowing dining room, at all her cousins and siblings, and never had she imagined feeling so very blessed.

Later that afternoon, Leo, Julian, and Peter escaped the festivities for the library.

Leo poured a brandy for each of them, then raised his glass. "To the wager."

"That the women won," Peter amended, shaking his head. "None of us could prove anything."

"I came out ahead—I bought the painting," Leo said, grinning.

"When the hell did you have time to do that?" Julian demanded.

"When I began to suspect the truth, I sent word to

have it done. It's a good thing neither of you studied the painting well, or you'd have known. But I can't discuss such private information," he added, when they would have demanded answers.

"So you won," Peter said in amazement.

"And neither of you are seeing my proof. The painting will only be for me and Susanna." They touched glasses and, wearing a wry smile, he added, "I think we all won."